DEADLY UNDERTAKINGS

OTHER BOOKS AND AUDIO BOOKS
BY GREGG LUKE

Altered State

Do No Harm

The Survivors

Blink of an Eye

Bloodborne

DEADLY UNDERTAKINGS

A NOVEL

GREGG LUKE

Covenant Communications, Inc.

Cover image *Pathology Department in a Hospital* © Team Static.

Cover design copyright © 2012 by Covenant Communications, Inc.

Published by Covenant Communications, Inc.
American Fork, Utah

Printed in the United States of America
First Printing: August 2012

18 17 16 15 14 13 12   10 9 8 7 6 5 4 3 2 1

ISBN 978-1-62108-074-9

ACKNOWLEDGMENTS

DEADLY UNDERTAKINGS IS A COMPLEX novel woven with an extraordinary amount of facts, information, procedures, and history. To complete such an undertaking, I had to rely on the expertise of many friends. I would sincerely like to thank Lynn Naylor, Michael Chatterton, Dr. Todd Brown, and Matthew Davidson for their contributions. In particular, I extend my appreciation to Dr. Jonathan Koehler, clinical pathologist, for his expertise and willingness to help correct and clarify numerous facts and procedures. Admittedly, I had to take artistic license with a few things, but overall the medical facts in this novel are accurate. I'd also like to thank Erika Luke, Brooke Ballard, Lemar Luke, and my amazing editor, Kirk Shaw, for editing the manuscript and offering many brilliant suggestions.

Finally, I would like to thank Rebekah Smith for letting me use her name, for being a constant source of encouragement and inspiration, and for being a good, good friend for many years. This one's for you!

CHAPTER 1

Monday

It was a curious phenomenon: There were only a few fluffy clouds in the hard summer sky, one of which cast a lone shadow over her mother's house. It did not darken the houses on either side nor the one behind it. Just her mom's. Curious.

Beth Mortimer knew exactly how she'd find her mother. Agnes Baugh would be in her recliner with a box of Cheese Nips and a Diet Dr. Pepper, participating in *Jeopardy!* by calling out questions to Alex Trebek's answers. Her snow-white hair would be fettered with pink sponge curlers, as if she were planning an outing later on. She'd be wearing a Hawaiian print muumuu and her fuzzy slippers—the ones that smelled like they'd absorbed three decades of foot sweat but were still "too comfortable to throw out."

Beth made the trip to her mom's house at precisely 1:00 Monday through Saturday, much to her mother's vexation. The 101-year-old was a strong-willed widow who fought tooth and nail for her independence. None of Beth's three brothers or two sisters helped in Mom's caretaking because they all lived out of state, so checking on Mom fell on Beth's shoulders. She didn't really mind. At seventy-eight years old, Beth had her own children who had all married and left Tremonton, Utah, for better jobs or a change of scenery. Checking on Mom gave her something to do, even if it wasn't fully appreciated. Besides, she felt she owed it to her. Forty years earlier, Mom had given Beth one of her kidneys due to bilateral renal failure. That was something she could never repay.

As she got out of her car, Beth again noted the curious cloud shadow. Hopefully, it would cool the house a tad. She let herself in the side door to the kitchen of the 1940s bungalow. The house was unusually quiet. She couldn't hear the TV . . . or sounds of *any* kind.

"Mom?" she called out.

There was no answer. The windows were still open. That wasn't right. Her mom always closed them each morning to trap the cool night air inside. Mid-August heat permeated the small house; the cloud shadow wasn't helping. Her mother refused to install AC or let anyone else install it. It was too expensive. Besides, the large poplar trees on the west side of the small house kept the majority of the summer heat to a tolerable level—or so she claimed.

"Not today," Beth grumbled to herself. The air was stifling.

"Mom?" she called out again. A knot of anxiety formed in her chest. *Don't worry yourself. Mom is fine; she's a brick; it isn't her "time." She still has a few good years, even at a hundred and one.* Beth swallowed against the dry heat parching her throat and called out again, "Mom, are you okay, dear?"

More silence followed. Perhaps this *was* her time.

Beth moved from the kitchen to the living room. The TV was off. It was cold. No static discharge crackled against her fingers when she touched it. She went to the hallway bathroom and found it empty too. The tub was bone dry, as was the sink.

"Mom?" she said before opening the door to Agnes's bedroom.

Agnes Baugh was stretched out in peaceful repose on top of her bed. Her hands were folded across her belly, her head centered perfectly on her pillow. The coverlet beneath her was crisp and wrinkle free. She wore a simple cotton dress that looked freshly laundered and pressed. A white linen handkerchief tenderly covered her face. The setting was so ridiculously precise it was almost comical—except that her mother wasn't breathing. It was almost as if she'd anticipated dying and had prepared everything to be just right. But why the hankie on her face? It didn't look . . . *natural*. In fact, nothing about the scene looked natural. Everything was arranged too perfectly. And then there was the smell. Not the stink of death or expressed body fluids but a lingering hint of olives and spice, and . . . and something else. Maybe an astringent?

Beth felt for a pulse on her mom's wrist. The skin was cool and dry. Her arm was stiff with rigor mortis. No pulse. She removed the handkerchief—and gasped loudly. On each eye lay a silver fifty-cent piece. She immediately called 911.

The EMTs arrived within minutes. As one technician went to work assessing the body, the other asked Beth several questions, which she answered as completely as possible. She'd discovered her mother at 1:05 p.m. Mom's meds consisted of a regular-strength aspirin, lovastatin for cholesterol, lisinopril for blood pressure, digoxin for her heart, and oxybutynin for bladder control. Mom's other children lived out of state; Beth had called them right after the 911 call. She was her mother's legal caretaker and executor—yes, she had paperwork to authenticate the arrangement. Mom had a signed and notarized do-not-resuscitate affidavit cosigned by her attorney.

Beth was not unduly upset about her mother's passing, but the bizarre condition in which her mother was found definitely bothered her. She stood back and listened intently to the conversations between the EMTs and the medical coordinator at Tremonton Hospital. The patient was extremely pale and unresponsive. Blood pressure was zero. The heart monitor read asystole: flatline. No carotid pulse. No breath. Her core temperature was eight-one degrees, slightly cooler than the ambient room temperature. Her mother's skin was semi-opaque—almost translucent. To Beth, it looked like single-ply tissue paper. The vessels that wormed their way along her forearms and hands were pale and pinkish, not the usual gray-green color she'd seen for over seventy years.

The emergency personnel told the hospital there were no obvious bloodstains or bowel evacuation, no vomiting or evidence of a coronary event. Her body showed minimal signs of first-stage decomposition despite the oppressive heat, and she was in end-stage rigor mortis. The last time anyone had contact with the deceased was Saturday afternoon. The preliminary estimated time of death was sometime between Saturday evening and Sunday morning, some thirty hours earlier.

Since the daughter had no idea why Mrs. Baugh had the coins on her eyes or the hankie over her face, they deemed the passing a suspicious event and called in local law enforcement. The sheriff arrived with a crime scene specialist who took photos of the entire house, all possible entries, and several shots of the bedroom and body. He questioned Beth at length and took down phone numbers of all her siblings. A forensics team was called in to check for evidence. The body was then transported to Tremonton Hospital.

The resident coroner gave a cursory examination but found no signs of blunt trauma on her head, face, neck, or arms. He next tried to take a blood sample for CPK and TN-1 enzyme levels, which would indicate a heart attack. It was then he discovered Agnes Baugh didn't have any blood. Her entire circulatory system had been replaced with an oil-based liquid.

CHAPTER 2

SALT LAKE COUNTY MEDICAL EXAMINER'S assistant Rebekah Smith frowned at the preliminary report on her computer screen. Although she'd seen more than her share of bizarre cases, this one seemed too strange to be real. It was forwarded from Tremonton Hospital. The local paramedics had delivered the body at 3:00 p.m. The deceased was a 101-year-old female from Tremonton, Utah. She was found dead in her home around 1:00 by her daughter, Beth Mortimer. Estimated time of death: approximately 11:00 Saturday evening. Possible cause of death: undetermined. Signs of trauma: a two-inch, sutured incision on the inside of her left leg, directly over the femoral artery and vein. Remarkable findings: no blood in body. Entire circulatory system filled with liquid resembling embalming fluid. Medical history: donation of one kidney to her daughter, Beth Mortimer. All children had been born at home. No other record of hospitalization.

The funeral home with which the deceased had prearranged her internment claimed they had no hand in it. The daughter had no clue who might have done such a deplorable act or why.

Agnes Baugh was a celebrity in her community, well-liked and respected. The suspicious nature of the death necessitated transferring the body to the medical examiner's office at the University of Utah Medical Center. An autopsy was scheduled for the following morning. In the meantime, Rebekah would ask her boyfriend, an investigator with the Salt Lake police department, if he had any information on the event.

"Exhume anything mortifying this evening, my beauty?" The voice was so close behind her that she felt it as well as heard.

Rebekah barely stifled a scream. "Dang it, Robert, you know I hate it when you sneak up on me in that slimy way!" She would have stood up to confront him had there been room, but her small cubicle was little more than a four-by-five partition in a bank of identical workstations. There was barely enough room for one body in each; with two, it was difficult to breathe.

Dr. Robert Lansing laughed and placed both unwelcome hands on her shoulders. "Well, you can't blame me for that, my dear. I *have* to sneak up on you." He leaned in and put his lips to her ear, as if ready to share a dark secret or plant a kiss. "Every time you see me coming, you seem to find some reason to disappear." His breath smelled like stale coffee, and his fingers felt like tentacles.

Rebekah jerked away from his grasp and closed the file on her computer. His comment was all too true—she'd like nothing more than to disappear—but she felt no guilt from the admission. She loathed the arrogant man and avoided him at all costs.

Glancing at her watch, she said, "Speaking of which, I have an engagement I can't miss. Excuse me." She pushed away from her desk, forcing him outside her cubicle. She clicked the shut-down feature on her computer, grabbed her purse from a nook over her desk, and turned to leave, but Robert had his hands on both sides of the narrow entrance, blocking her escape. His six-two frame loomed over her five-seven.

"Mmm, an *engagement*," he mused lasciviously. "Sounds stimulating. Is it with one of your refrigerated sleeping beauties? A little evening evisceration? Or are you hoping to reanimate dead Prince Charming with a kiss? They call that necrophilia, you know."

"You're mixing up your fairy tales again, Robert. Perhaps you should have your grandkids explain them to you one more time."

Lansing gave a low chuckle. It sounded like a panther preparing for a kill. "If the man *was* a fairy tale, then I wouldn't be so jealous. But I think he's real, and I call him one lucky stiff."

Having worked in the medical examiner's office for over five years, Rebekah had grown bored with Robert's countless, banal references to death. He worked them ad nauseam. What she hadn't gotten used to were his incessant flirtations.

Dr. Robert Lansing wasn't a physician. He had an advanced degree in healthcare administration . . . or something like that. He was one of the head honchos in the state ME's office. As such, Rebekah expected him to be a paradigm of decorum and professionalism. But that was not the case. The fifty-two-year-old was well-proportioned and classically handsome. He looked like one of those eye-candy doctors on daytime soap operas.

All of the women in the building swooned a little whenever he entered the room. Rebekah regurgitated a little—or at least felt like it. He had this perverted aura constantly oozing from his self-inflated demeanor. It wasn't hard to guess what he was thinking when they passed each other in the building. His leer almost has a stench to it.

Conversations with Robert were all the same. They'd start out talking about work, then he'd begin adding off-colored comments followed by sexual innuendos, all of which would lead to his asking her out again or suggesting a secret rendezvous with promises of "rewards beyond her wildest dreams." She had repeatedly asked him to stop his come-ons— there was no way she'd *ever* go out with him—but each request only deterred him a few days before he was back at his game. She debated going to his supervisor about it, but she didn't want to make waves or stir up interdepartmental animosity. Instead, she chose to fight fire with fire.

"Poor old Robert. You keep forgetting I have a boyfriend. Did you skip your Alzheimer's med again?" she asked as if talking to a five-year-old. "Run down to the pharmacy. I'm sure Gregg will loan you an Aricept or something so you can remember your way home."

His smug grin didn't falter. "Always ready with a smart remark."

"Around here one has to be. Actually, I'm meeting my boyfriend in a few minutes," she continued. "His name is Josh Logan, remember? And he's a real man in every sense of the word. I'm lucky to have found him. There is a critical shortage of real men these days, especially in *this* office."

She elbowed past him without apology and walked briskly down the hallway. She could feel his eyes on her the whole time. Still, it was better than being face-to-face, and having his eyes meet every part of her *except* her eyes.

Rebekah exited the building and checked her wristwatch. It was nearly eight. She didn't really have an appointment with Josh but she hoped to soon. She needed to get some things off her chest. The encounter with Robert Lansing wasn't nearly as disturbing as the Agnes Baugh case she'd just reviewed. There were several troubling aspects to the centenarian's death. The Box Elder County EMTs, law enforcement, and the Tremonton Hospital coroner were very thorough in their documentation. But it was something else—a passing snippet of information that brought up an event Rebekah wished she'd never have to remember.

CHAPTER 3

SPECIAL INVESTIGATIONS DETECTIVE JOSH LOGAN filed his last report, glad to have the day over and done. Mondays were particularly hectic in his department because half of the shift was spent sweeping up messes from the weekend. That was the nature of the business. He'd put in his time on the streets and knew that all the crazies came out on the weekends. It was his department that got all the cases no one else could figure out. Many of them were cold-case files—unsolved crimes committed several months (or years) earlier. Luckily, he had enough seniority and clout to pick which cases he handled.

Being the last officer to leave the office bullpen that evening, he switched off the overhead fluorescents and cast one last look over the small area. The glow of Salt Lake City's nightlife penetrated the tinted fourth-story windows, softening the angles of the desks, computers, printers, and other office paraphernalia. The droning hum of electric equipment on standby sounded deeply calming after the raucous tumult of the day. With mixed emotions, he acknowledged for the umpteenth time that this place was where he was supposed to be.

Josh grew up in an active LDS home. He did all the things he was supposed to do: He graduated from high school with good grades; he was an Eagle Scout; he attended his meetings, fulfilled his assignments, and was called to serve in the Louisiana, Baton Rouge Mission. A few months after he entered the field, Hurricane Katrina struck. When the incredible devastation weakened many people's belief in God's love, Josh used the opportunity to show Christlike love through service, friendship, and heartfelt compassion.

The humanitarian assistance from the Church was astounding. Unlike FEMA's, the Church's response was immediate. Thick in the Southern Bible

Belt, many of the local denominations were grateful for the organization and overall volunteerism of the Church. T-shirts emblazoned with *Mormon Helping Hands* were seen everywhere. Josh thought of his personal efforts as reenacting the parable of the Good Samaritan—only on a much grander scale.

Regrettably, Josh also saw a lot of un-Christian behavior in the aftermath of the devastation. Blatant vandalism, looting on an epidemic scale, even assault and rape in some parishes were commonplace in the wake of Katrina. Josh wondered how people could treat their fellowmen—their neighbors!—with such disregard, such heartlessness and lack of empathy. It was a turning point in his life, an epiphany.

It was then he decided to go into law enforcement after his mission. He loved serving people as a peacekeeper, even if many of those people looked on his service as an encroachment on their rights. But did bad people have the right to violate the rights of others by committing crimes against them? Of course not. That's where he came in.

After two years on the force, he was promoted to deputy. The following year he transferred to homicide. And two years after that, he accepted a detective's position with special investigations.

Just as Josh was shrugging on his blazer, his cell phone vibrated. It was a text from Rebekah: *Hungry?*

He smiled. He'd been seconds away from asking her if she was interested in a late-evening snack. Great minds think alike. He texted, *You read my mind.*

J. Wong's?

That was more than a "snack," but he didn't mind. Plus, it was only four blocks from his office in the Nonemergency Police Department building.

Sure, he typed in reply.

See you soon, Clouseau.

Josh shook his head. Because he was a detective, she loved calling him after Peter Sellers's bumbling character in the Pink Panther movies. But Josh was nothing like that. At least he hoped he wasn't.

He locked the office door and headed to his car in the basement parking lot. Sliding his briefcase into his Ford Escape, he glanced toward the exit. He desperately wanted to toss his blazer in too. The basement parking area was cool but sticky, and he knew outside would be even worse. But he had to keep his blazer on to conceal his shoulder holster. Technically he was now off duty, but he'd been in his career long enough that the only place he felt comfortable not wearing a sidearm was at home. You just never knew when aggressive *encouragement* would be necessary. Still, the odds of such instances occurring in special investigations were slim. And he found that his six-four, 210-pound frame often did the job without having to pull a weapon.

The next case on his docket, however, might be one that would challenge those odds. It had gang-involvement written all over it.

CHAPTER 4

THE CHINESE BISTRO WAS BUSY even at that late hour. As he approached, Josh was assaulted with myriad smells that had his mouth watering and his stomach rumbling. Perhaps he *was* in the mood for more than a snack. Admittedly, his eating habits were deplorable. His usual fare consisted of foods that had Rebekah lecturing him about esophageal ulcers, colon polyps, and carcinogenic visceral fat (whatever that was). J. Wong's bistro, however, was definitely above his pay grade.

Rebekah was waving at him from a booth midway into the restaurant.

"How'd you get a table so fast?" he asked as he kissed her cheek and sat across from her.

"Josh, we've been dating now for what—almost two years? I figured you'd be hungry after a long Monday shift, so I texted you *from* here."

"Okay, but I was only interested in a snack, not fine dining."

"If I'd left it up to you, we'd be picking through the leftovers from the deep fryer at a Flying J station."

He folded his arms defiantly. "Now you're exaggerating," he said, knowing she wasn't.

"Sweetie, of your six favorite places to eat, you can buy gas at five of them. That is neither fine dining *nor* snacking—it's self-destruction."

Josh couldn't help but smile at her cynical—but correct—way of putting things. She was that way with everything in her life. Perhaps that was part of his attraction to her.

They'd met over a corpse. Josh made a visit to the state morgue while investigating the death of a nameless blonde female found by Willard Bay. The woman was found clutching a dead chicken by the neck in each fist. No one knew how she died or how the poultry was involved. Rebekah was assisting the examiner on the case. Josh entered the autopsy room and saw her gowned in a paper smock and bloody latex gloves. The protective blue smock was splattered with dark, clotted spots. She lifted a mottled, reddish-brown organ with a few severed veins dangling beneath. She looked up at him and smiled. It was love at first sight.

Josh had seen his share of corpses and blood, but he avoided them whenever possible. He wasn't squeamish; he simply preferred working with the deceased on paper more than in the flesh—particularly when it involved copious amounts of body fluids. Therefore, the fact that this beautiful woman with chestnut-colored hair and fawn-like brown eyes didn't seem the least bit bothered to be handling someone's eviscerated liver intrigued him immensely.

Forgetting how the dead woman was found, he asked about the possibility of foul play with the Jane Doe they were dissecting. Rebekah laughed so hard she almost dropped the excised organ. It took a full minute before Josh realized his unintentional pun. He blushed, swallowed his pride, and asked for Rebekah's phone number. They'd been dating ever since.

A waiter showed up a few seconds later with a large platter of tangerine chicken, a house specialty. She'd obviously ordered before he'd arrived.

Josh leaned forward to deeply inhale the tangy-sweet aroma. "You're too good to me, Becks."

"Yeah, I know. So, I stumbled across a bizarre case today—one that'll probably be given to homicide tomorrow."

"Wow. Cutting right to the chase, huh? What's up?"

Using chopsticks with accomplished finesse, she popped a large piece of glazed chicken into her mouth and chewed with slow, prolonged passion. "Oh man, this is good. Hold that thought while I go propose to the chef, okay?"

"Hey, I can cook too, you know," Josh whined, feigning offense.

"Not like this, sweetie."

He stabbed a chunk with his fork and put it in his mouth. The flavor *was* amazing. "Wow. Maybe *I'll* go propose to him."

Rebekah smiled and blew him a kiss. She had one of those gorgeous smiles that could be an advertisement for the dazzling results of modern cosmetic dentistry.

They filled their plates with the various side choices and carried on light chitchat as they devoured the cuisine. She could brandish words and wits with just about anyone, but when she had an issue bothering her, she got this intense look in her eyes, one Josh had come to recognize as a something she needed to get off her chest.

"So, are you ready to tell me about this *bizarre* case?" he asked.

"*Bizarre* doesn't quite cut it. It's got homicide written all over it . . . and . . ." She took a sip of water and wiped her mouth.

"And . . . what?"

"I'm not sure."

"Was it murder?"

"Probably. I don't know yet. We're doing the autopsy in the morning. I'm going to assist. From what I've read, there are minimal clues from a CSI angle. I was hoping you could use your connections to look into that for me."

"Sure. What are the particulars?"

"A 101-year-old woman found dead on her bed at home by her seventy-eight-year-old daughter. The daughter has nothing against letting the investigators treat the house as a crime scene, but the police report says there was very little evidence of criminal activity—other than the dead body. As far as pathological evidence, we won't know until we open her up. Usually patients that age aren't even brought in for autopsy; they're assumed to have simply passed on from natural causes, and they go right to a funeral home."

"So what makes this case different?"

Rebekah locked eyes with him. "She was embalmed *before* the EMTs arrived."

Josh choked on a piece of dumpling. "Wh—at?" He swallowed hard. "That seems *extremely* suspicious."

"That's what *I* thought." She leaned back, furrowing her brow as she vocally rehearsed her impressions. "The deceased had prearranged processing and internment with Rogers and Taylor funeral home in Tremonton. She is survived by six kids, but only one daughter lives close by. The daughter's the one who called 911. And she was in relatively good health up until her death."

"Did the mortician get there before the daughter?"

"No. They didn't even know she'd passed away until the daughter contacted them. Besides, they don't do in-home embalming."

Josh set his fork on his plate and leaned forward. "Has anyone checked on the daughter? I mean, is she a person of interest yet?"

Rebekah's head cocked to one side. "You mean did *she* kill her mother?" She began to absently chew on her thumbnail. "I hadn't thought of that."

Josh grimaced at her actions. "Knowing where your hands have been all day, it always makes me cringe when you do that."

"Do what?"

He mimicked her chewing on her nail.

"Oh don't worry, Clouseau. I wash before and after each autopsy." She reached across the table and took his hand. "And I'm almost positive I wore gloves today."

Ignoring her goad, he said, "You know I hate that Clouseau name."

"Yeah. That's why I use it." She released his hand and began fishing through her purse.

"I got this," Josh said, leaning to one side, reaching for his back pocket.

She pulled out two twenties and laid them on the table. "Thanks, sweetie, but I know how much you make. Listen, I'm gonna run home and do some research online. See what you can find on whether or not the daughter is a suspect and what the CSI guys found. We'll compare notes after the autopsy tomorrow evening, say . . . over takeout at my place?"

"Why your place?"

"Because yours is a sty."

He slid his wallet back into his pocket. "You have such a blunt way of putting things, Becks. Really fires up the romance."

"It's not a date, sweetie, it's business. The fact that you get to spend an evening with a gorgeous, eligible, not-quite-thirty-year-old young woman is just a bonus." She rounded the table and gave him a quick kiss. "I'm serious about this, Josh. There's something going on here that . . . well, let's just see what we come up with, okay?" Worry fringed her eyes but left no room for argument.

"Okay, Becks. Sure."

"Love you, Clouseau."

Josh watched her exit the restaurant and turn quickly down the sidewalk. He couldn't help but gawk. She was definitely different from anyone he'd ever dated. She was quick-witted and intelligent but didn't rub his face in it. She was quirky and spontaneous but nowhere near ditsy. She was extremely pretty and could have the pick of any guy she wanted, but for some reason she'd chosen him. More importantly, she was honest to a fault. So when she said she loved him, he believed her without question.

Josh stared at the empty seat across from him. He knew she deserved the same. And he wished he could be more open with his feelings about her. He . . . he just couldn't. At least not yet.

CHAPTER 5

THAT EVENING, REBEKAH SAT IN front of her home computer, trying to steady her shaky hands. She'd been there for nearly an hour, entering words such as "organ donation" and "organ rejection." But each time she googled the keywords, her hands would tremble from anxiety and remorse. She would place her fists in her lap and chide herself again and again. How silly was it to get so worked up over a few words?—to start hyperventilating over a distant memory?

She was stronger than that. She performed work that would make most people gag. The stuff of nightmares was her daily bread and butter. She was not a macabre person; the gruesome and grotesque did not appeal to her. She simply accepted the way things were without putting any supernatural or horror-film spin on it. Therefore, it was silly to get so worked up over a coincidence.

Rebekah had never been squeamish. Her father was a retired Utah Highway Patrol officer. She'd grown up listening to graphic horror stories of traffic accidents over the dinner table. Not the most ideal mealtime conversation, but she took to heart the underlying messages of not driving distracted, drowsy, or drunk, and of always wearing your seat belt.

She was eighteen when her mother was hit by a drunk driver, which only solidified her father's resolve to keep the streets safe and his only child safer. That resolve became impenetrable when the drunk's insurance company was able to deny the claim because his blood alcohol level was reported at 0.078 percent, placing him within legal limit to drive. The police had found an open, empty bottle of Southern Comfort in the man's car, and they could smell alcohol on his clothes when they extracted his body from the wreck. Because he was pronounced dead at the scene, and with a documented legal blood alcohol level, only circumstantial evidence suggested he was at fault on that snowy December night.

Rebekah distinctly remembered that night, seeing her mother broken and battered in the emergency department. Several of mom's internal organs were badly damaged; along with a shattered pelvis, both kidneys were completely destroyed. She needed at least one kidney replaced immediately, and Rebekah's genetics and blood type seemed a perfect match for donation. But it didn't take. Words like "tissue insufficiency," "organ rejection," and "donor incompatibility" haunted her recovery. In spite of intensive dialysis and immunosuppressive therapy, her mother passed away three weeks later, on Christmas Eve. Rebekah's final words to her seemed feeble, inadequate. Her grief was profound, her remorse acutely guilt-laden.

Her donated kidney had not saved her mother. Everyone said it wasn't her fault, that it was beyond her control, but deep down she felt that *she* had failed to bring her mother back from death's door.

That's when Rebekah decided to attend the U and major in physiology, with the goal to someday work with the state medical examiner—to aid in organ donation procedures and to make sure people who intentionally hurt others didn't get off so easily. To her, drunk driving *was* intentional harm; it was categorically *preventable* recklessness.

Her father called in a favor and got her a summer clerkship with the ME's office, doing filing and some morgue clean up. She quickly proved to be a hard worker with a strong constitution, not afraid to tackle any assignment no matter how menial or ghastly. The clerkship turned into a part-time job when she entered the University of Utah. When she graduated with a bachelor's of science with honors, she accepted a full-time position with the ME.

The physicians and senior staffers constantly encouraged her to continue her studies into medical school, to become a licensed medical examiner or pathologist, but she was content with helping in her small way—which wasn't all that small. Everyone at the morgue knew Rebekah ran circles around all the other assistants, most of the interns, and even some of the doctors there. If she had a concern or saw something someone else had missed, her word alone would initiate a reexamination of the case. The chief medical examiner, Dr. Sandeep Mahesh, was perhaps her strongest supporter. Her word often became his word, which then became law.

Rebekah shook the memories from her head and left the search engine to log onto the ME's itinerary. Her anxiety abated when she saw Dr. Mahesh had assigned himself to the Agnes Baugh case. She closed her eyes, took a cleansing breath, and said a quick prayer of thanks. Just knowing her good friend would be managing the case lessened some of her angst. And yet, she wondered, for how long?

CHAPTER 6

Tuesday

Rebekah was at the office of Chief Medical Examiner Sandeep Mahesh, M.D., Ph.D., at precisely 7:00 the next morning. She knocked.

"It is open," the doctor answered in his rich New Delhi accent.

Rebekah walked in. "Morning, Sandy," she said informally. Because Rebekah had worked with him since day one, they'd dropped formalities long ago. "How are you today?"

"I am infinitely better than all of my patients combined," the doctor joked. It was an easy claim to make. "You are here very early, Sundara. What can I do for you?"

Sundara was the Hindi word for "beautiful." When he called her that, it had the complete opposite effect from when Robert Lansing called her beautiful. Dr. Mahesh was generous, nurturing, and kind, but he had a playful side too; he seemed to love making Rebekah blush. Robert's playfulness made her skin crawl.

"You have three autopsies scheduled this morning," she stated. "I'd like to assist on one in particular, if that's all right."

"Oh?" Mahesh said as he donned his reading glasses and looked at the manila folders in his *Today* tray. "Mrs. Mary Neuenschwander, Mr. James Carbine, or Mrs. Agnes Baugh?"

"Mrs. Baugh."

"Certainly you may. But may I ask why?"

Rebekah folded her arms. Although there were two reasons, she chose to list the most obvious. "I think there's something fishy going on with it."

His chuckle was closed-lipped and high-pitched. It never ceased to make her smile. "Obviously. Why else would *we* get her?" He waved her off before she could answer and took a sip from a steaming mug of tea.

"Of course, of course you may assist. Let me get settled in and I will meet you in the theater, say, in twenty minutes?"

"Thanks, Sandy," she said, smiling at his use of the old-school term for the morgue. "See you there." She picked up the manila folder and left.

* * *

Rebekah entered the autopsy room wearing a sweater under her smock. She usually didn't have to. Her healthy metabolism and constant movement kept her just warm enough to function without the constrictions of extra clothing. But today she was afflicted with a chill that ran deeper than the ambient room temperature. The sweater wasn't optional.

She looked around the morgue, realizing she was a bit odd for loving this place so much. Most people cringed at the thought of entering a room filled with cadavers, let alone touching a corpse. But it truly did not bother her. The human body was an intricate, elegantly designed, biologic machine whose main purpose was to house one of Heavenly Father's spirit children. Once the spirit was gone, what was left behind was a bag of organs, fluids, and assorted chemicals. She didn't consider herself callous or unfeeling. It was just a fact of life—well, of death. Even with that mindset, she always did her best to remain respectful of the deceased, if only for the surviving family's feelings.

Securing her long hair in a bun, Rebekah washed her hands, pulled on surgical gloves, and slipped into a blue, paper smock. She looked around once again to make sure everything was in order. The room was typical of any big-city morgue: sea-foam green linoleum floor, light gray walls, stainless steel everywhere. Operating lights and dangling microphones hung over four gleaming autopsy tables. One wall held an assortment of different-colored liquids used for preserving samples. The morgue was equipped to embalm patients if need be, but that task usually fell to the funeral home. The room smelled of formaldehyde, antiseptic, and bile, but powerful overhead fans drew most of the noxious air through filters, which helped keep odors to a minimum.

With firm resolve, she went straight to the stainless steel table that held the body of Agnes Baugh. Orderlies had moved her from the refrigeration unit to the table a short time earlier. Everything looked ready to go. Hopefully, they would be able to deduce what had happened to this poor old woman.

Mrs. Baugh lay naked beneath a single green surgical sheet. The report said she'd come in wearing a knee-length cotton dress. Her hair was washed and styled, and her body was freshly bathed. That was a pleasant change. The morgue rarely got clean patients.

Rebekah removed the sheet and began to examine Mrs. Baugh's exterior details. The first thing she noticed was the ten-inch lateral scar just over her left hip. Ignoring that, she moved to the two-inch suture over her left femoral artery. The tissue was still pink and swollen.

"So what do you think?" Dr. Mahesh asked upon entering the room. He headed to the sink to scrub up before slipping on a smock.

"This one's *really* strange. According to the report, she was embalmed and ready for burial *before* the daughter discovered her."

Mahesh frowned as he snapped on his gloves. "Who did the prep?"

"No one knows." She picked up the manila folder and slid out a few photos of the late Agnes Baugh. "These photos were taken during her hundredth birthday; this one's only a few months old. Look at how she wore her makeup and hair. It's very different from how she looks today. So whoever prepared her was not very familiar with her beforehand."

"Hmm. A brilliant observation, Sundara. What else?"

"It was done by someone who knew basic technique, yet there are a couple of irregularities that are more than simple mistakes."

Mahesh raised an eyebrow. Always the teacher, she knew he wanted more than a basic answer.

"Her lips are superglued shut, as is standard practice, but it doesn't feel like her jaw's been wired closed. There's no superglue on her eyelids. Instead, the embalmer used coins: a U.S. half-dollar over each eye to hold them closed. And there wasn't any cotton or eye cups under the lids to compensate for orb deflation. Also, the embalming portal over the femoral artery and vein is a bit larger than normal, which could indicate a novice mortician."

Mahesh gave Mrs. Baugh a cursory once-over. As he did, he asked, "And why are women typically embalmed at the femoral loci?"

"It's purely cosmetic. That way they can be viewed wearing a low neckline dress or blouse without a nasty carotid incision showing."

"Correct," he said as he poked at various areas of her body. He seemed rather intrigued by the elasticity of the veins in her hands. Rebekah had noticed something odd about them too. They seemed almost rubbery. He moved to the feet and poked at the veins along the top of each foot with the same result.

Moving to her torso, he ran a gloved finger along the scar across her side. "This is an old keloid."

"Kidney transplant," she said quickly. "Almost thirty years ago."

He nodded and then palpated the incision over her femoral artery. "Hmm. I agree with your first assessment: the suturing appears to be rather hasty work. Whoever did the embalming clearly has some experience, but he was not elegant in his technique." He pressed either side of the incision, causing a drop of amber liquid to escape between the stitches. He rubbed the fluid between his finger and thumb, then brought it to his nose and sniffed.

"This is incredibly interesting," he said with a frown.

"What?" Rebekah asked, moving closer.

"I do not believe this is embalming fluid."

CHAPTER 7

JOSH LOGGED ONTO THE STATEWIDE interdepartmental police blotter and brought up the preliminary report on Agnes Baugh. The observational details of the police and first responders were all there: No evidence of forcible entry, no substantial evidence of a struggle or violence, no fingerprints other than those of the victim and her daughter. Beth Mortimer had checked out clean. The police had questioned her at length, and she'd been very cooperative and had given straightforward answers. She had a solid alibi before, during, and after the estimated time of death. She had a key to the house, which allowed her unrestrained access, but the neighbors attested to the fact that Baugh never locked her doors anyway. Baugh left no major assets behind (other than her small home), and all of her children were fiscally sound, so there was little financial motive for her death.

Josh read the interview transcript three times, each time focusing from a different point of view: the questioning officer's, Mrs. Mortimer's, even Mrs. Baugh's. Nothing untoward jumped out. Tremonton law enforcement did not consider the daughter a person of interest, but Josh was going to keep that avenue open . . . just in case.

Mrs. Mortimer claimed nothing was missing from the house. Forensics was currently analyzing hair and fiber samples.

The Tremonton Hospital ME noted some swelling of Mrs. Baugh's lips, some dried blood inside the rim of both nostrils, and bloodshot eyes, but those could simply be attributed to the dry summer air and her significantly advanced age. The fact that she'd already been embalmed was the obvious reason to classify her death as "suspicious."

Josh stretched and yawned. He wasn't sure why Rebekah had a particular interest in this case—other than it being bizarre—but he'd try to help however he could. Until then, he really needed to get back to his current case.

He closed out the blotter and pulled up his docket for the day. Fourteen months earlier, a body was found behind a strip mall in downtown West Valley City: a seventeen-year-old Caucasian male named Paxton Harris. All evidence pointed to gang activity. Fatal gunshot to the back. Witnesses identified three suspicious vehicles in the area at the time of the shooting.

If it was in a high-traffic area of downtown West Valley, what made the vehicles suspicious? He'd go out there right after lunch to check things out. *Seventeen years old. What a waste of a life! Gangs. Why would any kid do that to himself?* There really wasn't a definitive answer, but Josh knew a majority of gang members came from troubled homes. It seemed that all gangbangers were doing was seeking the kinship they lacked under their own roofs. But gangs were a poor substitute for families.

He glanced over the West Valley police blotter, looking for any recent gang activity in the area. There was plenty. He decided he'd better just go out and start looking around in person.

As he backed out of the website, a tag from another entry caught his eye: the suspicious death of a senior citizen in St. George. Silas Snow, one hundred years old. Josh immediately thought of the Baugh case. The similarities were too stong to ignore. He linked into the site.

Mr. Snow had died in a gated retirement community: Mesa Roja. Estimated time of death: undetermined. Cause of death: undetermined.

Mesa Roja boasted a large social center that offered dining, recreational, and educational activities. Twenty-four condominium-style cottages lined either side of the social center, twelve on each side. All were within walking distance along beautifully manicured sidewalks across very flat terrain. Mr. Snow's cottage was on the north end of Sunrise Lane. The other street was named Sunset Lane. The housekeeping staff cleaned Sunrise on Mondays and Tuesdays, Sunset on Wednesdays and Thursdays. No one entered or exited the facility without checking through the guard kiosk at the gated entrance. They even had CCTV cameras along both sidewalks in case one of the residents took a nasty fall.

Mr. Snow had left the Sunday movie night event just before nine, saying he was too tired to finish the film. They had been showing *Ben-Hur*.

A housekeeper found him in bed Tuesday morning, very pale and unresponsive. She called the on-site nurse, who called 911.

Further details are pending.

To Josh, it sounded like the old guy simply passed away. It was certainly an "unattended" death, but why was it being labeled "suspicious?"

He called the Washington County sheriff's office. A middle-aged man answered. "Deputy Abramson."

"Hey, Glade, Josh."

"Hey, Josh," the officer replied with zero surprise in his voice. "You're calling about Mr. Snow, aren't you?"

"Wow, you're good."

"I have a crystal ball in my office."

Josh whistled low. "Ever use it down in Mesquite?"

"Nope. It doesn't work outside Utah. I think it's a Mormon crystal ball."

"I see," Josh chuckled. "So . . . is Mr. Snow destined to show up on my desk?"

"Maybe. It hasn't been determined unsolvable yet. Just suspicious."

"So what's so suspicious about it?"

There was a pause on the line. Glade Abramson was a good friend who usually didn't beat around the bush or drag his feet. If he was having difficulty trying to describe the event, something was definitely bothering him. Josh heard an intake of air then a catch. Apparently, this one had Glade on the ropes.

"So . . . the guy was found in his bed, right?" Josh prompted.

"Not in—on. Fully dressed in a suit and tie."

Another pause.

Josh cleared his throat. "Maybe he was dressed up to go to the temple that morning and just died in his suit."

"No way," Glade said with a scoff. "Mr. Snow was a character. He was a descendant of *the* Lorenzo Snow, but he had very little to do with the Church personally. He wasn't anti; he just felt he had better things to do with his time, he always said. He even looked kind of like his prophet ancestor: full beard, lots of wavy white hair, except Silas was skinny as a rail. That's because he used to walk everywhere, all the time. I never once saw him in a car or on a bus. In fact, he was the only contestant over ninety to finish the St. George marathon."

"Serious?"

"Yep. Saw him with my own two eyes. Truth be told, it was actually more of a shuffle than a run, but he made the whole twenty-six miles. I believe he was training to run it again this fall. Wanted to be the first person over a hundred to complete it. I believe he would have, too."

"That's fascinating, but what does that have to do with his suit?"

"The only clothing I've *ever* seen him in is jogging pants and a T-shirt—maybe a sweater now and then, but certainly nothing fancier. I didn't even know he owned a suit. Don't think anyone knew he did."

"Was he a loner?"

"Not really. He was always very friendly, outgoing. He loved to preach about the benefits of dry air and daily exercise. That's why his death is such a surprise."

Glade was speaking easily, but Josh sensed this was troubling him on a deeper level. "So they found him in a suit . . . ?"

"Housekeeper found him laid out clean as a whistle, as if in a funeral parlor. His beard was trimmed, his hair combed, suit pressed, even his hands were crossed over his belly. I took pictures an' all. The real freaky thing is that he had this napkin over his face."

Josh sat up straight. "A napkin over his face? Like a linen handkerchief?"

"Yeah, I guess. And get this: under the napkin—"

"He had a half-dollar coin covering each eye," Josh cut in.

He heard Glade draw a sharp breath. "Wait—how'd you know? I haven't even entered that tidbit in my report."

"Have you had the hospital ME check him out yet?" Josh asked in lieu of an answer.

"No. He's on ice at Dixie Regional Med. Should I?"

"Immediately. And tell me what you find the minute you do."

"Yeah, sure. What's up, Josh?"

"Just a hunch."

"Well, share what you got, buddy. I don't mind telling you, this one's got me pretty creeped out."

Josh's mind was racing. "If they find what I think they'll find, your 'suspicious death' just got a lot creepier."

CHAPTER 8

"IF IT'S NOT EMBALMING FLUID, what is it?" Rebekah asked.

"I am not sure. It smells like embalming fluid, but not the kind traditionally used in the United States. I do not smell any formaldehyde in it. It smells like . . ." Dr. Mahesh sniffed the substance again then wiped his fingers on his smock. "It smells like a mixture of oils and herbs used by pandits in my country."

"Pandits?" she asked, pressing against the incision and bringing the expressed oil to her nose.

"Hindu priests, basically. That is what we called them when I was a boy in New Delhi."

"So a pandit uses this stuff to prepare a body before burial?"

"In a manner of speaking. But Hindus are rarely buried. You see, in Hinduism, the individual soul, or *atman*, is what gives the body life. Once the soul is gone, all that is left behind is decomposing tissue. But as long as that tissue remains intact, the soul may still cling to it. That is why Hindus mostly choose cremation over burial. It speeds up the process and guarantees the soul will leave the body to ascend into heaven. It is the job of the pandit to see that all is done properly so the soul may go free."

"Do pandits do the embalming, too?"

"No, no. Most Hindus do not believe in embalming or organ donation. No, the oils I mentioned are used to anoint the body before cremation. They preserve a natural look to the skin until it is cremated. All of the blood and fluids are left inside the body, as they are part of the soul."

"Ah. Do they still practice that?—anointing the body with oil, I mean?" Rebekah asked, hoping she did not come across as cynical.

"Yes, they do. Even with our modern knowledge of pathogens and the importance of organ donation, many still follow the old customs."

"Okay . . . but Mrs. Baugh wasn't Hindi."

He nodded. "That may be true. I am not saying she was. I am merely stating that the embalming fluid in her smells like pandit oil. We will have the lab analyze the fluid more precisely later on. There very well may be more in it than meets the nostrils. Nevertheless, it clearly did a splendid job of preserving this patient. She shows very little sign of decomposition, do you not agree?"

"Yes. Maybe I should use some on my skin," she said with mock exasperation. "It's so hot outside I feel like *I* decompose just walking to and from my car."

"Ridiculous," he scoffed. "You should try this heat with the humidity of India. Then you would *smell* like you were decomposing too."

She punched him playfully on the shoulder. "Thanks a lot."

He winked. "So let us proceed to see if we can discover anything else out of the ordinary with this patient."

As Rebekah switched on the digital recorder, Mahesh repeated a much slower visual inspection of the body from head to toe, describing everything he saw. The only fresh breach in the skin was the embalming suture over the left femoral artery and vein. "Other than this old transplant scar, I do not see any abrasions, contusions, or lacerations. Do you?"

"No," she answered, doing her best to notice any flaw while avoiding the surgical scar. There were hundreds of liver spots and thousands of wrinkles, but nothing untoward on the century-old skin. "There are seven varicose vein clusters on her legs, two of which have burst, and some broken blood vessels on her forearms, but none of them look like they were from blunt trauma."

"I concur. Very good, Sundara." Mahesh then palpated the abdomen. "Hmm. It feels like whoever did this embalming did not perform a body cavity evacuation."

"There's no trocar incision," she said, referring to the hole made two inches above the navel to aspirate the "hollow" organs and internal fluids.

"That may be our lucky break," he said with another wink. "Let us take a look."

Using a scalpel, he made a Y incision beginning from each shoulder joint, joining over the breastbone, and continuing down to the pubis. He had Rebekah use a pair of leverage cutters to separate the ribs from the sternum. The breaks were clean with very little splintering, showing that Mrs. Baugh had strong, healthy bones.

The rest of the autopsy went without a hitch. For a woman over a century old, Mrs. Baugh was in surprisingly good shape. Her lungs were pink and free of clots, her liver was a dark, reddish brown color, her remaining kidney showed some calcification but no stones, and her heart had very little fat on it. It was difficult to determine the complete heath of her organs because there was only residual blood in them. Usually the amount of blood in each organ belied its overall fitness.

Rebekah then checked her eyes. "I think we've got something here. Both orbs are extremely bloodshot and distended."

Mahesh leaned in for a closer look. "What are you thinking, Sundara?"

"She suffocated—or *was* suffocated."

He swabbed a Hemoccult pad in each nostril and placed a few drops of reagent on the samples. "There is dried blood in both nares. That is two out of three for suffocation. All we need is a blood sample to test for CO_2 levels. But since there is no blood in her circulatory system, where might we find it?"

"The heart, obviously," she answered.

Rebekah knew that Sandy loved playing the teacher. As head of the pathology department, he regularly had University of Utah medical students rotate through his morgue. Some caught on quickly; others had to be continually coached. Over the years, he frequently told Rebekah that she was his favorite pupil.

"Clearly the heart is a logical reservoir," he said, "but if the embalming took place with high-pressure equipment, the heart may be devoid of blood."

She thought for a moment, scanning the various organs in the body cavity as she did. "Well, the liver filters all of the body's blood. I doubt *any* embalming system can express all the blood from it. How about we take a liver biopsy and extract blood from that?"

"Sundara, you are a very intelligent young woman. That is exactly what we shall do. If we get enough blood, we shall also run a toxicology screen." He removed the liver and weighed it, recording all his observations in the microphone. He had Rebekah prepare a biopsy of the tissue while he focused on the cadaver. "You know how greatly I think you should continue your studies into medical school. I can almost guarantee your admission."

"You're right," she said, hoping to circumvent the *go back to school* lecture she heard nearly every week. "I probably should. But I'm happy being a diener for the most brilliant pathologist in Utah." *Diener* was the Germanic idiom used for a pathology aide. She didn't care for the term because it sounded subservient, but she knew he liked it because it represented old-school concepts, traditions, and ideals—which was Sandeep Mahesh through and through.

"Just Utah?" he balked, feigning shock.

"Sorry. I meant the whole world."

His deep brown eyes twinkled. "You see how intelligent you are? I swear to Shiva if I had an unmarried son, I would insist he pursue you to the altar."

"Come on, Sandy," she chuckled. "You already know I have a steady boyfriend."

"Yes. And he is a bum!" he snapped with only mild humor. "He should have proposed to you a year long ago. What is his problem? Can he not see what a resplendent catch you are?"

She shrugged. "He was married once before. She died and . . . well, it was heartbreaking. He still has scars he's trying to smooth over." She shrugged again, not meeting the doctor's eyes. "Or maybe . . . he just has cold feet."

"I am terribly sorry, but I cannot accept either premise." He moved to the end of the table and lifted one of Agnes Baugh's ankles. "My patients have cold feet; your boyfriend is just a pigeon."

She gave a wan smile. "I think you mean a 'chicken,' but it's okay," she said, trying to keep her voice carefree. "I'm in no hurry."

"Oh, my dear Sundara. I am sorry for bringing up such a painful subject," he offered sincerely, obviously sensing her remorse. "Let us forget about him for the moment and concentrate on this unfortunate woman."

She nodded but said nothing.

"Let us first drain all the fluid from her circulatory system. I will take a sample to see if I can determine its composition. Then we shall take tissue sections from all the organs for analysis. If this woman was as healthy as she appears, then her premature departure from this life must be reasoned out. Perhaps your chicken boyfriend can help?"

His teasing was relentless, but it helped her to maintain focus. "I've already got him started on it," she said resolutely. "Hopefully, you, me, and the chicken can solve this murder."

"Ah, but *was* it murder? We know she was suffocated, but was it at the hand of a villain or was it accidental?"

Rebekah raised an eyebrow. "So she accidentally suffocated to death but was still able to put coins on her eyes and a handkerchief on her face?"

He guffawed. "Oo, once again you have outwitted me," he said with a deep bow. "I concede to your wisdom, Sundara. Now, let us proceed to uncover all elements of this intriguing conundrum."

CHAPTER 9

JOSH STOPPED TO GRAB A bite at the Maverik on the corner before heading out to look into the cold case assigned to his department. The West Valley police had a very complete file on the incident, but they'd exhausted all their leads and came up with little to show for it. The case was well over a year old. The young man would be eighteen now, living life to the fullest. Instead, he was six feet under in Valley View Cemetery. *What a waste!*

Paxton Harris was born and raised in the Salt Lake valley. He'd always been somewhat of a loner in school and in the neighborhood. His parents thought their son was simply the shy type. Then, just one week after starting high school, his popularity increased, seemingly overnight. His grades plummeted. He started coming home long after nightfall during the week, and sometimes not at all on weekends. During his sophomore year he got arrested for shoplifting beer. His probation was a hit-and-miss affair, with every miss resulting in an extension of his sentence. Every time his parents confronted him, they were met with animosity or rebellious apathy. His peers in the neighborhood said he was now involved in a gang at school, the Archangels. When his parents questioned him about it, his response was a belligerent, "So?"

Three weeks after beginning his junior year, he was found dead behind a strip mall in the heart of the city.

Josh reviewed the file three times, looking for anything that might lead to something previously overlooked. There wasn't much the police had missed. According to the report, no one heard or saw anything on the night in question other than a few suspicious vehicles. There was no mention of why they were considered suspicious. Ballistics said the 9mm slug was fired at close range, possibly from a semiauto pistol. The bullet shattered one rib before entering the heart. A list of suspects had been questioned. All had confirmed alibis. It looked like a dead-end case.

The strip mall was in a section of downtown that looked . . . well, *forgotten*. The shops included a check-loan company, a beauty supply outlet, a pet store that had gone out of business some years back, and a smoke shop. The four tiny shops sat between a national tire and lube franchise and a large dollar store that was owned by a family from Korea. The buildings were in various stages of disrepair, their exteriors tattooed with graffiti. The parking lot was pocked and strewn with litter.

A few Goth-clad teens stood outside the smoke shop casually dragging on cigarettes. Kids that age weren't supposed to have access to tobacco, but that rarely stopped them from acquiring it. There were three males and two females, although it was difficult to tell one gender from the other. They looked sullen, moody, and they treated anyone who passed by with the blatant disdain of youth.

When Josh stepped out of his SUV, all but the oldest-looking one stamped out their smokes. He wasn't in a uniform, but kids these days had a sharp eye for any type of law enforcement—especially the kids who were trying to avoid the law.

The stagnant afternoon air was sweltering. Waves of heat shimmered from the roofs of the cars in the small parking lot. The blacktop felt gummy. The pungent scent of motor oil and sun-baked rubber wafted from the tire and lube center.

Josh locked his car and headed toward the smoke shop.

"Sure is hot today," he said to the oldest one with several lip rings, inch-wide gauged earlobes, and a silver nose ring that resembled the kind a bull wears.

The young man stared at Josh with half-closed eyes. Tendrils of smoke drifted from his nostrils, weaving in and around the nose ring.

"You know, they've proven that smoking kills you," Josh said.

The young man regarded him a moment longer then took a long, defiant drag on his cigarette and let the smoke pour in thick plumes from his nose.

Josh smiled. "Has anyone told you it looks like your face is on fire when you do that?"

The girls made scoffing expulsions of air and rolled their raccoon-painted eyes. One of them made a comment just under her breath. Josh was pretty sure it wasn't a compliment.

"It's your funeral, sport," Josh said with a shrug, wanting to escape the thick, secondhand smoke. "By the way, if any of you kids are under nineteen, in addition to being stupid, smoking is a finable offense. Have a nice day."

He entered the shop and was immediately engulfed in a noxious fog that reeked of tobacco, incense, and something that smelled awfully close to marijuana. *So much for escaping the cancerous haze outside.* An oscillating fan in one corner kept the fog skulking around the small shop like a specter seeking living tissue to inhabit. Josh caught himself involuntarily flinching and holding his breath as it passed over.

A bald, sweaty, overweight man in ratty jeans and a Harley-Davidson tank top sat behind the glass display counter. The bar stool on which he perched looked dangerously close to collapsing under his weight. His goatee was big enough to qualify as a full goat. The glass case offered various items associated with drug use. The items themselves were not illegal, only their intended use; therefore, they were legal to sell. It was one of those gray areas of the law that irked Josh to no end. He perused the materials within the case a minute or two. "So . . . no AC in this place?" he asked without looking up.

"It's out," the shop attendant said in a guttural utterance that didn't quite qualify as articulated language. "You a cop?"

"An investigator," Josh said, removing his badge in a way that also exposed his shoulder holster. "Have you worked here long?"

"Long enough."

"I'd like to ask you a few questions."

"You can ask; don't know that I'll answer. Don't like cops much."

"And I don't like Harleys, but that doesn't mean we can't have a civilized conversation and behave like gentlemen."

The man drew in a long, reverberating snort followed by a thick hawking from deep in his throat. He turned his head to one side and launched a glob of mucus into a trash can.

"I stand corrected," Josh said, feeling a bit green in the face. He turned his back to the CCTV camera over the door, slipped his hand in and out of his blazer pocket, and placed it palm-down on the counter. When he withdrew his hand, a 2×2 ziplock baggie sat on the glass. It was filled with dried fragments of oregano and parsley—but the Harley dude didn't know that.

"Oh my," Josh exclaimed innocently. "Look what I just found in your store. I wonder what it could be."

"You just planted that, man," the attendant blustered.

"Can you prove that?"

The man stood and slid his hands into his pockets. "Look, man, I just work here."

"How long?"

He grumbled angrily. "Four years."

"Do you have a name?"

"Chet."

"So, Chet, you know the regulars who shop here?"

"I guess."

"You remember a kid named Paxton Harris?"

The goatee wriggled as he chewed on his lower lip. "Yeah. That was a bad scene all around, man. Pax was a good kid, ya know? Never gave me no flak . . . to speak of. He had his own battles, but he mostly kept them inside, ya know? I tried not to get involved, okay?"

"They say his death was gang related."

"Yeah," Chet shrugged. "So they say."

Josh looked around the small establishment with a critical eye. An adjacent counter displayed baggies of hooka, a spyce substitute, ephedra, and other herbal products meant to give the user a high. "You get a lot of gang traffic through here?"

"Some." Chet scratched at his hairy shoulder then shoved his hand back in his pocket. His eyes remained glued to the baggie on the counter. "Mostly kids, though. Not many bikers or bangers."

"Do you ever see any rivals mixing it up around here?"

The big man was breathing heavily now, from nerves or the exertion of standing, Josh couldn't tell. He removed a bandana from his back pocket and wiped his glistening pate. "Not really," he answered. "Some posturing, ya know? But it rarely leads to anything."

"Until Paxton."

"Yeah. Until Paxton," he said with some regret. "But that was over a year ago, man. Why're you digging it up again?"

Josh walked to a wall display of ninja throwing stars, samurai swords, butterfly knives, and other bladed weapons. "Just wondering if you might have remembered something you forgot back then. Like you said, Paxton was a good kid."

Chet sat back down, and his stool complained. "Yeah. Now that you mention it. Three, maybe four months after the shooting, a punk kid from the Oriental Posse comes in lookin' for some ninja darts. I had to special order them, which really made him mad 'cause it'd take about a week. He acted like he was gonna get in my face, but he was just a punk, and he knew it. So after a minute he has me order them. He comes back a week later with this seriously hot Asian chick in tow. I mean *seriously* tasty; the complete five-course Chinese takeout *and* a fortune cookie, ya know? So, while he was checkin' out the ninja stuff, this girl was scopin' the scene out the window. She was real nervous-like, right? Real fidgety, like she was gonna blow a gasket. Not hopped up an' twitchy; more like she was afraid of being spotted. At first I thought they were planning on rollin' the place, you know? But that's all they do: he's checkin' out the blades, she's checkin' out the parking lot. Anyways, after a few minutes she turns around and snaps at him. Says, "Let's go, Sun Lim. I don't like chilling in a KZ."

Josh slipped the baggie of herbs back in his pocket and asked, "How'd you know this Sun Lim was with the Oriental Posse?"

"Come on, man. They all have the same buzzed head and tats on the back of their neck. Every cop knows that."

Josh nodded. "By KZ she meant a kill zone?"

"What else?" the big guy grumbled.

"So what'd he do?—the kid, I mean."

"He says, 'The deal is cloroxed.' But when he said it, he held up his hands, like he was showin' *he* had no bloodstains, ya know?"

Josh nodded, comprehending that the perpetrator felt he was bleached clean. Josh then glanced up at the CCTV camera. "You got tapes for that?"

The Harley dude shook his head. "Nothin' that old. The boss wipes the hard drive every other month."

"Ever seen the Asian kid since?"

"Not in here. There's a whole nest of 'em next door, runnin' that dollar store."

"If I bring in some pics, could you look them over?"

Chet leaned forward, trying to act casual, and lowered his voice. "Man, I'm runnin' a shop here. Boss hears I'm cop talkin', I'm on the street, ya dig? Besides, they all look the same to me." He stood and folded his thick arms across his broad chest. "Why don't you go ask 'em next door? They're the ones that did it."

Josh cringed at the racial slurs. "You sure about that?"

"Oh yeah." Chet's voice hardened. "First they come in here an' offer top dollar rent for the place. Ronny Einerson had him a nice auto parts shop there. Decent guy tryin' to feed his wife and kids. Then they hop off the boat an' come in waving free government money they get just for being refugees; the owner sells up an' kicks Ronny out the next day. Now I hear they're tryin' to buy the rest of the mall." He let fly a number of expletives, some of which Josh had never heard before. "No one's job is safe these days—not with all these Hawmoong creepin' around."

"It's pronounced Hmong," Josh said with an edge of censure. "And they probably feel the same way about Harley dudes." He removed one of his business cards. "Call me if you think of anything useful. Regardless, if I don't hear from you in a couple weeks, I'll be back."

The shopkeeper looked the other way without further comment. Josh left his card on the counter and headed for the door.

The multipierced young man and his cronies had vanished. Josh went to his car and removed his blazer. It was easily a hundred degrees outside and 120 inside his Explorer. He sniffed his blazer and cringed. He vainly tried to beat the smoke shop stink from it. No luck.

He tossed his blazer in the passenger seat, cranked up the AC, and began looking for a one-hour dry cleaner. Six blocks later, success. While waiting for his blazer to be fumigated, he texted Rebekah, saying he had some juicy information to share. She probably hadn't heard about Silas Snow yet.

She replied, *Dinner at my place. I'll get pizza. You bring the beer.*

He knew she meant root beer—but not just any root beer. He had to get Hires Big H draft from the brewery on Seventh East. It would be the best part of their meal. Without a doubt she would order some thin-crusted, low-cheese, vegetarian excuse for a pizza. To Josh, if the cheese on one slice didn't cling tenaciously to its neighbor when removed, or if it didn't leave a triangle of grease after lifting it from your napkin, it wasn't real pizza.

The information from Chet mixed with the facts he'd read on Silas Snow. Although the two instances were not related, both stories had huge holes needing to be filled. He knew his focus should be on the Paxton case—that was officially his first assignment—but he also wanted to help Rebekah. Her interest in the Baugh case almost seemed personal. And strangely, somehow he felt one case would help him solve the other.

Josh picked up his phone and dialed headquarters.

"Caldwell, Homicide," said a brusque voice.

"Hey, Trevor, it's Josh. You got a minute?"

Trevor Caldwell had risen through the ranks with Josh. The two often worked together and had developed a mutual respect and camaraderie. "Yeah, sure, Josh. What's up?"

"I need in on the Agnes Baugh and Silas Snow cases."

"Um . . . okay. This crossing into a case you're on?"

"Not really," Josh said, followed with an awkward clearing of his throat. "I'm . . . well, I'm basically doing the state ME a favor. I don't want to step on any toes here; I just want to follow what you're doing and maybe chase down a lead when I find one."

Trevor chuckled. "You always were one for filling your plate with too much work." There was a brief pause on the line before he continued. "Yeah, okay. I'll send you my files. But you'll keep me posted on anything you find, right?"

"That's a promise. Thanks, Trev."

CHAPTER 10

REBEKAH LIVED ON THE TOP floor of an upscale apartment complex near Research Park on the university campus. Salt Lake's east bench afforded a spectacular view of the valley, but it also meant her apartment caught all of the afternoon and evening sun. Luckily, she had reflective glazing on her windows, which greatly reduced the amount of heat coming in.

True to Josh's prophecy, they ate vegetarian take-and-bake as they mulled over a dozen sheets of paper and a couple dozen photographs of the Agnes Baugh and Silas Snow crime scenes. Josh told Rebekah everything Glade had shared about Silas Snow, including the preliminary findings of the EMTs and the hospital. Some of the information was not yet released to the public, but as an assistant to the state ME, she had access to as much classified information as he did, if not more.

Examining the cases side by side made her brows rise high over her eyes. "Okay, now I'm really getting freaked out."

"The similarities are too close to be coincidence," Josh agreed. "Both were healthy senior citizens, both lived alone, both passed away without witnesses, both were embalmed in their own homes, both *look* like they were murdered, and yet no personal effects were missing from either home to indicate robbery or any other motive. In fact, both homes were left relatively undisturbed—except for a dead body, of course."

"Dr. Mahesh and I pretty much confirmed Mrs. Baugh *was* smothered, probably with her own pillow," Rebekah said without looking up. "We're matching the fibers from her pillowcase with those in her sinuses and lungs."

Josh wiped his fingers on his napkin. "Yeah, but wouldn't you find those anyway? I mean, I assume she slept with her face on the pillow every night, right?"

"You find pillowcase fibers in the nostrils but rarely all the way into the sinuses or lungs. As disgusting as they are, nose hairs are meant to function that way—to prevent stuff from getting into the lungs. Particles that far in means she was gasping for breath." Rebekah paused for a sip of root beer. "So, has the CSI team come up with anything from either house?"

"No, nothing." Josh took a bite of pizza and chewed doggedly before swallowing. "What concerns me is that the murders have the same MO and happened only two days apart. It's too early to call these serial killings, but the signs say it's the same guy."

"Are the two victims related to each other?" she wondered.

"I don't think so."

Rebekah stood and slowly paced the dining area while ticking off each fact with a finger. "Okay. So they were both smothered to death. They were both partially embalmed on the spot—but just their circulatory system, no evisceration of the body cavity. No signs of forcible entry in either home. Both victims were old but in relatively great health . . ."

"I feel like we're swimming in circles here," Josh said in frustration, tossing an uneaten slice of pizza back in the box and wiping his fingers. He fixated on the photos of the corpses. "Time to think beyond the bodies. Let's try tackling things like what the deal is with the coins over the eyes and the hankie on the face."

"I looked that up last night," she said, returning to her seat. "It's a practice from ancient Greece. A coin was placed with the dead to pay Charon, the ferryman, to take the deceased across the River Styx to the afterlife. Those who couldn't pay were forced to wander as specters in this world for eternity."

"Okay, but why on the eyes?"

"Dr. Mahesh said that's the way ancient morticians kept the eyes closed during viewing of the body. Nowadays they mostly use superglue; sometimes they'll use custom eye cups under the lids to hold them closed and give them form because the eyes tend to dry out and shrink. Before that they used to sew the eyes shut, which is why early cartoons represented dead people with Xs over their eyes. And before that they used coins or flat stones."

"So whoever did this has some knowledge of modern *and* ancient burial practices."

"It would appear so."

"And the hankie?"

"Anthropology 101, Clouseau. It's part of a burial shroud. Long ago they wrapped the deceased in a shroud and covered the face with a napkin. Some religions still do so today. Even you guys in the police force traditionally cover the faces of victims at the scene of the crime until the EMTs get there. I thought everyone knew that."

"I guess so." Josh wiped his fingers again even though he hadn't retouched his pizza. All this talk of burial practices had him feeling grimy. "I just thought there might be something more to it."

"Like what?"

He shrugged. "Just grabbing at straws, Becks. For instance, neither victim owned the type of hankie found at the scene. We weren't able to lift any prints off the fabric, but we did analyze the material and found it's some high-end linen—not your average cotton snot rag."

"Your tact is underwhelming, Clouseau."

"Thanks. Anyway, we're having the weave analyzed with hopes of locating the manufacturer. If they sell to specific retailers, then it might lead to who's been buying it."

"That seems like a stretch. Lots of people use linen handkerchiefs."

"That's basic forensics," he said with a shrug. "Gather a bunch of threads until you form a pattern that weaves into a blanket that covers everything."

"Wow, good looks, a respectable career, *and* a talent for metaphors. You're quite the catch, detective."

Instead of a smart reply, he picked up both patient demographic reports. "Do you think there's a connection with both victims being Caucasian?"

She leaned back and stretched. "Nothing's out of the question on this one, but I doubt it. My big quandary is why they were only partially embalmed. From a pathological standpoint it doesn't make sense to only drain the circulatory system."

Josh looked up suddenly. "That's it!"

She sat forward. "What?"

"No blood. There was no blood at either crime scene." He stood and began pacing just as she had moments before.

"Well, yeah. Their circulatory systems were filled with homemade embalming fluid. So?"

"So where is the blood?"

She cocked her head to one side. "Ah. You mean someone killed them so they could *harvest* their blood?"

"Precisely."

"But . . . why?"

"I was hoping you could tell me."

CHAPTER 11

Wednesday

THE FOLLOWING MORNING, REBEKAH PULLED up the file on Agnes Baugh and reviewed the first analyses. Although there was minimal volume found in her system, they were able to extract about 3ccs, enough to get a blood type and test for possible toxins. The latter proved negative—her blood containing nothing dangerous or unusual, other than strange fluid in the rest of her circulatory system.

Her blood type was AB-positive, which was the second rarest among U.S. Caucasians—only about three percent of the population had it. A-positive and O-positive were the most common, with AB-negative the rarest.

Mrs. Baugh's blood type was the second factor with which Rebekah felt an unwelcome connection. She knew it was mere coincidence—that it didn't mean a thing—but a sharp twinge of angst hit her stomach without warning. She closed her eyes and tried to concentrate on something else—anything else. *Don't go there, Rebekah*, she commanded herself. *Not again.* But it did no good—her repressed anxiety lashing out like a cobra strike. Pressing her head between her palms, she focused on controlling her shallow respiration—only to realize she wasn't breathing at all. Memories flooded her mind, strangling her logic and sensibility. She pushed back from her desk and plodded to a drinking fountain. Swallowing large gulps of cold water helped only a little. With her head bent over the fountain, she forced herself to breathe in and out. Each inhalation felt like a hundred-pound weight rested atop her chest—like she was expelling razor blades. She burst into an adjacent restroom and splashed cold water on her face. Then, steeling herself, she stood close to the mirror and stared into her eyes.

"It was not your fault," she said through clenched teeth. The image staring back at her did not believe her. She hardened her scowl and repeated, "It was *not* your fault."

Little by little, as the negative thoughts dissipated from her mind, her anxiety began to abate. Her pupils gradually contracted, and her chest slowly relaxed. She took a step back from the mirror and repeated, "It was not your fault." Her voice was still tense, but it was also reassuring. When her shoulders loosened and her breathing steadied, she took a third step back. "It was not your fault," she reiterated, this time with a calm assurance that filled her with confidence. "Now get back to work."

She left the restroom and headed back to her desk with a purposeful stride. Keeping busy was the best way to keep the past in the past.

She started lining up facts, examining details, comparing anomalies and similarities. The Baugh case was rife with unknowns. What she needed was to bounce her thoughts off someone with an eye for these things.

She called Josh at his office.

"Hey, gorgeous. What's—"

"Mrs. Baugh was AB-positive," she said, cutting him off.

"Wow, jumping right in again. I don't know why that continues to surprise me. By the way, I'm fine. How's your day going?"

"This is important, Josh. Her blood tests are significant. There were no toxins or byproducts of poisoning in her system, but she *did* have a high amount of CO_2, which confirms she suffocated."

"AB-positive, huh? That's a universal donor, right?"

"The plasma is universal but not the red blood cells. ABs are usually thought of as universal *acceptors*. It's the O-types that are universal donors," she explained.

"Okay. So why's that important?"

"I—" She stopped cold. Why *was* it important? Other than it being a unique blood type, she hadn't decided that it *did* factor into the mystery. "I'm not sure why . . . but I know it is. Look, from a mathematical standpoint, it's enormously against the odds. I mean, the chances of someone reaching a hundred years old are rare enough. But the chances of someone being AB-positive are even rarer because there're so few of them. Put those two together in the same person and you've got a statistical anomaly."

"Okay, I think I see where you're going with this. Hang on a sec." There was a pause on the line through which she could hear the tapping of a keyboard. "Son of a gun. Call your bookie, sweetheart, you're about to hit the jackpot."

"What?"

"Guess what blood type Silas Snow was?"

"No way. AB-positive?"

"Bingo." He paused again. "Out of curiosity, there isn't a national shortage of AB-positive blood, is there?"

Rebekah felt a renewed surge of anxiety but forced it down by concentrating on Josh's question. "Not that I'm aware of. There's always need for A and O, but the demand for AB is not that great because they can accept from A *and* B *and* O, and yet they can only *donate* to another AB."

"What about the plasma, then?" he asked. "You said they can donate plasma without a hitch."

She nodded, even though he couldn't see the action over the phone. "Yes, mostly. Plasma is readily obtained from all blood types because there's rarely a rejection to it. It's the antigens on the red blood cells that create the antibodies associated with rejection. That's why there's no reason to specifically seek out AB-positive plasma."

"Huh?"

Rebekah could picture Josh's face scrunched in concentration. It was such a cute face, whatever the expression.

"But this blood-type angle *does* give us a good place to start," Josh continued. "Do you have a database that lists known blood types per county in Utah?"

"I think so. The Red Cross keeps track of that stuff, and I think all the hospitals in the state do too. I'm pretty sure most of it is confidential per HIPAA, but I'll look into it. Why? What are you thinking, Clouseau?"

She heard a chuff of air across the line. "First, I'm thinking you need to find me a new nickname."

Rebekah's former angst was all but gone. It felt like they were actually onto something. Besides, talking to Josh *always* made her feel better—especially when she had him on the defensive. "A new nickname? Okay. How about 'snuggle bug' or 'cinnamon bear'?"

This time she heard a gag. "We'll discuss that later. In the meantime, I'll search the police files for any other cases that involved people with AB-positive blood. I have a strong feeling something's going to tie into these two deaths."

"Murders," she corrected.

"*Alleged.* But I think you're right."

"Call me the minute you get anything."

"Sure thing, Becks. See you for lunch?"

"Can't, sweetie. I'm booked all day here."

She could feel his disappointment over the phone. It was endearing.

"No problem. Call me if anything changes, okay?"

"Definitely. Love you, Clouseau."

Rebekah disconnected and immediately began searching her database for records of known blood types throughout the state. The Red Cross had a list of all blood banks in the Intermountain area, but it didn't list quantities or types available at each site.

Since the ME had accessibility to all hospitals in Utah, she entered a search for known quantities of AB-positive blood available per facility. When the search ended, her hand reflexively came to her mouth. "You've got to be kidding," she whispered aloud.

CHAPTER 12

JOSH HAD TEAMED UP WITH Rebekah on several cases in the past. Mostly it was the sharing of information the other couldn't speedily access. This time Josh knew they were on equal ground, and yet he felt like he was still trying to catch up. His angle, of course, was criminology—hers, obviously, medical. Only, she seemed to be attacking this case with extra emotion. Normally she accepted criminal actions of this sort as proof of humanity's steady deterioration. But with the Baugh case, it seemed more personal.

"Yo, Logan, you comin' ta the game tonight or what?" Nick Lonardo asked from a desk diagonal to his.

Nick was an implant from New Jersey who plied his native accent like an artist wielded a brush—especially when trying to be extra charismatic. He'd been with the department just over three years. He and Josh had worked well together, but the friendship didn't extend beyond the office. Nick was a sports enthusiast whose world revolved around the Jazz, Real Salt Lake, and the Bees. Josh enjoyed the odd game now and then, but he wasn't a diehard fan of any team. Some of that had to do with Rebekah. Sports weren't high on her list of pastimes either.

"What game?" Josh asked.

"Jazz verses Trail Blazers, ya gumba." Nick smacked his own forehead in frustration. "You remember the Jazz, right? They play basketball in that big arena a few blocks from here?"

"Oh yeah," Josh said, hoping he could avoid another lecture. "Not tonight, thanks."

"Please tell me you's not gonna spend another evenin' with CK. Man, don't she make yous feel like one of the living dead when she's aroun'?"

Josh shook his head—but he was smiling. "No, she doesn't. And, coincidentally, if she ever finds out you call her the Crypt Keeper, we're both dead men."

With an air of condescension, Nick rounded his desk and sat on the edge of Josh's.

Here comes the lecture.

"Dude, you should just marry her and get it over with, ya know what I'm sayin'? Once she's hitched, yous're off da hook and can spend more time with your bros."

Josh frowned at the logic—or lack thereof. He favored Nick with a look of bewilderment. "Do you realize how little sense that makes?"

"No, I mean it. Listen to me. Yous're with her all da time because yous're tryin' to woo her, am I right? I mean, I know I calls her the Crypt Keeper 'cause she works with dead guys, but everyone knows she's A-1 primo merchandise, if ya don't mind me sayin'." He hummed *um-um* while snapping his fingers with a whip of his forearm. "You see, when yous just dating, yous're pretty much bagged, *capisce*? Gotta do everything just right, 'cause single women're always scannin' for mooks in boss's clothing, ya know what I'm sayin'? One mistake and you show up like a bogie on the radar: *ping*! Loser alert! Loser alert!" he said in a staticy voice, as if coming from a loudspeaker. "But! Yous puts a ring on her finger, it jams the radar, my friend. And then ya won't have ta work so hard tryin' ta get her 'cause yous already got her. And then she *has* ta cut you some slack—even if yous ends up *being* a lowlife gumba."

Josh closed his eyes and pinched the bridge of his nose. "Nope, that didn't help either. Sorry. You go to the game without me. I'll take my chances with Rebekah."

Nick raised his hands toward the ceiling. "May the Blessed Virgin help ya, *mio amico*. Yous're *so completely* bagged. Totally whipped. Admit it. Call me a liar."

Josh smiled and shrugged. "Nope. You're right."

Nick pantomimed slapping handcuffs on his wrists and, with his arms stretched out in front, led himself back to his desk.

Josh knew what his friend was trying to say, but he wasn't going to admit it to him. Ever since he'd started dating Rebekah, his man-friend time had become almost nonexistent. But he didn't mind. His time with Rebekah was filled with one surprise after another, each one better than the last. And yet, Nick *did* have one valid point. Why *didn't* he ask her to marry him?

He knew the answer: Loren.

Josh and Rebekah came from such different backgrounds, and yet they had so much in common. Both of their lives started out ideally, but both ended up marred by tragedy: she lost her mother at eighteen, the year of her graduation; he lost his wife at twenty-three, one year after their honeymoon.

Josh had returned from his mission to what was supposed to be a life filled with happiness. He met Loren at Salt Lake Community College. They dated for eight months before marrying in the Jordan River Temple. They went on their honeymoon to Acapulco—a gift from her parents. On their way home, Loren began to experience intestinal pains. Her doctor suspected traveler's diarrhea. He put her on antibiotics and antidiarrheals, told her to keep hydrated and to simply "ride it out." But the pains and cramping increased in frequency and intensity. When her stool sample tested positive for tapeworms, he prescribed Vermox tabs. They didn't seem to help. Then came the headaches—severe to the point of vomiting and passing out. She lost weight exponentially. Her head constantly felt like it was going to explode. She became disoriented, delusional.

One evening she got up from the couch, stumbled, and hit her head on the end table. Just a bump—not even hard enough to break the skin—but she crumpled to the floor and within minutes stopped breathing. The EMTs could not revive her. It wasn't until her autopsy that they found several hydatid cysts in her brain, one of which had ruptured. The doctors called it polycystic echinococcosis, a "hyper tapeworm." They figured she picked it up from eating contaminated food in Mexico. Drugs were almost useless against the parasite. Surgery was normally the best option for removal, but it was also the most dangerous. The chances of rupturing the delicate cysts were high and almost guaranteed subsequent death. The medical examiner concluded that the cyst had burst when Loren hit her head. He also said he found several smaller cysts in her liver, spleen, and lungs. In an attempt at consolation, he said it was best she died so early in the infestation. Some polycystic infections last for years and cause constant, excruciating pain.

But that did little to comfort Josh. And the thought of losing someone that close again terrified him.

CHAPTER 13

Josh's cell phone rang. It was Rebekah. "Hey, Becks. What'd you find?"

She gave a short laugh. "You're not going to believe this."

"Try me."

"Utah has one of the highest incidences of AB blood in the U.S. The highest is California, but that's probably because they have the highest population base. Then I found out which state has the highest number of centenarians. Guess who wins?"

"Utah?"

"Nope, California again—but not across the entire state. Loma Linda, California, has a citizenry that cranks out the centenarians like crazy."

"Really?" Josh though for a moment, trying to mentally line up the facts. "Is Loma Linda some place up in the mountains, like where the giant redwoods grow?"

"That's Sequoia National Park, Clouseau, up above Sacramento. Loma Linda is a city just east of LA," she said with a snort of incredulity. "So much for 'clean environment' playing a role in longevity."

"That *is* strange. So what is it, then—some sort of retirement community?"

"Yeah, sort of. But get this: the states that have the most centenarians *per capita* are Iowa, South Dakota, and Nebraska."

"Good old wholesome Midwest stock, huh?" Josh supposed aloud. "So where does Utah fall on the centenarian chart?"

"That's what I can't figure out. We're near the *bottom* of the list. You'd think with our predominately LDS population living the Word of Wisdom, we'd live longer than most others, but apparently that's not always the case. I haven't looked into why just yet, but I'll try to before I leave today. I'm assisting Dr. Mahesh on another autopsy, and I have a ton of lab work I need to process before I leave tonight. So . . . can we give this evening a miss?"

Josh sighed. "Sure, babe. I'll just run down to the 7-11 for some Cheez Whiz and crackers."

He heard a clench-toothed hiss across the line. "It just occurred to me why some Utahns are at the bottom of the centenarian list. And we claim to be such a 'healthy' people."

"Hey, I'm *very* healthy. It's probably my superior genetics and my wholesome mind."

She snorted again. For one so pretty, it was a decidedly unattractive sound—and yet, kind of endearing at the same time. "Right. Now I know why there aren't any former homicide investigators succeeding as stand-up comics."

He laughed. "Okay, okay, I get your point. I'll eat at Denny's instead."

"Ugh. I give up. You really know how to drive a girl batty, don't you?" Without waiting for a response, she asked, "Have you found any other homicides involving AB blood types?" Her voice was suddenly hesitant now—almost as if she didn't want to know.

"Afraid not. I've been juggling three different cases today, one of which is the Silas Snow investigation. You should be getting him tomorrow evening, by the way."

"Yeah, I saw that on the roster," she acknowledged. "The Washington County ME estimates his time of death late Sunday evening or early Monday morning . . . but they didn't find him until Tuesday?"

"Yeah."

"Well, his report didn't mention any tissue decomposition or lividity in spite of the fact that it's been averaging 110 degrees down there."

"He probably had AC in his apartment. I'll check it out," Josh promised. "Hey, something you said a minute ago gave me another thought. Looking for a specific blood type in the homicide archives is going to be needle-in-a-haystack stuff. Maybe I'll put a rookie on it. In the meantime, I think I'll look into deaths of centenarians in general. There may be a few that slipped through the cracks."

"What do you mean?"

"You know—those who died suspiciously but were not handed over to homicide."

There was a slight pause. "But I thought all 'suspicious' deaths went to you guys."

"Not if the local law enforcement takes care of it to their satisfaction. Quite often, families of the deceased don't want the publicity. You know how invasive paparazzi can be."

"Oh yeah—only too well. Well, let me know what you find, Clouseau. It's important."

"Sure, Becks." He stalled as he tried to figure the best way to ask his next question. Their relationship had always been open and honest. Few were the times they had held anything back from each other. But Rebekah seemed to be doing so now. "Hey . . . you want to tell me *why* this case is so important to you?"

Her pause this time was uncomfortable. He knew she was there; he could hear her breathing. The inhalations were sharp, the exhalations tight. "Becks?"

"Yeah. Um, give me some time on that one, okay?" It was a plea—not whiney or plaintive, but still asked with the same intensity. More of a request between close friends than an appeal.

"Sure, babe."

"Thanks, sweetie. You're the best."

Josh closed his phone and stared at it. Because they'd been dating for so long, he knew quite a bit about Rebekah Smith. He knew her mother's death still pained her on a level deeper than the loss of a loved one usually did. He knew her likes and dislikes, her strengths and her foibles. He knew just how much he could tease her on some subjects and when to back off.

This was one of those times. And because it bothered her so much, it bothered him. He hated seeing her so troubled, so pensive. Perhaps discovering more about the two bizarre deaths would help heal the wound she'd been protecting all these years. That's what she needed to do—bring it to the surface and face it head on. But perhaps doing so would open her wound afresh and cause her even more pain . . .

He clenched his fists and banged them on his desktop. Who was he to lecture *anyone* about not dealing with repressed sorrows? He would give her the time she needed because *he* still needed some time for his own demons.

Josh went to Google to begin his search. He was determined to give Rebekah something she could latch onto with confidence . . . for both of their sakes.

CHAPTER 14

LESTER JOHNSON WAS A CELEBRITY at Avalon Manor. Having just turned a hundred, he was the assisted living center's oldest resident. As such he'd been visited by more people that day than he had in the last ten years: News reporters, a ninety-three-year-old sister, a couple of distant relatives, the entire nursing staff, and housekeeping personnel. Even the mayor of Sandy, Utah, made an appearance—most likely to preen in front of the cameras. Regrettably, none of Lester's children, grandchildren, or great-grandchildren showed up.

A huge sheet cake resembled a bonfire. The pyrotechnic confection boasted white frosting with blue-gel lettering declaring, *Happy Birthday Lester. Best wishes on the next one hundred years!* The centenarian gave three heroic attempts to blow out his candles. Yet despite his wheezing exhalations accompanied by generous flecks of spittle, nearly two-thirds of the candles remained lit. Nevertheless, the small crowd in the dinning hall applauded his efforts. The first piece of cake went to the birthday boy. No one jumped to accept the second.

Damien Slade, Avalon's newest LPN, was surprised the overhead sprinkler system hadn't triggered. He stood in the background, not wanting to attract too much attention. It wasn't hard. At five seven, 150 pounds, with thinning red hair and thick, black-rimmed glasses, and pasty skin, he was as unassuming as a wart on a toad's back. The only thing that set him apart was when he spoke. Ever since he could remember, and much to his chagrin, he stuttered—especially when he was nervous. It'd been the brunt of endless teasing growing up, and still continued when around heartless, mean people. That's why he liked working in nursing homes. The old folks rarely gave him flak about his disability.

"Speech, Lester!" one of the nurses hollered.

Lester waved her off with a motion that came close to an obscene gesture then returned to his cake. Everyone laughed good-naturedly.

Damien's fake smile hid his true concern for Lester. The centenarian's birthday cake was wishful thinking. With uncommon luck, the old guy *might* live another year or two at best. The LPN had seen enough senior citizens at this stage of life to know the signs of a life near completion.

Lester had been a resident of Avalon Manor for nearly eleven years. His children had placed him there because none of the four had the wherewithal to take care of him. At least that's what they claimed. But Lester wasn't a time-sapping invalid. For a hundred years old, he was surprisingly lucid and fit. With the aid of a walker, he regularly went for strolls around the manor's courtyard, identifying birds by their individual songs, flowers by their petals. When not nature-watching, he always had his face in a book. He especially loved Louis L'Amour. Lester said his two remaining pleasures in life were the outdoors and reading. He didn't make friends easily, but the ones he had were friends for life. It wasn't that he was off-putting or cantankerous; he merely liked his private time as much as random socializing.

That's why the chaotic clamor in the dining hall that evening was wearing on him, Damien surmised.

"What's your secret to a long life?" was the ubiquitous question.

"An honest day's work," was his pat answer.

As Lester answered maudlin questions between bites of cake, Damien continued to smile at the nurses and other residents. The LPN turned down one offer after another for a piece of birthday cake, claiming he was watching his blood sugar levels. In reality, he was keeping a close eye on Lester. As the newbie on the staff, everyone was surprised at how easily Damien had gained the old man's confidence. But he wasn't surprised. He'd always had a way with people of that generation.

As soon as he'd finished his piece of cake, Lester gave Damien a knowing glance. The LPN moved behind the wheelchair and offered apologies on behalf of the birthday boy. It's near his bedtime, you see. Too much excitement is bad for his constitution. He always takes his heart medicine at this hour. No, he can't take it here; it's not administered orally.

Wheeling Lester to his room, Damien whistled "Red River Valley." He knew the old man loved the tune. Lester Johnson was a dry farmer from long, long ago, just like his daddy and his daddy's daddy. He'd worked hard all his life on the family farm. Grandpa had started out by growing wheat on a high Colorado plateau. By the time Lester began to run the operation, they had developed an amazingly hearty strain of wheat that could withstand early frost, drought, and wind. It even proved insect resistant. The entire 1,000 acres of prime Colorado topsoil was worth a fortune, but the patent to their wheat seed was worth even more. A decade and a half past standard retirement age, Lester finally decided his farming days were over. He deeded the farm and shares of ownership of the registered seed equally among his four children, hoping one of them would carry on the family legacy. Within a year, the land, the house, and the patent were sold. Lester was placed in Avalon Manor in Sandy, Utah, because his sister lived nearby. He didn't feel the need for assisted living, but his children had all moved to million-dollar seaside estates, and he didn't want to leave his beloved Rocky Mountains. Besides, the kids had contracted with Avalon Manor to care for Lester as long as he lived—and he wanted to make them pay for a long, long, *long* time.

No one had expected him to make it to a hundred.

"That was one b-big mess, eh, Lester?" Damien said, leaning in close.

"You're tellin' me, son," he replied. "Never did cotton much to birthday parties. What's the big dag-burned deal about gettin' old anyhow?"

"You g-got me."

"Well, just get me back to my room pronto. I'm in the middle of another Louis L'Amour, an' it's a hoot an' a holler better'n listenin' to a buncha numbskulls cacklin' on about how wonderful it is to get old."

"I b-bet Mr. L'Amour would know how t-to handle them."

"Dang tootin'. Jus' like this book I'm a-readin' now. Six cattle rustlers have just sauntered into Luke's campsite pretty as you please, an' all he's got is his pappy's Henry rifle with only one bullet and a Comanche tomahawk."

Damien chuckled. "Lester, y-you've read each one of those b-books at least a d-dozen times. You know how it's g-gonna end. Where's the ap-peal anymore?"

"The appeal comes from a good, uncomplicated story where the nice guy always wins, where the women are wholesome an' pert, and the men are *real* men. And they ain't gettin' naked every other page neither! You should read 'em sometime, son. I got me just about every L'Amour ever written."

The LPN patted his charge on the shoulder. "T-tell you what. You leave them to m-me in your will, and I p-promise to read them. Okay?"

"Then you'd best learn how to read in the dark and breathe dirt," Lester chided. "I'm havin' 'em buried with me when I check out."

Damien burst out laughing. "Oh, r-really? Well, w-what if they won't let you r-read Louis L'Amour in heaven?"

"Then dip me in million-proof sunblock before you plant me, an' I'll gladly go the other direction. Can't be much worse than the last dozen years here."

As they turned in to Lester's suite, the centenarian struggled out of the wheelchair and moved to a recliner next to the window. The view was a third-floor panorama of downtown Sandy. The somber shades of dusk could barely be discerned beyond the brightly lit soccer stadium and glaring billboards. Harsh traffic sounds penetrated the glazed window. Below, cars and trucks moved like noisy molasses.

"Talk about havin' no appeal," the old man grumbled. He shook his head as wistful reminiscence filled his eyes. "This is just like my hometown back in Colorada. I still remember how it used to look back in 1922 when I was just a tyke. The town was alive and neighborly then. Everyone was your friend—didn't matter who you were. Nowadays everyone is afraid of their own shadow—especially here. I visited this place a time or two back in the day when we was selling grain. Right neighborly place back then. Now just look at it! All them big modern buildings and that silly falderal they play kickball in."

"It's called soccer," Damien corrected.

"I don't give a flying fig what they call it. The place looks like a covered wagon with a glandular problem. I'll tell you something, son: all them flashy cars and trucks? Seems like everyone's in too big'a dag-burned hurry to care a lick about the guy next to him. Nobody'll look you in the eye. An' nobody'll be your friend unless they get something out of it."

Damien moved behind him and helped him stand. "Come on, Lester. Let's get you into b-bed. This day is supposed to be happy, not rem-morseful. D-don't think of everything that's g-gone bad over the years; think of all you've b-been able to experience that so m-many others haven't. I know a lot of p-people who are jealous of your l-longevity."

Lester harrumphed, but his eyes reflected gratitude toward the young man who'd become such a good friend in such a short time. "You're right, Damien. Maybe all's I need is a good night's sleep."

The hundred-year-old struggled into his pajamas, placed his teeth in a soaking solution, and slid under the covers. The LPN tucked the sheets tightly around him and drew the curtains to block out the annoying lights and traffic noises. He then returned to the centenarian's side.

"Read to me, will ya, son?"

The younger man looked down with soft eyes. He felt such compassion for the old man. "Sure, L-Lester. Where's that L'Amour b-book?"

He pointed a bony finger to the nightstand.

Damien opened the drawer and found the well-worn paperback with a bookmark indicating Lester's place in the story. He drew up a chair and began reading. Westerns were usually not to his liking, but he did his best to put emotion into the characters and narrative. Despite that, Lester fell asleep within a half hour.

"Good night, old m-man," the LPN said with moist eyes. "Ton-night, your life will cont-tinue in ways you never dreamed possible. I p-promise."

CHAPTER 15

Thursday

REBEKAH ASSISTED DR. MAHESH WITH the autopsy of a John Doe, but she just couldn't get into the cadaver. She snorted. Better rephrase that. Her hands were *in* the cadaver—she just wasn't into the procedure. Her movements were mechanical, her responses rote.

They were working on a homeless man, approximately sixty years old, who'd been found in an alley in downtown Salt Lake. The police report indicated no apparent cause of death at the scene. He was dressed in ratty slacks, a T-shirt, no shoes. He was five ten, 117 pounds. There was no drug paraphernalia or indication of foul play, but there were a number of empty wine and liquor bottles and spent cans of beer. He carried no identification. No one in the area knew him.

When they completed the dissection, weighed and replaced the various organs, Dr. Mahesh asked, "Where is my Sundara this morning?"

She looked up. "Sorry?"

"You seem terribly preoccupied."

"Oh. Sorry," she repeated with a sigh. "Did you ask me something?"

"Yes. We need to confirm the cause of death of this John Doe. Do you have any suppositions thus far?"

She shook her head. "I guess I'm not into playing the student today. If we can just finish—"

"We are all students," he interrupted. "We all seek wisdom. But remember, as a great teacher of mine once said, wisdom is like a nanny goat's udder. You get nothing out of it unless you give it a good tug."

She returned a slight smile, genuinely appreciating her boss's efforts to help her focus. "If that's some ancient Hindu maxim for encouragement, you'll have to do better," she smirked. "Exactly what are you saying?"

"Seeking the answers to one mystery may answer the questions of another."

"Wow. That's deep."

"No, it is *San*deep. I just made it up. Tell me, isn't it the most extraordinary thing you have heard today?" His dark eyes twinkled with self-amusement.

"My life will never be the same."

He barked out a laugh. "That is fantastic. Now that we are on the same page, tell me what happened to this old man."

She looked at the man's organs, the condition of the body, and other indicators of death, but nothing came to mind. Every little detail reminded her of Agnes Baugh—and Agnes Baugh reminded her of her past.

She shook her head to concentrate. "Okay, let's see . . . He was found near several empty liquor bottles, so one could assume alcohol poisoning. And yet his initial tox screen showed only a slightly elevated blood alcohol level." She paused for a full minute, her eyes searching but finding nothing. She exhaled slowly. "I'm sorry, Sandy. I'm just not seeing it."

Sandy shifted his weight and cocked his head to one side. "Sometimes, if you do not see what you want, first see what you do *not* want."

Her eyebrows lifted in an expression of regret. "I'm sorry. I'm afraid I'm just not with it this morning. What should I *not* want to see?"

"The first rule of the medical examiner: If the cause of death is not obvious, eliminate what is." He passed his hand, palm up, over the body, like a jeweler displaying his wares. "How did this patient *not* die?"

"Ah. Well, the external examination didn't reveal any stab or gunshot wounds, or excessive bruising or strangulation marks, so we can assume Mr. Doe wasn't a victim of random or premeditated violence." She leaned down for a closer examination of the skin. "There are some tiny lacerations on his feet and arms, but they don't look like needle marks, and the urine dip didn't show any drug use . . ."

"The cuts are very small and v-shaped, are they not?"

Reexamining his feet, she nodded. "Yes, for the most part."

"Those are rat bites. I suspect they happened fairly recently because they do not yet show signs of infection. But does it not also suggest that he was motionless for some time?"

"Ah—the rats lost their fear of him."

"That is precisely correct. The advanced lividity along his back and the lack of rigor mortis reveals he has been dead for at least three to four days. So then how *did* he die?"

Rebekah was quickly warming to Sandeep's coaching. "Well, there *are* some scrapes and bruises on his elbows and knees, but that could be because he lived on the streets. And there was a small contusion on the back of his head but no skull damage or brain hemorrhaging, so he may simply have fallen."

"Very, very good, Sundara. But did a bump to his noggin kill him, or is there more to this baffling conundrum than meets the eye?"

She inspected each internal organ with renewed concentration. "There was excessive fluid in his lungs and his CO_2 levels were elevated . . . but according to the police report, he wasn't found near any water, and his clothes weren't wet, so he didn't drown . . . but he may have asphyxiated. His liver was only slightly cirrhotic, but it is too soon to tell if he was a chronic alcoholic, despite the fact that he was inebriated when he died. We'll know for sure when the complete toxicology labs come back. I see no internal hemorrhaging . . . and the intestines were nearly empty, which means he hadn't had a decent meal for at least three days before his death."

"Yes, yes, that is all very correct. Now look closely at the vessels of his heart."

She again looked and noticed the blood vessels were distended, some broken. That *could* mean a coronary event of some kind . . .

"You recognized the bite marks on his feet, but did you also notice his ankles are swollen and discolored beyond normal lividity?" Mahesh prompted. "And his lungs were filled with excessive fluid . . . ?"

It suddenly came to her. "Ah. Congestive heart failure."

"I concur. And so we can conclude that this old man died of natural causes."

"And all alone," she added softly.

Mahesh asked her to close the body and excused himself to prep for his next patient, but Rebekah could not bring herself to finish the procedure. She asked another assistant to stitch up the Y incision and prepare it for cremation. She washed up and returned to her desk, still very curious—and apprehensive—about Silas Snow's upcoming autopsy.

Her computer manifest indicated that he would be delivered at 1500 hours. It was currently just past noon. *Shoot.* That didn't give her much time.

She was slogging through a stack of autopsy manifests when her cell phone rang. It was Josh.

"Hey Clouseau, I hope you have some good news for me," she said with despondency.

"I do . . . sort of. What's wrong?"

"Oh, we just confirmed the death of another old, lonely homeless guy."

"Getting personally involved again, huh? How many times have you lectured *me* about that?"

She placed her forehead in her palm and closed her eyes. "You're absolutely right. You got me."

"Wow. I'm going to mark this in my journal as the day Rebekah Smith admitted *I* was right and *she* was wrong."

"Don't push it, detective. I merely said you were right; I didn't say anything about me being wrong. Now, how about giving me that good news?"

"Okay. But just remember *I* didn't say it was good, you did. We have another embalmed centenarian."

Her eyes flew open. "Say that again."

"I just got a call from the Sandy police. A nursing home down there just found one of their patients dead in his room, all dressed out and ready for a viewing. The EMTs came and verified he has no blood in his veins. Plus, he had a hankie over his face and coins on his eyes. Looks like we've got an honest-to-goodness serial psycho on our hands."

She was on her feet. Her heart slammed against her sternum. "Tell them not to move the body or touch it or anything else in the room," she almost shouted.

"O—okay," he stammered. "It's now officially a crime scene, so no one will go in without authorization. Why? What've you got?"

"Nothing. But I'll let you know when I find out."

CHAPTER 16

SKIPPING LUNCH, REBEKAH HEADED TO Avalon Manor. She wasn't sure what she hoped to find at the assisted living center, or even if the trip would be worthwhile. But she felt she *had* to go.

Avalon Manor sat back from the west arm of Dimple Dell Park in Sandy. The faux plantation façade faced the park and boasted a full porch that held lots of white wicker furniture and numerous hanging baskets overflowing with petunia, sweet pea, and fern. Mature willows lined a 300-foot driveway accessed through a wrought-iron portico. It was the picture of Southern comfort and elegance. The backside of the building, however, was expressionless white stucco that overlooked an expanse of urban sprawl.

Rebekah entered the main lobby and halted. She assumed an edifice with such an ostentatious façade would have an equally flamboyant interior. Quite to the contrary, the lobby was unpretentious and efficient. The waiting area offered functional furniture, and cream-colored walls held impressionistic artwork. A plaque behind the reception counter showed a picture of the Resident of the Month—in this case, eighty-one-year-old Alice Sizemore. The woman was pale and wrinkled, but she had a brilliant twinkle in her blue eyes that belied a still-youthful mind. Several other plaques displayed certificates of quality and professionalism bestowed on the assisted living center over the years. One was from the National Endowment for the Aging.

"M-may I help you?" asked a thin man in scrubs from behind the counter.

Rebekah refocused her attention to the task at hand. She flashed a badge that showed she worked for the state medical examiner. "I need to see the body of Lester Johnson, please."

The man blanched then picked up a phone and spoke in whispers. He grunted a few times and stuttered a lot. The poor guy was probably scared. Nursing homes were frequently audited for adherence to state licensing standards. Having a government official arrive unannounced was a sure way to put any staff member on edge.

"Yes, m-ma'am," he said into the phone before hanging up. "If y-you'll p-p-please take a seat, Dr. Smith, someone will b-be right with you."

Rebekah probably should have corrected the nervous guy about her true title, but she kind of liked the sound of "Dr. Smith." Besides, she never actually *said* she was a doctor, so they couldn't nail her for impersonating a state physician.

Glancing at his nametag, she said, "Thank you, Damien," and moved to the waiting area.

After only a few moments in a magazine, she heard a firm voice say, "Dr. Smith?"

Rebekah stared up at the most formidable woman she'd ever seen. The matron stood only about five three and probably weighed in around 250 pounds—but very little of it looked like fat. She had a small head resting on broad shoulders, stout legs, and close-set, ferret-like eyes. She looked like a block of granite, as thick as any of those shaping the Salt Lake Temple. A lanyard hung from her nonexistent neck identifying her as Ms. Mossberg.

Rebekah stood, offering her right hand while flashing her ID with the left. "Hello, Ms. Mossberg, I'm Miss Smith, from the state medical examiner."

She did her best to sound confident, but she couldn't hide a quaver of uncertainty in her voice. Ms. Mossberg remained fixed to the floor, her sturdy legs planted like tree trunks, her balled fists resting on unyielding hips. After a long, breathless pause, she took Rebekah's hand in a bone-crushing grip.

"So it's *Miss* Smith, not *doctor*. I see. Pleased to meet you," she said in a tone that challenged the word *pleased*. "I'm Ms. Mossberg, director of operations at Avalon Manor. Follow me."

Passing the reception counter, they entered an office as austere as the woman occupying it. Her desk was Spartan, her shelves utilitarian. She pointed to a seat and rounded her desk to a chair of her own.

"What can I do for the ME's office?"

"I'm here to see the body of Lester Johnson. I assume he's still in his room and that the room is secured?"

She hesitated. "Yes."

"Good. I'd like to see him now, please."

Her second hesitation was accentuated with narrowed eyes. "I'm afraid that's not allowed," she said with an arrogant chuckle.

The belligerence in the director's reply triggered Rebekah's ire. "Perhaps I wasn't clear. I'm with the state medical examiner's office, Ms. Mossberg—"

"I saw your credentials, Miss Smith. I *can* read. However, I was given specific instructions by the Sandy police not to allow *anyone* near the body—"

"The medical examiner has jurisdiction in these matters," Rebekah cut in harshly. "You may call the ME's office or Salt Lake Homicide if you wish to confirm my authority here."

Mossberg's expression remained impregnable. "Why was I not given notice of your impending visit?"

"Because it was not required."

A thin layer of Mossberg's coolness seemed to thaw as she mutely took measure of her visitor. Rebekah decided to throw her a crumb. "Listen, I apologize for the impromptu nature of my visit, but it *is* vital to this investigation."

"And as director of this facility, I need to ascertain your full intentions, Miss Smith. I am not questioning your authority. This entire incident is appalling on multiple levels. Foremost, Mr. Johnson had just celebrated his hundredth birthday wherein he received statewide notoriety. He was still very healthy, all things considered, so we can only hope he didn't suffer when he passed."

"When he was murdered," Rebekah corrected.

Mossberg stiffened. "That remains to be seen. Secondly, in light of Mr. Johnson's recent celebration, this incident could look extraordinarily bad for Avalon Manor. We have a solid reputation for happy, healthy residents. If word gets out someone *was* murdered—if that is indeed what happened—we will have a very difficult time convincing the other residents that they are safe."

"Not to mention future paying customers," Rebekah said evenly.

She saw Mossberg's jaw muscles clench and loosen repeatedly beneath her thick jowls. Were Ms. Mossberg in a cartoon, Rebekah was certain she'd see smoke coming from Mossberg's ears.

"Our number-one concern at Avalon Manor is and always will be patient comfort and safety," the director huffed, clearly offended by Rebekah's last comment. "Suggesting we are here solely for monetary gain is slanderous, Miss Smith."

Rebekah nodded. "Very well. I promise to be very brief and discreet. You have my word on that."

Mossberg considered her promise with wary eyes. She stood and removed a large ring of keys from her desk. "Follow me, please."

The two women walked to the elevators and hailed a car.

"Do you mind if I take the stairs?" Rebekah asked, wanting to work off some of the remaining embers of anger.

Mossberg's ferret eyes narrowed to two tiny black dots. She gave a curt nod and headed to the first landing. Counterbalanced by the swinging of her arms, she began a shifting waddle that had her moving up the stairs with robotic efficiency. Rebekah had trouble keeping up with her—mostly because it was all she could do not to laugh. By the time they reached the third floor, Mossberg was red-faced, but her breathing was deep and steady, not short and winded as Rebekah had expected.

The large woman paused at the stair head and daubed her face with a tissue. Rebekah hadn't asked her to take the stairs but was impressed that she had.

A moment later, they walked to the end of the hall where a small wall plaque read, *Lester Johnson*. The door was locked.

As Mossberg selected a key from the ring, a sudden knot of anxiety rose in Rebekah's stomach. She forced it down and hoped it didn't show on her face.

"The police have requested that no one touch anything until they get results from their forensics team. I trust you will honor that request?"

"I am only here to record pertinent environmental facts. I'll assist in the autopsy when Mr. Johnson's body is brought to the ME later this evening," she said in lieu of a direct answer.

Mossberg nodded and unlocked the door.

The small room was designed for self-sufficiency. It had a double bed with a nightstand, a private bathroom, a sitting area, a large LCD TV, and a wet bar with a small refrigerator. The single window overlooked the Real Salt Lake sports complex and other large buildings in the downtown district. There was a slight hint of spice in the air. Rebekah noted the room's features for only a moment before fixating on Mr. Johnson.

He was laid out in peaceful repose with his hands crossed just below his sternum. His eyes were closed and slightly collapsed; his mouth was an expressionless, straight line. His face looked clean shaven, his nails freshly trimmed. She knew that many people thought hair and nails continued to grow after death, but what actually happened was that the skin dehydrates and pulls away from the hair and nails, giving them the *appearance* of growth. Mr. Johnson's skin looked moist and fresh and had a slight sheen to it, attesting to the use of some kind of moisturizer. If it was pandit oil, he'd be added to the list of serial murder victims.

She looked closely at his hands. The veins were pink and full. She snapped on some surgical gloves and pushed against his veins with her finger.

"Ms. Smith, I thought I made it clear you were not to touch him," Mossberg said in a tone that left no doubt her request wasn't open to debate.

"I am performing an on-site environmental examination, Ms. Mossberg," Rebekah said without looking up. "I thought *I* made that clear. If being in the room at this time makes you uncomfortable, please feel free to leave." Without waiting for a response, Rebekah removed a small digital recorder and began dictation of her initial analysis: "The deceased is fully clothed: black suit, white shirt, black tie, socks, and shoes. He has thin white hair, closely cut. No facial hair other than bushy eyebrows. His skin looks clear and flaccid. The blood vessels are distended but not to an extreme. Of note, they look pink in color, not the typical green-gray hue. His eyes are closed . . ." she reached over and opened one of them, "but not glued shut. The sclerae are receding and are very bloodshot—almost completely red. Possible suffocation. The lips are bluish-pink and . . ." she tried to separate them with her thumb and forefinger, "are sealed shut, possibly with superglue. The body seems intact and has a pleasant, spicy odor about it. No hint of isopropyl alcohol or formaldehyde. It smells somewhat like . . . like . . ."

"Linseed oil," Mossberg suggested.

She turned to the matron. "Yes, that's it. Linseed oil. Thank you."

The stout woman remained statuesque.

"Did Mr. Johnson ever wear cologne?" Rebekah asked.

"No. Not that I am aware of. We have a strict policy limiting the use of perfumes, as many of the residents are allergic to such fragrances."

"I see." She returned to her recording device. "The vessels of the hand are not pliable, and the knuckle joints are very stiff. Lingering rigor mortis suggests Mr. Johnson's been dead less than three days." She began to loosen the knot in his tie.

"Ms. Smith, please, I must insist you stop at once," Mossberg said with a stomp of her right foot.

"I'm just checking his left carotid artery, Ms. Mossberg. If my suspicions are correct, there will be a two- to three-inch incision over the artery and vein. And . . . yes. You see? Just as I thought. The deceased was embalmed through the left carotid vessels." She pressed the incision, causing a few drops of oil to purge, and brought it to her nose.

"Ms. Smith, must you?" The stout woman had lost much of her stoicism and actually looked a little green.

"Don't worry, Ms. Mossberg. I'm not going to open him up until I'll be able to remove and examine each organ individually."

Mossberg's color paled.

"For now, I need to know what you did with the coins placed on his eyes and the linen handkerchief covering his face."

Her color changed from green to white in a fraction of a second. "How—how did you know about those?" she asked in a hoarse whisper.

Not wanting to divulge too much, Rebekah said, "Mr. Johnson's eyelashes are bent unnaturally, like they've been compressed; therefore, I figured something must have been laid over them when he died. Coins are traditionally used, but I've read accounts where ancient people used polished stones or precious metal amulets. The handkerchief was just a guess, but it goes right along with the eye weights."

Mossberg nodded dumbly and shuffled to a bureau where she opened the top drawer and removed two ziplock baggies, one containing the handkerchief, the other holding the two fifty-cent coins.

"What were they doing in there?" Rebekah asked in a sharp tone. "All suspicious deaths are technically crime scenes and should be left as is until a forensics team can evaluate the situation. That was even one of *your* stipulations, as I recall." She grabbed the baggies as if taking away a child's toy.

The last remnants of Mossberg's piercing gaze vanished as her focus dropped to the floor. She moved to the window and stared out at the hard summer sky. "I didn't want rumors to start."

"Rumors?"

"That strange things are going on here. If word of this gets out . . . well, as you said, it'll ruin us." Her voice was strained, imploring.

Rebekah pocketed her recorder, removed her gloves, and laid a gentle hand on the woman's shoulder. "Even though Mr. Johnson's death *is* suspicious, I still believe in confidentiality and discretion. Don't worry, Ms. Mossberg. I'll keep this under wraps as best I can."

A smile Rebekah didn't think was physically possible spread across the woman's face. "Thank you," she gushed.

Glancing at her watch, Rebekah said, "Well, I'm running behind. I'll take these notes to the ME and get things prepped for the autopsy. Thank you for your assistance."

Mossberg nodded but continued to stare out the window with an empty expression.

As Rebekah quickly stepped into the hallway, she bumped into a body. It was the thin, redheaded man from the reception counter. "I-I'm so s-s-sorry," he stuttered.

"No, no. I'm sorry," Rebekah offered quickly. "I shouldn't have burst out of the room like that."

"What are *you* doing here, Mr. Slade?" Mossberg snapped, coming up behind Rebekah, her domineering persona returning at once.

"I w-was j-j-just seeing who w-was in here. I'm n-n-not doing anything—"

"That's right. You're not doing *anything*—useful or otherwise," she growled. "Now get back to work. This is a private matter."

The man ducked his head but favored Rebekah with a final glance as he passed by. It was a bashful expression, cast with pale, depthless eyes. He was undoubtedly embarrassed over the lambasting he'd received from Commandant Mossberg. She obviously ruled with an iron fist.

"It's okay, really," Rebekah said. "Thank you again for your time, ma'am." And with that, she headed down the stairs as fast as her legs would carry her without breaking into a run.

She had to get out of the building and show Josh her findings. In her pocket were the baggies holding the hankie and the two coins. Hopefully, it would be some time before Mossberg discovered they were missing.

CHAPTER 17

"THESE WERE FOUND ON LESTER Johnson's face," Rebekah said, handing Josh the baggies.

"Dare I ask how you got them?" he asked, looking up from his desk.

"They were handed to me," she said with an air of innocence. "I was hoping you could courier them to the forensics lab ASAP so we can compare them with the others."

"Um, sure. You know, we could drive them over ourselves then grab a late lunch."

"Sorry, Clouseau. I'm already late for the Silas Snow case. Rain check, okay?"

He sighed. "Okay."

She smiled mischievously. "If you're feeling neglected, you can always come help me with the autopsy."

"Um, I'm going to file that suggestion under *Eew*," he said, faking a gag reflex. "The only time I'm getting near one of your tables is when I'm *on* one, thanks."

She cradled his face between her hands and pulled him into a gentle kiss. "I hope that time never comes." Then, holding him there, she added, "Take these to forensics, please, Josh. This is important to me."

He initiated a second kiss. "Anything for you, Becks."

After she left, Josh began wondering just how common centenarian murders were. He quickly pulled up the files of deaths deemed suspicious in Utah over the past three years. Out of ninety-two, he found only one that involved anyone over a hundred years old—and even then, his age was questionable. The body of a Navajo tribesman from Blanding was discovered by some hikers on a weekend excursion. The corpse was found sitting cross-legged in the center of a medicine wheel carved centuries earlier atop a sandstone plateau. Dressed only in a buckskin loincloth and a few ceremonial beads, the old man was bent forward with his elbows resting in the crook of his knees. His head hung low, allowing his long silver hair to caress his ankles. His back and shoulders had been exposed to the merciless southern Utah sun. They were blistered and cracked, exposing muscle, sinew, and bone. Flies swarmed around the body, yet curiously, no animal had dared take a bite.

It was estimated that he'd been there for about three weeks. No one knew his real name. He carried no ID. The local Navajo population said he was known only as the Story Talker. The man had no verifiable address or worldly possessions, but it was rumored that he knew of a hidden cave laden with pre-Columbian artifacts, including some Nephite gold. The tribal council refused to let the state ME autopsy the body. They believed allowing any non-Navajo to touch a dead tribesman would enable his spirit to return from the underworld to haunt their village. After some political jockeying, the ME was allowed to do a brief external examination before the deceased was buried. He saw nothing that suggested a homicide, but he couldn't be sure without an autopsy. Still, his supposed knowledge of hidden treasure could create motive, and his death wasn't witnessed; therefore, it was labeled as suspicious.

Josh closed the file and rubbed his eyes. He felt like he was wading through molasses. He had a serial killer loose in Utah, but the random clues were not definitive enough to reveal where he might strike next— other than a hundred-year-old with AB-positive blood. It was an uncommon blood type, so the likelihood of another centenarian having it was minimal. But that person would likely be the next target.

Josh flipped back to the latest three cases to look for similarities.

According to the ME's estimates, Agnes Baugh had died early Saturday evening, Silas Snow died late Sunday evening, and Lester Johnson late Tuesday evening. The drive from Mrs. Baugh's house in Tremonton to Mr. Snow's condo in Washington County was about six hours, depending on weather and traffic. The killer obviously had to have everything preplanned to accomplish unseen, back-to-back murders that also included partial embalming. Then there was transporting the blood from the harvesting location to . . . to where? The man had to have some kind of headquarters with a quality refrigeration system. Would he also need a refrigerator van . . . or would a Styrofoam cooler suffice? It was anyone's guess what he was doing with the blood. Even with the rarity of the type, Josh doubted it would be a lucrative venture for the black market.

What Josh needed was more "solid" evidence. The coins and handkerchiefs were a great start, but just one additional find would significantly increase his odds of finding this creep. He wanted to solve this case for Rebekah. He'd seen her get emotionally attached to cases before but not like this. Even though she hadn't said as much, he knew this case scraped against an emotional scar she'd buried deep in her past. Sometimes such scars remained hidden forever. At other times a single occurrence could irritate them to the point of reopening the wound.

He harbored deep scars of his own. He knew they were what prevented him from taking his relationship with Rebekah to the next level. One of these days he'd have to face those scars and risk reopening them. But perhaps that was the only way he could truly help Rebekah deal with hers.

CHAPTER 18

DR. MAHESH AND REBEKAH TOOK their time going over the body of Silas Snow. She noted that Mr. Snow's sclera were extremely bloodshot and that his eyelids were not superglued shut but his lips were. Again, just like Agnes Baugh and Lester Johnson.

She carefully examined every fold of skin, every liver spot and bruise, anything that looked out of the ordinary for a centenarian in perfect health. That was the key to this autopsy—the fact that Mr. Snow *was* in perfect health and should not have died. Murder was the only explanation.

"I hope I am as fit as this man was when I reach one hundred," Dr. Mahesh said. "Just look at his buttocks. There is very little sag to them, whereas mine look like two elephants wrestling in a sleeping bag."

Rebekah laughed. "You're in fine shape, Sandy." She glanced up at the microphone dangling overhead. "You sure you want comments about your backside on file here?"

"As chief medical examiner, it is my responsibility and privilege to review all autopsy transcripts. I also have the authority to edit anything I deem irrelevant to the case." He winked. "So if you wish to comment on my astonishing pathology prowess or the seductive way in which I remove a spleen, be my guest."

"If I ever do see a seductive spleen removal, I may be too shocked to speak."

"Do not be afraid to share your wildest dreams with me, Sundara," he teased. "After all, everybody has one or two." He cleared his throat. "Now, then. Do you notice anything untoward about this patient who, according to the report, was very healthy and active?"

She sobered and concentrated. "Well, his physique attests to his athleticism, but I'm seeing hundreds of petechiae on his skin. He may have a blood disease like thrombocytopenia or vasculitis. Since he doesn't have any blood in his circulatory system, we'll have to extract what we can from the heart or liver, like we did with Mrs. Baugh, to see if there was toxin involved."

"Excellent. And we shall do exactly that. But could not these tiny blood seepages also be caused by the pressure of the embalming fluid being forced into his circulatory system?"

"Ah. True. Speaking of which, have you found out anything on the composition of the pandit fluid we extracted from Mrs. Baugh?"

"I have indeed," he said with obvious pride. "It is a unique mix of ingredients I have not seen anywhere else, even in New Delhi. But this is not uncommon. Morticians often have their preferred recipes that vary according to the condition and ethnicity of the deceased." He depressed the stitch over the carotid artery until a drop of fluid seeped out. He sniffed it and then held it out for Rebekah to smell. "It smells the same, do you agree?"

She sniffed the spicy, sharp odor and nodded. "Yeah, that's the same stuff. But I doubt this creep is a real mortician. He's probably just some psychopath with a Bill Nye chemistry set in his basement."

"Agreed. He may be exactly that."

"So what's in it—the embalming fluid, I mean?"

"Well, if the embalmer's intent was in preserving tissue, he did not do his homework. From what I have determined, the solution contains magnesium phosphate, sodium chloride, manganese, antimony, and balsam in a linseed oil base, with a pinch of arsenic for flavor."

"Tasty. But I don't think I'll try it on a salad anytime soon," she said, playing along.

"Nor should you use it for embalming. It has a wonderful ability to keep tissues malleable, but it will only forestall putrefaction for one to two days at best." He paused, thinking. "I believe it is mostly a cosmetic substance. It is terribly inefficient as a preservative, but it does have an intoxicating fragrance, does it not?"

"Magnesium, manganese, balsam—it sounds like common bath salts to me," Rebekah mused. "It'd probably do more good outside the body than in."

"Precisely, Sundara. The addition of linseed oil would make it very moisturizing, do you agree?"

"As long as it doesn't go rancid."

"On the contrary, linseed oil has a very long shelf life due to its biochemical structure. But we shall leave that lecture for another day."

"I quiver with anticipation," she said with unmasked sarcasm.

"As do I," Mahesh said as he began making the Y incision down Mr. Snow's torso.

As Rebekah drained the peculiar embalming fluid and labeled it for identification, Mahesh removed and weighed Mr. Snow's organs, again noting that the only anomaly in them was how healthy they were. Using a large troche, Rebekah sucked the bile and other fluids out of the individual organs and then did the same for the body cavity. Luckily, she was able to extract nearly five ccs of blood for tox screening. As she returned the organs to the cadaver, Sandy completed his removal of the brain for later examination. She then closed the body cavity with sutures and reattached the skull plate and scalp tissue. She'd done the procedure so many times she could almost do it by feel. As her fingers nimbly worked the needle and suture, her mind filled with images of silver coins, linen handkerchiefs, and of a dark-eyed alchemist mixing strange potions in black cauldrons over a low fire. She doubted the person behind all this looked like that, but the description fit the bizarre circumstances.

She next filled Mr. Snow's circulatory system with standard embalming fluid and his body cavity with saline solution then checked for leaks. Normally, these procedures were performed by the mortician, but owing to the suspicious nature surrounding these deaths, the ME staff did it all, just in case something stood out that would give them a clue.

"So, do you think the embalming fluid is traceable?" she asked as they washed up.

"I do not. The ingredients can be purchased from any chemical supplier. Therefore, I am afraid that path leads nowhere. But do not be distressed. I am certain your boyfriend will be able to reason out a murderer for you in no time."

"I hope you're right," she said with heartfelt sincerity.

CHAPTER 19

Damien Slade was used to being a loner. That was okay. Even while at work, he talked to patients only when he had to. His stutter strangled his self-confidence. He preferred the silent company of his heroes, the men he venerated because of their contributions to medicine. He loved reading about them—not only about their research but also about their personal lives. They motivated him, guided him, *inspired* him. And although most were decades in the grave, he felt a personal connection with them. They spoke to him, pleading for him to continue their work.

When his shift at Avalon Manor ended at eight, he returned home, nuked some chicken nuggets, and logged onto the Internet—one of his favorite pastimes. He loved to search for listings of people over a hundred years old. There were actually quite a few. One study estimated that one in every 3,000 people will reach that ripe old age; and one in 10,000 of those will make it to super-centenarian: someone who lives to 110 and beyond. He'd been surprised to learn that most centenarians live in the United States. Considering the unhealthy lifestyle of Americans, the numbers seemed awfully high. But the reason they were living longer had little to do with lifestyle. It all came down to modern medicine and long-term care facilities. Those interventions did not necessarily mean the old-timers were healthier or happier. They simply lived longer. Regardless of that, people kept alive by machines and modern drugs were not the ones he was seeking.

He switched his browsing to a website reserved for government officials monitoring all healthcare activities nationwide. Few people had access to such comprehensive, highly personal information. Thanks to the Unified Healthcare Reform enacted by the federal government, a centralized database contained all records of every patient seen by every licensed healthcare practitioner nationwide. The list also contained which practitioners were employed at each facility, and which ones interacted with each patient. Because the lists were exhaustive, each offered internal search engines to expedite requests.

Damien had acquired access to the database from his mentor—a man who had legal admission privileges. The man also had an enormous ego—but so did many brilliant people. More importantly, the man shared in Damien's ideas and gladly supplied him with the passwords, files, and drugs necessary to complete his mission.

Out of curiosity, Damien accessed the interdepartmental files from the University of Utah Medical Center, where the state medical examiner's office was housed. After hopping through a few connections, he pulled up the autopsy files and read the chart notes on Agnes Baugh. There were a lot of speculations, some educated guesses, but so far they had not figured things out. Good. The other one he was looking for was Silas Snow. Five autopsies later he found him. His autopsy had been performed at 4:00 p.m., but his exam notes had yet to be entered. He wondered why it was taking so long. They should give centenarians priority consideration. Anything less was disrespectful.

It was so sad to see the passing of someone who had beaten the odds of average longevity. There were so many that were kept alive by machines. That was undignified, shameful. That wasn't beating the odds—it was cheating. Agnes Baugh had been one of the elite, one of those who deserved respect and admiration, perhaps even veneration. So was Silas Snow. Damien's heart went out to the families of the recently deceased centenarians. They were the true losers in the winless game of mortality. He wished he could have gotten to know Mr. Snow personally. Think of the stories he could tell!

Damien closed his eyes and placed his right palm against the flatscreen monitor, willing the electronic signal to allow him preternatural sight into the autopsy room. The screen was warm, but no static discharge snapped between his skin and the liquid crystal display. Still, he felt a connection—he felt himself pulled into the monitor as if through a portal and whisked along miles of communications wire, like traveling through a wormhole in space at incomprehensible speeds, colors streaking by in a kaleidoscope of undulating waves and streams. Then, as suddenly as his meteoric journey began, it ended. Yet he did not feel the whiplash of gained kinetic energy. He was now hovering above an autopsy table, looking down on the corpse of Silas Snow.

He remembered him well—the images were still fresh in his memory. The man had been unexpectedly strong. He was one of the few who'd put up quite a bit of fight. His body was sinewy and hard. His skin was thin and saggy (they were all saggy), but not to the point of being brittle. Nor did he have all the blemishes, broken blood vessels, and non-healing sores that so many old people had. What a perfect specimen!

Then doctors materialized, dressed in surgical smocks and gloves. As the autopsy commenced, Damien was awestruck with the overall health of the dead man. His organs were in textbook condition, almost as if he was still in his thirties and had led a puritanical lifestyle. He noted the flawlessness of the intestines, the deep, rich color of the liver, the clean, pink lungs, the lack of fattiness around the heart. Most of his muscles still held tonicity, and there was little atrophy or flaccidity. His beard still looked nicely trimmed, just as Damien had groomed it; his mouth was set and proud; his eyes—

Damien cried out. Silas's eyes were open, staring at him, piercing his soul with indictment. He tried pulling his hand from the monitor, but it seemed glued in place. He tried looking away but couldn't. A frown sharpened Silas's glare, focused it until it burned like the sun's ray through a magnifying glass. His mouth opened. *Impossible!* It was superglued shut! The bluish lips began to move, to articulate words. Damien couldn't read lips, but somehow the power that held him in this trance also gave him that skill.

The dead man mouthed, *Murderer.*

Damien shook his head. *No, you don't understand. You were going to die soon anyway.*

Unblinking, the eyes flared with hatred. *Murderer!*

No. Your sacrifice will save millions of lives.

The dead man pointed an accusatory finger of tendon and bone at him. *MURDERER!*

No! Damien yanked his hand from the monitor with such force he fell out of his chair. His breathing came in sharp gasps that burned his lungs. It was like inhaling caustic sludge. His heart thundered in his chest.

He rolled to his knees but kept his head lowered. This was ridiculous. He knew he hadn't actually traversed space and time to witness the autopsy of Silas Snow. He knew he was just imagining the scene—which meant he was also imagining the reanimation of the late Mr. Snow. But his mind was so adept at creating such scenes that his body reacted as if he had actually experienced them in person.

Fumbling to his feet, he lunged toward the sink for a drink of water.

He was *not* crazy. And he wasn't doing anything wrong. He was on a quest, perhaps the greatest quest in all history. Soon his name would be heralded on every continent. People would worship him. Women would throw themselves at his feet. Parents would name children after him. So why then did he have that hallucination? Why had Silas Snow accused him of murder?

Moving back to the computer, he gazed slowly across the screen. Patient names, demographics, doctor names, medical histories all swirled in front of him in a maelstrom of words and numbers. Nothing stood out from the deluge. But there had to be *something*.

He removed his glasses and screwed his eyes shut, willing the images to stop their dervish dance. When he opened them again, the screen displayed motionless information, the cursor blinked innocently. Within the mosaic of digits, one name stood out from the rest. Donning his glasses, he saw it was listed under "Support Personnel."

Instantly, he understood. It was that woman—the one visiting the nursing home. She actually *did* work for the medical examiner's office. He had no clue what she was up to, but he was certain it wasn't routine for her job. She was sticking her nose where it didn't belong. That could spell trouble very fast. Normally he would simply up and leave—move to a new state with a new identity, pursuing new donors. That's what his mentor had made him do before. But he couldn't this time. His mentor was close to a breakthrough. He needed to stay close.

And yet, because Silas had accused him so harshly, Damien knew his secrets were dangerously close to being discovered.

Then a new revelation burst into his mind—one that brought with it understanding, tranquility. The dead man wasn't accusing him, after all. Silas Snow was *warning* him—warning him about Rebekah Smith. She was up to no good. And it would be up to him to do something about it.

CHAPTER 20

THE HALLWAYS WERE THINLY LIT. The offices were dark, the frenzied hum of the day having vanished shortly after six, along with most of the morgue's employees. A janitorial crew came in around 3:00 a.m. Until then, only a support staffer and a med student rotating through his pathology requirement occupied the office, manning the morgue's drop-off.

Rebekah sniggered. She could never get used to the fact they had an actual *drop-off*. But what else would you call it? If the morgues throughout Utah overflowed, the extra bodies were often sequestered to the ME's refrigeration units. Most unclaimed corpses ended up there anyway.

Having finally completed her extensive to-do list, Rebekah typed Lester Johnson's name into her database, along with his date of birth and social security number. His demographics flashed onto her screen. She tried to read his brief life's history with a forensic eye. She tried to focus on the facts that may have led to his murder. But she found it impossible to treat the man as merely a collection of data. What kept filling her mind was that Lester Johnson had been more than a statistic, more than a body currently lying in a fridge in the morgue. He had probably been a good son, a hard-working husband, a father concerned for the future of his children. He had lived on this earth, tended to it, and returned to it sooner than his Maker had planned, she was certain. The man had made it to one hundred years, for heaven's sake! Just think of the wisdom he could have imparted. Just imagine the lessons he could have taught. Just think of the mistakes he could have helped others avoid—the mistakes *she* could have avoided.

She grabbed a tissue and squeezed it in her fist, forbidding tears to form. She shook her head, not wanting the images to appear. *It wasn't your fault. Now focus!*

Lester Johnson: born December 6, 1912, in Colorado Springs, Colorado. Son of Justin Johnson and Doris McConkie Johnson. Married to Martha Folks of Stratmoor, Colorado, in 1933.

Rebekah skipped the rest of the demographics, scrolling quickly to the medical stats. Height: six two. Weight: 176 pounds. Blood type: AB-positive. No known allergies. Standard maintenance meds like digoxin and furosemide. Nothing stood out that might lead her to a potential suspect.

Then another thought came to her: Perhaps Avalon Manor had a list of who'd recently paid him a visit. Maybe he'd had a visitor who'd killed him, partially embalmed him, and then left without anyone noticing. She snorted. *Ridiculous.* Of course they'd notice. No one got in or out of the facility without checking in at the reception counter. It'd be too obvious.

Then—as if a light clicked on in her head—she thought of a more plausible scenario. What if it was someone *at* the facility, an employee whom no one would take notice of because he or she was *supposed* to be there? It could be a long-time employee or a new hire—it didn't matter.

Her mind was churning. She was getting close to something, but she couldn't tell what. It was like groping through a thick fog where amorphous shapes coalesced and dissipated, surged and ebbed with no discernible regularity. Before she could pinpoint something, it would fade away or be obfuscated by a wash of white on white. But it was there—the answer she so desperately sought. She *knew* it was. If only she could distill the random—

The harsh crashing of a metal tray on the tile floor startled her from her thoughts. All around her was dark, save for the meager light from the hallway and the glow of her monitor. She thought she heard cursing. One of the med students coming to the office at this late hour? Her desk clock read 1:10 a.m. Med students were famous for keeping insane schedules, but visiting the morgue past midnight was pushing it. Even *she* should have been home hours ago.

The sound of metal scraping against tile echoed toward her as the intruder apparently had some difficulty picking up the tray. Then the grating noise ceased as suddenly as it had begun. He or she must have successfully placed it back on the counter or was still holding it. Less than ten seconds passed before it crashed again, followed by more vile cursing—a man's voice . . . with a familiar timbre.

A fluorescent light flickered on in the hallway. A shadow grew on the floor, perpendicular to her room, as the man moved toward the junction.

She considered turning off her computer to hide in darkness then shook off the silly notion. She was just being paranoid. It was ridiculous to think she was in any kind of danger.

Rather than wait for the intruder to make an appearance, Rebekah decided to take the initiative. "Hello? Who's there?" she called.

The shadow froze. It was not well-defined, but the shape was clearly that of a man . . . fairly large . . . holding something in his right hand. The tray? No, it wasn't that bulky. The shadow moved again, growing.

"Hello?" she called once more. "Are you lost?"

The body of the shadow passed the doorway. She could now see the indication of two legs. Still growing. So close. Maybe she should run—

He appeared in the doorway—a dark silhouette, slightly hunched. His head turned to face her. He was tall, broad-shouldered, trim. In his hand gleamed a large knife. She recognized it as one from the autopsy room.

"Good evening, you beautiful creature," the man slurred.

"Robert?" Her voice was tight with dread. "What are you doing here so late?"

Dr. Lansing walked slowly toward her with a definite wobble in his gait. Even before he was ten feet away, she could smell the alcohol.

"Robert, you've been drinking," she said in a scolding tone. She rose to her feet, glaring at him. "You need to get home and get some sleep. I'll call a taxi—"

"Shut up and sit down," he barked, pointing the knife at her. "You think you're so much better than me." His voice was strained, lost somewhere between sorrow and anger. "Just because you get to use scalpels and suture and—and—and get to cut things." He squinted at the knife, as if wondering why it was in his hand, but he kept it pointed at her.

Rebekah sat but kept her glare strong. "Robert, you need to put down that knife—"

"I'm a doctor too, you know! *Doctor* Robert Lansing," he cried as his final awkward steps brought him looming over her. One word slurred into the next as he continued. "I know howta use a blade, but I don' haveta b'cause ulimat—uluminate—ulim—in the end, the pen is mightier than the blade."

"*The sword*, Robert. The pen is mightier than the sword."

"That what *I* said!" he bellowed, raising the knife and bringing it down with deadly force.

His aim was clearly off, but Rebekah still flinched. The knife tip penetrated her desktop and stuck. When he tried to pull it free, he collapsed forward, landing against the desk, then crumpling into a fetal position on the floor.

Filled with indignation, Rebekah left her chair to turn on some overhead fluorescents. Lansing shielded his face and whimpered at the brightness. Returning to her desk, she heard him repeating a mantra, as if trying to justify his actions. "I'll still be here. You'll see. I'll still be here. When you're gone, I'll still be here. I'll outlast you all."

She wasn't about to ask him what he meant. Frankly, she couldn't care less. She picked up the phone and called campus security. She tried to pull the knife free from her desk, but the tip was securely embedded. Her failed efforts amplified her anger.

"Why were you carrying a knife?" she demanded.

Lansing continued whimpering his little chant, oblivious to her presence.

"Robert! You could be in serious trouble here. You could lose your job over this. Tell me why you had the knife."

His chanting changed slightly. "I'm not afraid of blood either, you know. Everyone thinks you're so special, but I am too. And I'll still be here. I'll still be here. I'll still be . . ." His words trailed off to mere whispers as he curled up tighter.

She stood over the forlorn man, feeling little pity for him. He'd had a rough life—of his own making. He was currently single but was always on the prowl for "fresh meat," as he'd once called his marriages. What number was he looking for now? Wife number four . . . or was it five? He'd probably be able to hang onto a marriage if he didn't also have four or five girlfriends at the same time.

The campus police showed up minutes later. Rebekah wanted to let Robert get just what he deserved, but instead she found herself pitying the man. Yes, he was an insufferable sleazebag; but she always had a soft spot for a good sob story—even one that was self-inflicted. Thankfully she'd had the presence of mind to remove the knife before the police arrived.

"I found Dr. Lansing on the floor like this," she told the officers while showing her ME badge. "He's obviously intoxicated, but I'm certain the drinking took place off campus. He's never had alcohol in his office."

"And why are you here at this hour, ma'am?" one officer asked.

"We've had a full docket lately. This is the only time I have to catch up on paperwork."

"I know just what you mean," the second officer said with a nod. "So, what would you like us to do?"

"If you could just get him to his office, he can sleep it off on his couch," she said with a disarming smile.

The police helped Robert to his feet and escorted him to the elevator. He grumbled and complained but didn't put up a fight. Rebekah hoped Robert's office was unlocked. If it wasn't, well, she'd let the police worry about that.

Deciding she'd had enough excitement for one evening, Rebekah logged off her computer and headed for her car. She tried to refocus on Lester Johnson and his upcoming autopsy, but Lansing's words kept echoing in her mind: *I'll still be here. Even after you're gone, I'll still be here. I'll still be here.*

CHAPTER 21

Friday

JOSH HATED TYPING REPORTS. HE'D never learned to type in middle school and had gotten by in high school because he could hunt-and-peck reasonably fast. He'd invested in a program that typed dictation, but the number of police terms, acronyms, and personal names he used kept registering as spelling errors. It was simply easier to hunt-and-peck and deal with the disparagement he took from his fellow officers who typed with aplomb.

He finished his reports from the day before and submitted them electronically. He then skimmed through the gang task force reports. He was hoping something had developed from the information he had gotten from the smoke shop employee on Paxton Harris. The GTF had already interviewed a few suspected members of Asian gangs, and a new roster was being created of potential suspects—all of which were known members the Oriental Posse. He cringed, knowing it would only add accelerant to an already volatile environment. But he wanted to find out more about the young Asian couple Chet had mentioned. There was something about his story that didn't ring true. Josh then uploaded a photo file of known gangbangers onto his phone. He'd make another trip to West Valley to see if Chet could recognize any of them. But he didn't hold out much hope. The man was clearly a bigot and would not recognize anyone because he said they "all looked alike."

Josh pulled up the business licenses of the smoke shop, the failed auto parts store, and the subsequent dollar store. Just as Chet the Harley dude had said, a man named Ronny Einerson had an auto parts store that operated for about two years before closing. A family named Mongkut leased the building from Bridger Capital Ventures, an investment group based out of Cache Valley, Utah. They owned the strip mall and the buildings on either side, as well as several other properties along the Wasatch front. They were local boys—not the Asian takeover conspiracy Chet alleged.

Josh chuffed, shaking his head. He loved these kinds of cases. They tested his wits, his intelligence, but, most importantly, his intuition. He had learned long ago to trust his instincts. He liked to think it was the Spirit prompting him in his efforts to do good. And the more he thought about the smoke shop employee's allegations, the more suspicious the employee himself looked. Josh began to doubt there'd even been a young Asian couple talking about Paxton's murder. It sounded too perfect, too convenient.

He took a large gulp of Mountain Dew and reexamined the file from the beginning. Yeah, something smelled fishy. Following his instincts, he cancelled the round-up of Oriental Posse members and asked for a full profile on the smoke shop owner and all his employees, especially one named Chet.

His phone rang, disrupting him. It was the forensics lab. "Logan here."

"Josh, Ricky. Those coins you brought me yesterday? I lifted nothing useful off them," Ricky Danforth, the forensics guy, stated plainly. "There's some residue of acetone in the ridges, which means he cleaned them up some before using them. And there are some flat smudges on both sides, which usually indicates the guy wore latex gloves. Cloth gloves would have left fibers, depending on the material."

Ricky was a science geek Josh had known since high school. The guy was meticulous to an extreme. There was little that got past him.

"So it's a dead end, huh?" Josh assumed.

"I didn't say that. There may be a lead. They have identical mint marks to the coins on your other two stiffs."

"Mint marks?"

"Yeah, shows where they were struck. See, these coins aren't just any half-dollars. These are 1917 Walking Liberties. They have a silver content of ninety percent, which makes them worth a lot more than fifty cents each. But each stiff had coins with the *identical* mint mark covering each eye: an S on the left eye, a D on the right, and both marks are on the obverse side of the coin."

Josh rubbed his eyes with his free hand. "You just lost me, Ricky. Does all this mean something?"

"Bet your sweet patootie it does. Those are rare coins, dude. 1917 S and D obverse Walking Liberties are the only ones with the mint mark on the obverse of the coin."

"'Obverse' meaning?"

"The face of the coin. Most mint marks are on the back of the coin."

"Okay, so the guy owned a half-dozen rare fifty-cent pieces. Tell me how you think there's a tie-in?"

"Well, your perp is not a very smart numismatist to be wasting his collection on dead people."

"A what?"

"A numismatist—a coin collector. To me it doesn't figure. Maybe he's showing off because he's got a lot of rare coins. Maybe those particular coins have something to do with each stiff. Or maybe he's leaving a sign. You know, like a calling card. A lot of serials do that."

"Okay. Thanks, Ricky. I owe you."

"I was hoping you were going to say that. Listen, if the families of these guys don't claim the coins, can I have them?—after the investigation is closed, of course."

"Are you a num-hypno-tist?" Josh stumbled over the word.

"Numismatist, you jughead. Yeah—ever since I was a kid. I've got some real beauties, too. I got a 1913 Liberty nickel and ten Indian head pennies of various dates, and a 1928 half cent classic head. My old man got me started back in middle school. I'll show you my collection sometime, if you like."

Josh couldn't think of anything more boring than gawking at old coins. "Maybe later. Thanks again, Ricky. Let me know of you dig up anything else."

"You got it."

Josh hung up and stared at the info he'd written down. As boring as it was, there *was* something there. He was sure of it.

CHAPTER 22

REBEKAH ENTERED AVALON MANOR JUST before one in the afternoon. She flashed her badge and asked the receptionist for a complete list of the center's employees, including nurses, aids, volunteers, maintenance personnel, and administration. The young girl balked, her eyes filling with worry. She glanced around as if seeking help from someone with more authority. "Um, that's confidential information. I'm not allowed to—"

"I know it's confidential," Rebekah cut in, flashing her credentials a second time. "In case you didn't notice, I'm with the state medical examiner's office. This request involves the case we've opened on Mr. Lester Johnson."

"But I'm afraid Mr. Johnson is not at Avalon Manor anymore," she said nervously.

Rebekah rolled her eyes. "Yes, I am aware of that, Miss . . ." She glanced at the girl's nametag and frowned. *J-A-Z-Z-M-I-N*. "Jazzmin?"

The receptionist's expression spoke equally of embarrassment and resignation. "My parents are overly obsessed basketball fans. I was doomed before I was born."

"Well it's . . . unique. Look, Jazzmin, we know Mr. Johnson is no longer here. He's at the morgue. I checked him in myself. I'll be doing the autopsy later this afternoon. There are some minor things I need to clear up dealing with this facility, seeing as it was here that he died. And it would greatly speed things up if I had a point of reference."

Jazzmin reached for her phone. "Ms. Mossberg is at lunch, but maybe I can get her on her cell—"

"I talked with Ms. Mossberg yesterday," Rebekah said, glancing at her watch, "and I'm running late. She gave me her full cooperation. I can only assume that cooperation would continue until our investigation is complete."

Jazzmin gnawed on the end of her pen a moment before pecking at her keyboard. A few seconds later, the printer cycled out four sheets of paper. She gave them a quick once-over before handing them to Rebekah.

The stats were complete: name, address, phone, date of birth, date of hire, position at the center, and a few other facts pertinent to their position.

"Thank you, Jazzmin. This is perfect. May I call on you later if need be?" she asked, flashing the girl a reassuring smile.

"Um, sure."

"Thanks."

Rebekah returned to her car and drove to the Bangkok Thai restaurant in south Sandy. She grabbed some beef dumplings in curry to go and headed back to the university. The autopsy of Lester Johnson was scheduled for four under the scalpel of Dr. Savage. He was a brilliant pathologist with a dry sense of humor and an indelicate name for a pathologist. She liked working with him, but she wished Dr. Mahesh was assigned to the procedure. He would understand the importance of the case to her.

A few minutes later, Rebekah entered Sandeep Mahesh's office holding the open container of Thai food in front of her like a sacred chalice. "I bring you epicurean endowments of enticement," she said formally.

Dr. Mahesh's eyes widened. "What have you got there?" he asked just before inhaling deeply. "Oh you evil, evil temptress. Is that forbidden nourishment you hold, Sundara?"

"If it's nourishing, how can it be forbidden?" she asked innocently.

He inhaled again. "I smell curry . . . and soy and . . . beef? You *are* an evil temptress! I should change your name to Kali, the dark destroyer."

She smiled devilishly. "Oops, did I accidentally get *beef* dumplings? I know you don't like the taste of beef. I should have double-checked the order." She stabbed a dumpling with a plastic fork and bit it in half. "Umm. Too bad. This is the most tender, delicious, savory beef I've ever had. One could almost mistake it for lamb or—"

"Stop. Stop this very instant! You are a fiendish, evil woman! But it . . ." He paused and inhaled a third time, relishing the aromatic ambrosia. "It was an honest mistake, I am certain. Here, allow me to remove the burden of your error," he said, reaching.

Rebekah handed him the Styrofoam container and pulled up a chair. "Sandy, there is an autopsy this afternoon that I'd really like to assist in, but it means bumping another case until later."

"Then assist. You have authority to help in any case you wish, do you not?" he said around a mouthful of dumpling.

"Yes, but Dr. Savage is the ME on staff this afternoon."

He swallowed. "You don't like Dr. Savage? I thought you were good friends."

"We are. It's just . . ." She paused, not because she was acting or baiting him but because she knew what Dr. Mahesh would ask next, and she wasn't sure how to answer him.

"Sundara?"

She decided to lay it all on the line. "It's the Lester Johnson case. He has the same suspicious death profile as Agnes Baugh and Silas Snow. They were all partially embalmed before anyone found them. And they each had a napkin over their face and coins on their eyes. It stands to reason they will all be filled with the same pandit oil. I know I can wait for the reports, but I'd like to be there in case I see something someone else might miss."

"Dr. Savage would be offended to hear you say that," Mahesh teased.

"That's not what I mean. He's an excellent pathologist. I just mean . . ." She stalled with her mouth open. She wasn't sure *what* she meant. That was precisely the problem. The three cases were obviously connected. But what did that mean? There were so many whys to these events that it was hard to pinpoint a single uniform question.

"You mean you would like me to do the autopsy with you so we can reason out the mysteries together, am I correct?"

She nodded. "Would you mind?"

"Mr. Johnson is scheduled for four o'clock. Because we want to be extra vigilant on the case, it will take the better part of four hours. We could be here terribly late."

Rebekah lowered her eyes. "I know. But it's important."

Dr. Mahesh stabbed another dumpling and held it up, using it as a focal point. "You realize, of course, this could be misconstrued as a bribe," he said before popping the delicious treat in his mouth.

Rebekah placed her hand on her chest, feigning shock. "The thought never crossed my mind."

"Of course not. But now that you have intentionally tainted my eternal soul with your devious ways, I am uncontrollably under your spell. I will ask Jeff if I can take the Johnson case. I am confident he will comply. He will be able to go home that much sooner, which will be compelling to him because he has a secret project that is near completion."

"A *secret* project?" she asked, intrigued. "He's not trying to reanimate dead tissue, is he?"

He raised a thick eyebrow. "In a manner of speaking, yes. He has confided in me that he is writing a novel. Can you imagine?" he chuckled. "A forensic pathologist writing a novel?"

Rebekah offered a worried smile. "I certainly hope it's not a children's book."

"Or a romance novel," he said with a wink.

"Oh—I know, it's a how-to book for do-it-yourself autopsies."

Mahesh tipped his head back and roared with laughter.

Rebekah stood and kissed his balding head. "Thanks, Sandy. You're the best."

He stabbed the last dumpling and brought it to his mouth. "No. Thank *you*, Sundara. I will see you at four."

CHAPTER 23

"I THINK WE MAY HAVE overlooked something," Josh told Rebekah over the phone. "I'm on my way to the state's evidence building to check on it."

"Cool. What have you sniffed out?" she asked.

He huffed. "You know, every time you say that you make me sound like a dog."

"When was the last time you took a good look at your apartment, sweetie?"

He palmed his forehead. "Okay, okay. I'll do a thorough clean sweep tomorrow, I promise. Care to help a desperate soul in need?"

"I'll see if I can pencil in some time for you. Until then, tell me what you've found."

"The coins."

"You mean the ones I brought you yesterday?"

"All of them. I think they may be more of a clue than we suspected. In serial cases like this, the perpetrator often leaves a signature or calling card. Most psychologists think they do it as a means of self-adulation."

"Ah. So they don't want to be caught but they definitely want to be recognized. And this creep uses fifty-cent pieces. Does that also mean he's going to do this fifty times?" she wondered.

"Let's hope not," he said, again impressed that she'd thought of an angle he hadn't. "But I *do* know there's something unique about the particular coins he's using. All six are 1917 silver half-dollars from the Denver and San Francisco mints."

"And the significance is . . . ?"

"I'm not sure. But like everything else in this crazy business, any clue can be the piece of the puzzle that bags the bad guy."

"Gosh, I love it when you talk cop."

"I'm serious, Becks. I'm thinking that because the coins are fairly rare, we might be able to narrow our search using coin collector sites."

There was a pause on the line. "I like it. So how do you know where they were minted?"

"Most coins have a mint mark," he explained. "There's a tiny capital letter somewhere on the coin. In this case, the letter is on the front. There were only about 900,000 minted from San Francisco and 700,000 from Denver."

"Only?" she said incredulously. "That's over one and a half million coins, Clouseau. How does that *narrow* our search?"

"Ricky down at forensics says most coins run in mints of two million or more from *each* facility. The big mints are in Denver, Philadelphia, and San Francisco. Plus these were made in 1917. Many of them are lost or melted down for their silver content. I think if we dig deep enough, we might get lucky."

"Okay. I've got a four o'clock autopsy on Lester Johnson—and we're going to take our time so we don't miss anything. I'll call you when I'm done, but it may be very late."

Josh pursed his mouth. "Okay, but . . . I, um . . . I was kind of hoping to see you tonight."

He heard her sigh. "You're so cute when you try to be romantic. How about we start with breakfast first thing tomorrow?"

"Okay, but it's my turn to cook."

"Really? You did say *cook,* right? That usually implies more than pouring milk on cold cereal, you know. Are there any clean dishes at your place?"

"Man, you make me sound like such a slob. I do have *some* culture, I'll have you know."

"Sweetie, your knowledge of *culture* stops at frozen yogurt," she said in a patronizing tone. "But I love you anyway." She paused then added, "Still, would it offend you if I showed up in a hazmat suit?"

"Funny. Ever wonder why pathology assistants never become stand-up comics when they retire?" he mimicked.

"Oo, touché. Good one, hon. Okay, I'll be at your place at about seven?"

"In the morning?"

"We did say *breakfast,* right? That's what time *I* usually eat breakfast."

"Um . . . okay, sure. Seven. What would you like me to make?" he asked with hesitation.

"Boy, you sure like walking on thin ice, don't you," she sniggered. "Oh never mind. Whatever you make is fine, as long as it's warm but not deep fried, and it doesn't come out of a box with the word *toaster* on the label."

"I'll see what I can do," he grumbled.

"Hey, great job on the coins. Now see if you can root out anything on the linen hankies, okay?"

"First 'sniff out,' now 'root out.' Boy, you're just hitting a bull's-eye with your animal metaphors today."

She laughed. "I honestly didn't mean it that way. But since you brought it up . . ."

"Never mind. I'll see you in the morning, Becks."

"Love you, Clouseau."

"Back at ya," he said with a sigh of resignation. He hung up and immediately decided to stop by the store before returning home. As far as what to make . . . his mind was a total blank.

CHAPTER 24

Rebekah had an hour before the autopsy of Lester Johnson. Normally she'd be in the theater room preparing everything in her thorough fashion. But there was an uneasiness hounding her that she needed to muzzle.

She pulled out the list of personnel from Avalon Manor and began reading through the information. She didn't know what she was looking for but decided to start with the two newest employees: Jazzmin S. Black and Damien Slade. Although she could not imagine a young girl like Jazzmin committing such a heinous act, she reviewed her file as if reading the journal of Lizzie Borden. The girl was previously employed at T.J. Maxx as a salesperson. She'd held that position since December of the previous year. She left because she'd just completed the first year of LPN training and wanted to work in a setting that utilized her blossoming skills. She had graduated from East High with average grades, but she had glowing references from professionals throughout the community. She'd started at Avalon Manor one month ago.

But an ax-wielding Lizzie Borden wannabe? Not likely. She snorted and moved on to the next employee.

Damien Slade. Rebekah had trouble thinking of him as a serial killer too. The twenty-something redhead was not much to look at. He was shy, unassuming, a little strange but not to the point of threatening. In a word, he was, well, wimpy. His stutter was almost debilitating, bless his heart. Just thinking of him made her want to give him a hug. His résumé, however, was very impressive. He was an LPN accredited in five states. His employment history listed experience in nursing homes, assisted living centers, and hospitals in Utah, Colorado, Iowa, Texas, and Florida. He had several letters of recommendation, all with rave reviews. He'd started at Avalon Manor just shy of two months earlier, and to date the only negative mark was his recent requests for time off.

Well what's wrong with that? she wondered. Everyone needs a day off now and then. She then noticed the criticism originated from Ms. Mossberg. *Figures. That woman wouldn't know a happy day if it came up and slapped her across the face.* No—Damien Slade may be strange, but he did not impress Rebekah as someone who would intentionally kill anyone . . . or anything.

Perhaps the killer was someone who'd worked at Avalon Manor a long time, a staffer who knew the ins and outs of the facility, including the best time to murder Lester Johnson without detection. But then, how did he also know about Agnes Baugh and Silas Snow? And when could he find time to "harvest" their blood?

Rebekah grabbed at her neck muscles, pulling on them with such force that the vertebrae in her neck popped; but it didn't hurt; frustration dampened the pain.

The killer obviously traveled from town to town seeking out centenarians with AB-positive blood. He was collecting it and . . . what? Selling it? Storing it? Drinking it? The vampire craze was still going strong in the entertainment industry. Perhaps some sociopath thought he was the embodiment of Count Dracula with a penchant for AB-positive blood. But who would be privy to such confidential information on individual blood types? Surely, it would be someone within the health professions . . . which led her to an almost infinite number of suspects, including those who worked at Avalon Manor.

Ugh! She was going in circles. Her gnawing uneasiness was not going away. She pinched the bridge of her nose and tried to ignore the thumping at her temples. Each thread of logic ended up twisted and frayed. She simply needed more information.

During yesterday's autopsy, Sandy had told her to look for what *didn't* cause the death of the patient as a way of discovering what *did*. That concept morphed into the idea that she could get critical information from those personally involved with each victim *before* their demise: Mrs. Baugh's daughter and neighbors, Mr. Snow's neighbors and the Mesa Roja staff, and Mr. Johnson's acquaintances at Avalon Manor—in particular the timid LPN Damien Slade. Somehow, she felt he knew a lot more than most people suspected.

CHAPTER 25

DAMIEN GAZED AT THE MARBLE busts of Thomas Holmes, Richard Lower, and Karl Landsteiner with a mixture of reverence and idol worship. Holmes was one of the fathers of modern embalming, noted mostly for his work during the American Civil War. Lower was credited for performing the first successful blood transfusions on animals. And Landsteiner was the Nobel Prize–winning physician who discovered the different blood types in humans. Together, these men had built a foundation that would eventually grant Damien superhuman longevity and perhaps even eternal life.

The three marble luminaries stared sternly into the converted basement laboratory from atop a length of open-faced cabinets. At times, Damien thought they exuded an air of censure; other times they seemed awestruck at the strides he'd made from their groundwork. Ultimately, their immortalized expressions were ones of jealousy and envy. Like with many great men of science, their true contributions were not fully appreciated until long after their demise. In one hundred years, Damien would not only be heralded in the annals of science and medicine, he'd actually *be there* to accept the praise.

Damien Slade was a medical school dropout—but that didn't matter. Many truly brilliant men throughout history did poorly in structured academia. He came from a wealthy, obdurately traditional family who said he *had* to become a doctor or he'd be written out of the will. He'd tried three times to get a decent MCAT score, each time scoring worse than his first abysmal performance. Finally, he was accepted as first alternate at the University of the Caribbean Medical College. As such, he had to wait for one of the registered students to drop out before he could get in.

Six months before the term began, he flew down to Puerto Rico then took an island hopper east to Anguilla to become familiar with the campus and the island on which it stood. He watched as students began to trickle in to acclimate themselves to the campus. One shy girl in particular caught his interest. She was very reclusive and, according to her medical history, suffered from deep clinical depression. A week into the first term, the girl came up missing. Her body was later discovered in an isolated coral cay on the far side of the island. Investigations showed her blood was saturated with large amounts of benzodiazepine and alcohol. Both products were available without prescription in the Caribbean. As no evidence of foul play was discovered, it was assumed she took a massive dose of Valium and rum to ward off depression and had subsequently drowned. As first alternate, Damien was admitted into the medical college the following week.

Despite being the brunt of countless jokes regarding its quality of staff, facilities, and students, the four-year college had an accredited, rigorous, comprehensive medical curriculum. Damien was soon overwhelmed with the classes and was placed on academic probation after the first year for failing grades. He struggled through his second year, barely passing most classes and having to retake others. The one course he excelled at was histology. He loved making slides of various tissues and organs; in particular, the preparation of blood samples. Perhaps it was his prowess at lab work that kept the administration from booting him out.

During spring break of his second year, rather than going home, he explored the adjacent island of Puerto Rico, where he learned the *real* history of Juan Ponce de León and the Fountain of Youth. Most scholars believed Ponce de León's quest for the elusive fountain was actually a search for gold. But Ponce de León's personal historian told a different account of private travels to the Bahamas, Hispaniola, Florida, and many points in between. There, strange events such as encountering huge primordial creatures in Florida's swamps and seeing bizarre sheets of colored light skit across the skies of the Bahamas led scholars to believe Ponce de León's historian was a chronic alcoholic.

The tales that piqued Damien's curiosity were those of encountering fair-skinned natives who claimed to be hundreds of years old. The translations were sketchy, but when Ponce de León asked about the secret to their longevity, the natives responded with claims of having "living water" and "living blood." For years, the Spanish governor searched for those living waters but never found them. His exploits became known as the legend of the Fountain of Youth.

A legend definitely, but Damien knew there had to be *something* to it. All legends were based on *some* actual fact. After extensive searching and questioning, he found a local shaman who claimed to have a roll of parchment that revealed the truth about "living water." Damien's quest became an obsession. He spent so much time investigating Ponce de León's "living water" that he let his already tenuous grades go unattended. Six months into his third year he was expelled from medical school. But it didn't matter. He was onto a discovery for which people would pay billions.

Damien moved to the marble figures cresting his cabinets. They'd each come so close to understanding the concept of living water. He clambered onto the countertop and respectfully placed his palm on their foreheads, one after the other, saying a little prayer of thanks as he did. He felt power surge into his hand as the luminaries shared their wisdom with him. Tears pooled in his eyes as he studied the details of each face. Such noble men, such enlightened minds. That he could carry on their work was an honor he could barely contain.

Wiping his eyes, he hopped down and went to the plasma cooler unit on the opposite wall. The digital thermometer read 38 degrees Fahrenheit. Excellent. The cryopreservation unit next to it was steady at -321 degrees, the point at which nitrogen becomes liquid. Perfect. The cadaver fridge was kept at a constant 40 degrees.

The money needed to maintain such equipment was substantial. But so was the monthly stipend his family dumped into his offshore account. The money would continue as long as they thought he was still in medical school. No problem. They never visited anyway—never called or texted. Everything was proctored through e-mail. He knew his family was embarrassed to be associated with him because of his stutter. Well, that didn't matter anymore. Soon the whole world would be knocking at his door, venerating him as a god.

Next to the refrigeration units was an autopsy table mounted with casters for easy mobility. On the gurney-like table lay a homeless man. He was still alive—but just barely. Damien didn't hold out much hope for him. Like countless others before him, he was sure to die within a few days of his transfusion. But Damien and his mentor were close to a breakthrough, he was certain. And when he found it, immortality would be his.

As he glanced at the reflection of the three marble luminaries in the glass of the plasma fridge, his breath caught. Their somber expressions had changed. They were now *smiling*. At him! He *must* be close. Somehow *they* knew.

His vision again misted with tears. It was a sign.

CHAPTER 26

JOSH'S EYES BURNED WITH FATIGUE. He'd spent the last four hours online researching different types of linen. It was incredibly complex . . . and incredibly boring. How did someone discover all the steps required to make that fabric in the first place? And from a plant that, to Josh, looked like a weed. Terms such as winnowing, retting, and scutching clogged his mind like hair in a barber's drain. He knew it was important to identify the specific linen used in the embalming murders, but to do so he had to slog through veritable quagmires of mind-numbing information. He was not opposed to study—he simply didn't like having to delve into such a tedious topic.

In the end, he discovered that *pure* linen was a fabric made solely from flax fibers. Because producing pure flax linen is labor-intensive, most manufacturers blend linen fibers with cotton, hemp, or fine wool. Linen blends were cheaper to make, but ultimately they were an inferior product when compared to the pure material.

The majority of flax was grown in France, Belgium, and the Netherlands, then sold to mills throughout Europe and China. It was during the milling process that the quality of the final product was determined. According to the crime lab, the hankies used at all three crimes scenes were long-fiber, ivory-bast from Ireland. Additionally, they were all from the same mill: Baird McNutt out of Ballymena, Northern Ireland.

Josh found that while you could buy directly from the mill, the majority of pure linen products came from Brooks Brothers Ltd. out of Enfield, Connecticut. They had stores nationwide and an online warehouse. That was not good news. It meant that thousands of people could place orders for pure linen hankies any given day. Still, he doubted there would be many buyers. Even the plainest pattern available was exorbitantly expensive. That meant whoever was purchasing them had ample financial backing—a feature most serial killers did not possess.

He pulled up images of the handkerchiefs from each crime scene. They looked identical. He enlarged the images to better see the particular weave. The edges were finely hemmed, but the cloth was basically patternless. He flipped back to the Brooks Brothers page and enlarged the image of their plain handkerchiefs. Close . . . but he couldn't be sure. Granted, his computer monitor wasn't high-def. The budget department hadn't approved his office for that upgrade yet. He'd have the IT nerds compare images of the hankies with ones from several websites to see if they could find an exact match.

In the meantime, he had to come up with a breakfast for tomorrow. His watch read 10:22 p.m. And she wanted to eat at 7:00 a.m. Ugh. Good thing a number of stores never closed. He'd cooked for Rebekah a few times in the past but never breakfast. She was pretty picky about what she ate. It'd been a long while since they'd spent an entire day together, and he wanted to make sure it started off right. He hoped working together would help alleviate some of her anxiety over the embalming cases.

He decided to try his hand at French toast. Better be sure to get real maple syrup, not that artificially flavored corn syrup stuff she said caused circulatory problems. Orange juice—with lots of pulp, of course. Maybe some bacon? He shook his head. No, better not. She'd ride him all day long about that particular indulgence. *Alas.*

He loved seeing Rebekah excited about . . . well, about anything. Although she seemed ubiquitously cynical, she had this bubbly nature that fairly glowed when she talked about her work, some new discovery, or a good book she was reading. It was infectious.

Josh rarely got excited about anything—at least not since Loren's death. But ever since he'd started dating Rebekah, he found himself opening up to the idea that he could be happy again. Not a forced, artificial happiness but a deep, satisfying, fulfilling joy. At first, happiness had confused him and ultimately made him feel guilty. It didn't feel right that he should experience those emotions again. It wasn't fair to Loren or her memory. But with Rebekah, it came so naturally, so uninhibited and free, that he didn't even realize he was falling in love until it was too late. Maybe Nick was onto something. Maybe he *should* take the next step in their relationship. Although Nick's logic defied logic, he *was* right.

Josh turned off his computer with a disgusted punch of the switch. He couldn't believe he'd just owned up to that. *As true as it is, there's no way I'm going to admit Nick Lonardo has anything to do with my relationship with CK—I mean Rebekah. Ugh.*

CHAPTER 27

Late that evening, Damien sat in his basement studying the Internet hits he'd acquired throughout the day. His software ran 24–7. The complex algorithm brought up several potential centenarian donors, but it did not delineate those who were on life support or were dependent on a significant level of chronic care. He'd have to dig deeper for that information.

Damien felt blessed to have found two out of the three Utah centenarians living by themselves. That always simplified things. Less exposure. And the procedure had gone flawlessly with each. The other benefit was being so close to his mentor. He'd been corresponding with him for almost two years. It was a godsend, no longer needing the use of overnight delivery services. Using such carriers increased the likelihood of exposure. At this point in the grand design, the less others knew of him, the better.

He had planned on turning in his two-weeks' notice to Avalon Manor tomorrow. His work there was done, but he knew he couldn't simply quit. It would raise suspicions. He wasn't concerned about having worked there only a few months. The turnover at such facilities was generally pretty high. But he knew the ME was investigating the death of Lester Johnson, and quitting right after the man's generous donation would cause a stir. He wasn't about to make that mistake again.

Damien stood and stretched. The tiny house he leased in South Salt Lake City was perfect. It was as unassuming as he was. It sat in a small service area at the end of a narrow alley separating a dry cleaner and a defunct butcher's shop. Large, unkempt lilac shrubs and half a dozen bristling junipers nearly strangled the small house. Weeds proliferated from cracks in the neglected blacktop surrounding it. From the street you could hardly tell it was a house.

Barely a thousand square feet, it was little more than a box, with mottled-brown tarpaper siding and a disintegrating asphalt roof that had long ago turned from black to gray. An exterior brick chimney provided a generous canvas for local graffiti artists. The house was elevated just enough to allow four quarter-sized windows in the foundation walls to peek above ground level, two on opposite sides. They did little good, however. In addition to the overgrown shrubbery, Damien had masked the windows with duct tape to thwart prying eyes. The basement boasted a set of double doors at the end of a downward-sloping service ramp, just wide enough for a standard pickup truck. There was no access from within the house, but a backdoor opened onto a narrow wrought-iron staircase that zigzagged down to the sloping drive.

The landlord said the building was the butcher's home back in the forties. He'd used the basement as a temporary meat locker. Damien loved the irony. His contract said he could use the space for whatever he liked, but he was responsible for all upgrades and damages.

The ugly little building was probably one citation away from being condemned, but because the basement was already wired with 220 industrial current, it was perfect for Damien's needs. Thanks to the service drive and the double doors, getting the refrigeration units down there was a breeze. The cryo-unit had to be perfectly level, which proved to be more challenging than expected. The basement floor appeared to have been poured right over ungraded dirt. But in the end, he had a passable lab in which to perform his divine tests.

The upstairs was more like an apartment: a small living room, a smaller kitchen, one bedroom, one bath. Once he had moved in, Damien actually had spent more time in the basement than upstairs. He was more comfortable down there, away from the harsh sun and harsher world.

He paused and frowned at the thought. Did that make him a creature of the underworld—a being of darkness thriving on the misfortune of others? No. He was doing something good for humanity. And if not for humanity, at least for himself. Just think of it: never needing to fear death. Having suffered belittlement and humiliation all his life, he certainly deserved to discover a secret hidden from the world for centuries.

Damien stretched again and took in the makeshift lab. All of his experiments to date had ended poorly. But they weren't failures. Trial and error equaled discovery and eventual success. And he was so close to success. Thanks to the three recent donations, he currently had enough

AB-positive blood to try again. And with the recent acquisition of a new volunteer, he could begin testing immediately. He loved large cities with their indigenous homeless populations. New volunteers were so easy to come by. The major drawback was that most of them were not very healthy to begin with. Oh well.

Damien checked on the transient he'd picked up the night before last. The man had been grimy, unkempt, and malnourished. Damien had sedated him and fed him parenteral IV nutrition, then he scrubbed him from head to toe. It was a disgusting job, but, having worked with so many old people over the years, he was used to it. The man's vital signs had stabilized overnight, enough to begin the transfusion.

Damien drew a sample of blood and tested it for type and Rh factor. He'd done so when he'd first acquired him, but he always liked to double-check his initial findings.

"Ok-kay, Mr. Doe. Let's see what we c-can see," he said, reading the display on his Beckman-Coulter blood analysis system. "Oh good. You're B-positive. I've always said you should t-try to b-be positive." He snickered and winked. "Hmm. Your white cell count looks a b-bit high; plasma pH is low. You really should t-take better care of yourself, Mr. D-Doe. You know, eat more fruits and veget-tables and get p-plenty of exercise."

Along with having an IV draining into his left arm, the unconscious Mr. Doe was hooked to a heart monitor and a respirator. The IV solution contained a special mix of nutritional essentials, anticoagulants, antibiotics, and the unique antirejection compound he'd acquired from his mentor.

Damien held a large-bore to the median cubital vein in Mr. Doe's left arm. "Okay, you may feel a little p-pressure here," he said just before sliding the surgical steel into the thin tissue. The old man grunted. "Okay, couple more p-p-pokes and we're done." He pushed a similar needle into the vein on his right arm and taped it in place. The second needle was attached to a tube with a valve that regulated the rate at which the man lost blood. "There. Now that w-wasn't so b-bad, was it? Of course it wasn't." He'd had lots of practice on his donors.

Using his embalming pump, Damien began to fill the man's system with AB-positive blood at the same rate he lost his B-positive blood. Both the inlet and outlet of blood were metered very slowly to allow the body time to compensate for variances in pH and osmolality. It was well known that changing the blood too quickly would send the system into shock and could lead to metabolic acidosis and death. As far as blood type incompatibility, his mentor's unique compound should prevent antibody rejection, which would allow Mr. Doe's system to accept the new blood.

To date, their precautions hadn't done much more than delay the fatal reaction. Damien would know how this John Doe would fare in about two days. That's how long the total-body transfusion would take. Good thing it was the weekend.

Once again, Damien snuck a look at the marble figures above his cabinets. They were still smiling. The bust of Richard Lower nodded, causing Damien's breath to catch. Like a lighthouse sending life-saving direction through a storm, the father of modern blood transfusion was giving him his approval, his blessing.

Overwhelmed with emotion, Damien fell into a chair, took Mr. Doe's hand in his, and sobbed with gratitude.

CHAPTER 28

Saturday

JOSH WAS UP AT SIX—which struck him as an unpardonable sin on a Saturday. But he had a lot to do. He showered, dressed, and then swooped through his apartment, cleaning and organizing as he went. The place was not a sty, but it did need a thorough going-over. Okay, so the laundry hamper was erupting . . . and his bathroom smelled like a locker room . . . and his kitchen cupboards were suffering from Old Mother Hubbard syndrome. But at least the carpet didn't crunch when he walked on it . . . anymore. That was something, wasn't it? Just in case, he had purchased some carpet freshener along with the breakfast fixings.

He prepared the French toast using a recipe off the Internet. It smelled heavenly. The table was set for two. The butter was softened just right. The maple syrup was warm. He even sprang for a small bouquet of daisies. Just as he was about to remove the first batch from the griddle, his doorbell rang.

Nick stood outside wearing shorts, sneakers, and a sleeveless tee. "Mornin', boss," he said cheerily. He looked Josh over. "Whoa, I thought fo'sure I'd get you outta bed. I didn't know yous was a mornin' person."

Josh blinked a few times. "Nick?"

"Yeah, so I was just on my way ta the community center for some round ball. Thought I'd drop this by," he said, handing him a large manila envelope.

"What is it?"

"Remember yous asked me ta look inta murders of old folks over a hundred? So I modified a couple of standard department searches and did a nationwide scan. I got me some freaky weird hits on it."

Josh looked at the folder with renewed interest. "Weird things, huh?"

"Yeah. Take a look. Might be connected, might not."

"Thanks, Nick."

"No problemo, boss. Hey, ya wanna come play some b-ball?"

"Can't. Got a date this morning."

Nick stood on his tiptoes to look over Josh's shoulder. "Is that right? She already here? Or, should I ask, *still* here?"

Josh shook his head. "No to both. But she will be any minute, so . . ."

"*Pisano*, it's not CK again, is it?"

"Who's CeeKay?" Rebekah asked, walking up behind the young detective. "Hey, Nick."

"Hey, Rebekah," he said sheepishly.

"Nick just dropped off some new info on our investigation. Thanks again, Nick," Josh said dismissively. "Have a good ball game."

"Uh, yeah, thanks," Nick said, edging away from the door.

Rebekah smiled. "See ya, Lonardo."

Josh ran back to the kitchen to rescue the current batch of French toast, tossing the envelope onto the table as he passed.

"So what'd he give us?" she asked, closing the door and following him to the kitchen.

"Don't know. Why don't you open it up and take a look? Breakfast will be ready in about three minutes." He removed the nearly scorched French toast from the griddle and replaced them with four fresh slices.

She sat and opened the envelope. "So who's this CeeKay—some secret Puerto Rican girlfriend you're hiding from me?"

He chuckled. "Sort of."

She looked up. "What's *that* supposed to mean?"

"It's the initials C. K. It's a nickname Nick's given you." Right when he said it, he wished he hadn't.

"Really? Initials for . . . ?"

"'Cute Kid,'" he lied.

Her eyes narrowed. "Nick Lonardo—the Jersey Gigolo—saying 'cute kid'? Come on, detective, you can do better than that."

"I really can't remember," he mumbled, flipping the toast.

"Right," she harrumphed, removing a stack of papers from the envelope.

"I hope you're hungry. I think I made too much—" He stopped midsentence, staring at Rebekah. She was gawking at the papers in her hands. Her eyes were wide, her face ashen.

"What's wrong?" he asked.

"You are not going to believe this," she said in a tense voice.

"Try me."

"Our guy's been going from one state to the next. Utah appears to be about number four on his list."

Josh looked at the paperwork and saw the same pattern Rebekah was referencing. Over the past three years, five centenarians in Florida had passed away suspiciously. In Arizona, two centenarians and one super centenarian had died in the same manner. And Iowa had lost two citizens older than one hundred. All of the deceased had had their blood replaced with an oily preserving solution lacking formaldehyde.

"Why hasn't the FBI jumped all over this?" Rebekah wondered aloud.

"I don't know," Josh replied. "Maybe no one has thought to correlate their deaths from one state to the next."

"I wonder if they're all AB-positive?" she said, turning the next page. "I hope that's in here. I'd hate to have to call the state MEs to ask." Her voice was shallow, as if she was forcing herself to say what she'd rather keep private.

"Are you okay, Becks?"

"I have a terrible feeling this is only the beginning of something much bigger." She went to the sink, filled a glass with water, and gulped it down.

Josh moved behind her and gently gripped her shoulders. Leaning down, he whispered, "You want to tell me why this is bothering you so much?"

She set down her glass and turned to embrace him. Josh loved the feeling of her arms around him, and his around her. But this embrace felt cold. Not the chill from a lack of affection. Rather, her body radiated an icy aura of . . . *fear*. He sensed that she clung to him out of desperation—out of a need to feel safe, protected.

"Rebekah?"

"I guess you wouldn't know," she whispered into his shoulder.

"Know what?"

"My mom had AB-positive blood."

"Oh." He kissed the top of her head. "But you're not, right?"

"I know. But . . ."

"But what?"

"AB is a universal acceptor. They can receive blood from *anyone* without antibody rejection."

"Okay . . ."

Forcing her words through a wall of emotion, she said, "So why did her body reject the kidney I gave her? It's a blood organ. Why wasn't it enough to save her? Why couldn't I have kept her from dying . . . ?" Her voice trailed off as she buried her face in his chest.

"Rebekah. Sweetheart. That wasn't your fault. You've said so yourself. You know you had no control over that. We've talked about this before. You risked your life donating that kidney. That was an enormous sacrifice—especially at eighteen."

"But I failed!" she cried into his shirt.

"No, Rebekah, you didn't."

Josh held her tighter as her body trembled uncontrollably. They *had* talked about her mother's death before. He knew it was a bitterly tender subject, even after all these years. She was a strong woman with impenetrable confidence, but when it came to the memory of her mom, her chainmail-reinforced willpower had a huge chink in it.

Josh took a steadying breath. He'd never seen her react this intensely before. But he understood why. Stroking her hair, he said firmly, "Rebekah, listen to me. Agnes Baugh, Silas Snow, and Lester Johnson have nothing to do with your mother's death. She was killed by a drunk driver, not by a psychopath seeking out centenarians with AB blood. The fact that Agnes Baugh donated a kidney for transplant just like your mother did is mere coincidence."

"I know," she said, wiping her eyes on his shirt. "I know I'm just being silly. I guess it just triggered all the old doubts. I know all the medical facts behind tissue rejection and all that. But it still doesn't stop me from wondering why."

"I wonder why too, sweetheart. I guess this is just one of those times we need to bow our heads and say, 'Thy will be done.'"

She nodded and held him tighter. She then looked up and pulled his face to hers. She gave him a lingering kiss. When they parted, her eyes registered acceptance and gratitude. Releasing him, she said, "Thank you, Josh. I wish I could be as strong as you."

He chortled. "You kidding? You're the one who picks apart dead bodies all day long. My stomach isn't half as strong as yours."

She smiled. The chill in the air was gone. Color had returned to her face. "Yeah. Speaking of strong stomachs, let's try some of your French toast."

He pushed her away playfully. "You're ruthless."

"No," she said smiling. "Just honest."

CHAPTER 29

DAMIEN AWOKE EARLY AND CHECKED on Mr. Doe. He was still alive, but his vital signs were dangerously weak. He had no clue what was in the vial he received from his mentor, but he followed the directions to the letter, injecting ten mLs of the yellow liquid into Mr. Doe's drip line every day.

The vial was labeled with letters and numbers forming a code he could not decipher. Having been a med student, he was familiar with a lot of medical nomenclature. But the coded vial was not available to the public, which meant it had not gone through FDA procedures for new drug development. This was pure "bathtub" pharmacy. It was how many drugs were developed before the government began regulating everything back in the fifties. It was how things were done back in the days of Ponce de León.

His mentor said it was a hormone-carbohydrate polymer that inhibited the IgM and IgG immunity triggers which coded antibodies from the antigens on red blood cells . . . or something like that. It was supposed to prevent the immune system from creating the antibodies that would reject transfused blood. He developed it specifically for the AB antigens, but it could have application in other blood types if it proved successful.

Damien rolled his eyes. Other blood types didn't matter. And as far as knowing exactly how the compound worked, he couldn't care less. He got Cs and Ds in biochemistry and immunology, respectively, so he wouldn't understand. But understanding the chemistry behind it all wasn't what he needed right now. What he really needed was another volunteer to receive a full blood transfusion. The current Mr. Doe was clearly not worthy of the procedure. His body was rejecting the superior blood. However, having just obtained a wonderfully fresh supply of AB-positive blood, Damien felt he could run two procedures at once anyway. He'd keep his eyes peeled for a new recipient—hopefully a healthier one this time.

His watch indicated he had almost an hour before his shift at Avalon Manor, so he decided to check his computer for hits. No new names had popped up, but he did see a few threads from other people searching similar parameters. He followed one that led to someone searching for a ninety-nine-year-old man with a rare blood type who once lived in Maine. The thread started in New Mexico and had passed through most of New England before triggering Damien's program. But it led nowhere—as did most random search strings.

Then one thread in particular caught his eye. It originated in Salt Lake City. Now who would be searching for the same thing he was seeking *and* in the same city *and* at the same time? He opened the link and traced it back to the University of Utah. Really? He traced the search parameters and was able to pull up the login signature of the person initiating it. Rebekah Smith, pathology assistant from the state medical examiner's office.

A quiver ran through him—not the giddy thrill of discovery but the glacial fingers of foreboding. This was the second, perhaps the third, time he'd come across her name. Add to that the warning Silas Snow had given him from the grave, and he was convinced she was following his activities. Or was trying to.

He looked up at the stone busts of his heroes. Their expressions were uniformly ambivalent. That was a relief. If they weren't concerned, then neither was he. Besides, he always covered his tracks after each donation. Many investigators in a number of cities had tried to find him—obviously with no luck. To Damien, it was confirmation that he was doing a hallowed work, a righteous endeavor. Even his mentor had said the concept was heaven-sent, and he was a brilliant man.

But this Rebekah Smith woman was showing a persistence that was significantly greater than that of all the other investigators. She might cause more trouble than he could deflect. If she stumbled across his name, she could zero in on the fact that he'd been associated with old people all his life. Worse, she had talked with him face-to-face. That added a significant amount of risk.

He continued to follow her search string and found she had specifically looked for information on Agnes Baugh, Silas Snow, *and* Lester Johnson.

Not good. The glacial fingers tightened on his spine. He'd better let his mentor know he needed to lie low for a time. He had such a sweet setup with his Salt Lake hideaway; it would be a shame to have to move to another location and waste the countless hours invested in securing it. If he just went into hiding for a while, he could still use the house and simply travel to find new acquisitions—both donors and recipients.

He glanced at the clock. He only had twenty minutes before work. Damien made a snap decision and stopped the flow of drugs to Mr. Doe. It was an old batch anyway. The old transient would simply have to make it on his own. The beeping heart monitor remained slow and weak, sounding more like a death knell than an acknowledgment of life. It wouldn't be long.

Damien exited the basement in a funk. He hated it when things didn't go the way he wanted. His mentor had promised him a new compound that had yet to arrive. Worse, that pest Rebekah Smith was prying into his experiments. Well, enough was enough. Things were going to change. He'd make sure they did.

CHAPTER 30

AFTER BREAKFAST, JOSH AND REBEKAH looked over the materials Nick had dropped off. His search brought up a lot of information they probably didn't need, but it gave them a better perspective on centenarians worldwide.

A large number of one-hundred-year-olds lived in Okinawa, Japan, and in Sardinia, Italy. The largest *percentage* of centenarians per population base, however, was in France. Many experts attributed the longevity of foreigners to diets of fish, vegetables, whole grains, very little processed foods, and daily consumption of red wines.

"And here we sit eating cholesterol-coated carbohydrates smothered in fat and sugar," Rebekah said.

"Hey, it's *French* toast, remember? They must know what they're doing," he argued.

"Except that French toast didn't come from France. The English invented it to use up dried old bread."

"Really?"

"It doesn't matter. It's still pretty bad for you. That's probably why it tastes so good."

"Ah-ha. I knew you'd start to see things my way," Josh teased.

They finished the breakfast and cleared the table. She was feeling much better since Josh had helped her through her brief panic attack. The big breakfast didn't hurt either. While Josh stacked the dishwasher, Rebekah gave Nick's printouts a closer inspection and compared them with those that Josh had brought from his office. The information on linen surprised her.

"Wow. A hundred bucks for three linen handkerchiefs?" she exclaimed, looking at the Brooks Brothers page.

"Ninety-eight fifty, plus shipping, but yeah, that was my reaction too."

"Seems like an expensive way to blow your nose. What's so special about them?"

"Maybe they hold more snot than cotton?"

She grimaced. "No. I mean what's so special about *Irish* linen?"

"I'm not sure," he said. Then, snapping his fingers, he added, "Hey, let's go down to that shop on Main Street that imports Scottish and Irish stuff. We'll ask them."

She laughed and rolled her eyes. "What're you going to say? 'Excuse me. What is the booger-holding capacity of your hankies?' That type of investigation is below even *your* standards, Clouseau."

He returned to the table. "No, I'm serious. Look, we keep picking up all these little clues about blood types and statistics on old folks, but we have yet to figure *why* they link together. Sometimes it's better to look at things from a completely different angle."

"Now you sound like Dr. Mahesh," she said with her head cocked to one side. "But I like it. Maybe we should figure out why he wants *this* blood in particular?"

"Or . . ." Josh paused and scratched his head. "Or maybe there's something special about the *people*, not just their blood. For all we know he could be dumping it down the drain."

She leaned over the table and kissed him. "That's why I love you, Clouseau. I tell you what: you go to the import shop and check out the hankies, and I'll go to Avalon Manor to ask some specifics about Lester Johnson."

"But . . . well, I thought we were going to spend the day together," he said with a hint of complaint.

"We've had all morning together. And look at how productive it's been."

"But—"

"Listen. Let's do this one thing, then we'll meet again in a couple hours and drive up to Tremonton to see if we can meet with Agnes Baugh's daughter. Even if we get nothing from them, at least we've had a good country drive together. And we can have lunch at that famous steak place up there."

"Maddox?"

"Yeah, Maddox."

She watched him consider his options, knowing he'd agree. Josh usually bent to her will. She was flattered to have that kind of control over him, but she rarely abused the power. She was above that kind of behavior. But it was still fun to wield it every now and then.

She found it intriguing that Josh had suggested the same tactics as Dr. Mahesh. But then, it made sense that he would. Both men held jobs in which they had to determine causality from minimal information. And both men were good at their jobs. Perhaps that's why she enjoyed their company so much. Of course, her association with Sandeep Mahesh was on a strictly professional level. It was the same with Josh in some ways but much more intimate in others.

Then something else Sandy had said popped into her mind. *He should have proposed to you a year ago. Can he not see what a resplendent catch you are?*

Was she a resplendent catch? Or was she a quirky, unbalanced, headstrong woman who dissected cadavers for a living and who still carried emotional baggage about her mother's death? Maybe Josh *was* dragging his feet for those very reasons.

Or were there others?

CHAPTER 31

"He's on the clock right now," a middle-aged receptionist named Tina told Rebekah. "We're not supposed to have personal visits while we're working."

"This isn't a personal visit," she replied.

Tina appraised Rebekah's casual attire with a dubious expression.

Rebekah showed the woman her state ME identification. "Look, I was here yesterday and the day before. I've already been cleared. I just need to ask a couple more questions."

"You're dressed oddly for a medical examiner on official business," she said, leaning back and folding her arms.

"I know what I'm wearing," Rebekah snapped. "I don't have to be in a pencil skirt and blazer to do my job."

"Of course not," the woman said, completely unfazed by her small tirade. "Please have a seat while I check with Ms. Mossberg."

Before Rebekah could object, the receptionist had the center's manager on the line. Rebekah stepped over to a reflective surface and appraised her casual jeans, blouse, and vest. Although her outfit looked great, it was definitely not "professional" attire. But it was Saturday. Everyone dressed casually on Saturdays, didn't they?

In less than a minute, Rebekah saw Ms. Mossberg storming up behind her. She straightened her posture, smoothed her vest, and turned. "Oh good. It's you, Ms. Mossberg. Now I won't have to start at the beginning. We've had a breakthrough at the ME's office. I just need to clarify one or two points with a specific member of your staff."

The solidly framed woman stood with arms akimbo as she scowled at Rebekah. "Ms. Smith, I am surprised that you came back considering you breached patient confidentiality, violated company HIPAA policies, and stole personal possessions from a dead man. I have already lodged a complaint with the state medical board and the Sandy police. Please leave immediately or I shall call security."

Rebekah stood speechless. Her first impulse was to fight fire with fire, as was her style. She recognized that doing so with this woman might be like shooting a rhinoceros with a .22; it would only make her mad. Still, it was worth the shot.

The injunctions levied against her were serious, but they would not hold up. As an ME employee, she had access to all of Mr. Johnson's records, she was fully HIPAA qualified, and she hadn't stolen anything . . . well, anything that Josh wouldn't eventually have ended up with anyway. She was merely expediting the process. That's the sole reason she was there now—to talk to LPN Slade and expedite the investigation.

Mossberg stood planted where she'd stopped, solid and immovable—almost daring Rebekah to challenge her. Well, *challenge accepted.*

"Ms. Mossberg, I am shocked by your accusations. I have full authorization from the chief medical examiner, Dr. Sandeep Mahesh, and the State of Utah. You may call anytime to verify my credentials. I am also working directly with the head of special case investigation, Detective Josh Logan. I had a meeting with him just this morning, in fact. We deemed it prudent to interview a certain member of your staff regarding the Lester Johnson case. Any interference on your part will be considered an obstruction of justice. Last time I was here you asked that we keep things under the radar so as not to cast an ill light on your facility. I have honored that request, but if you force me to get warrants and subpoenas, I promise you it will become very public."

Mossberg's menacing stance faltered. Her thin mouth opened, but no sound came out.

"Do we have an understanding?" Rebekah asked, still very much on the offensive.

The center's manager gave a slow nod.

"Good. Now please have Nurse Slade meet me in your office. We are not to be disturbed. Do I make myself clear?"

Mossberg trudged to the reception desk and spoke brusquely to Tina. "Get Damien out here immediately."

While Tina spoke into her phone, Mossberg preceded Rebekah to her office. "We are short staffed as it is," she said with no measure of apology. "Please be brief so Nurse Slade can return to his duties." She left without further comment.

Rebekah eased into Mossberg's desk chair and couldn't help smiling. It's amazing how often fighting fire with fire worked. Of course, when it didn't, you usually got burned.

After a few moments, Damien Slade leaned his head around the doorjamb. His eyes widened, and a grin started to spread across his face then stopped abruptly. To Rebekah it seemed an odd reaction to her presence. She decided to maintain her professional air, but she would be a lot easier on the poor stutterer than she was on Master Sergeant Mossberg.

"Come in, Mr. Slade. Please close the door. It's good to see you again."

The fleeting smile crossed his face a second time.

"I need to ask you some questions regarding Mr. Lester Johnson," she continued as he took a seat, "particularly about the time you spent with him before he died."

He shuffled his feet restlessly under his chair. "Okay."

"You have nothing to fear from me. I promise you will not be held accountable for what happened to Mr. Johnson."

The LPN snorted and covered his nose. It sounded strangely like a mix between a laugh and a sneeze. "S-s-sorry, ma'am. Allergies."

"It's okay. I don't believe we were properly introduced last time. My name is Rebekah Smith. I'm with the state ME's office. I was wondering if you noticed anything unusual the days before Mr. Johnson's hundredth birthday."

Damien's eyes darted back and forth under a furrowed brow. She suspected the guy's nervousness was making it hard to concentrate. "N-no, Miss Smith. Nothing."

"Please, call me Rebekah. According to your employment record you've only been here a few months, but your résumé shows you've had lots of experience in geriatric centers across the country. Comparing this facility with the others, have you noticed anything out of the ordinary?"

The man scratched at his cheek. "No . . . n-n-not really. Why? Is there s-something in p-particular you're l-looking for?"

Rebekah wondered if she should share her suspicions with this shy man. Giving too much information could lead him to create circumstances or embellish facts. She needed pure, honest assessments from him. She'd better keep it simple.

"I am part of an investigation involving Mr. Johnson's unusual death. I take it you are familiar with the way in which he died?"

He shook his head. "We've been told n-not to t-talk about it. B-b-but I know something strange happened to him. It k-kind of scares me."

Rebekah smiled warmly. "You have nothing to be afraid of, Damien. May I call you Damien? I'd like to think of you as my friend, and I could sure use your help."

He nodded. The quirky smile came and went again. He glanced at the door behind him. "M-ms. M-m-mossberg will be angry if I s-say anything," he said worriedly.

Rebekah understood his anxiety. She wondered if Mossberg was listening in from a two-way speaker system. Not wanting to jeopardize his job, she asked quietly, "Would you feel more comfortable discussing this elsewhere?"

"Y-yes, please." He sounded truly relieved.

"By agreeing to this, I take it you have something important to share with me?"

He nodded. The smile returned.

"Can we meet later this evening, say about seven o'clock?"

The smile widened. "Yes, ma'am."

CHAPTER 32

Josh drove to Edinburgh Castle, the Scottish import shop on Main Street. He'd passed by it many times before, but this was the first time he'd been inside. He knew some of his ancestry hailed from Scotland, but he wasn't into genealogy or family history, nor did he care for the few selections of Celtic music he'd heard. It all sounded the same to him. He recalled the first time he tried eating haggis. It ended up being the last time, too. He couldn't hold onto it and spent the rest of the afternoon bent over his toilet.

The small import shop was filled with more plaid clothing, more Scottish novelties, and more clan crests than he knew existed. Bagpipe music played softly (another first) in the background.

"Welcome, sir. What clan are you from?" asked a young man with sandy-red hair and green eyes. Josh expected him to have a thick Scottish brogue or a mellifluous Irish lilt, but such was not the case. He sounded Utahn, born and bred. His nametag read *Brian*.

The question caught him off guard. "My clan? Logan, I think. That's my last name."

"Highland or lowland?"

"Excuse me?"

"Logan is a huge clan. It's separated into two branches: the highland clan and lowland clan. They were contemporaries of Robert the Bruce. This is their tartan," he said, pointing to a swatch with a tic-tac-toe pattern of red and green panels surrounded by wide blue stripes crisscrossed with thin blue lines. "They actually share a tartan with the clan MacLennan. That's this one." He pulled out a similar swatch, but this one added thin yellow stripes boxing in smaller grids of blue and green with red stripes. Both designs were far too busy for Josh's liking. They reminded him of a headache. Crank up the bagpipe music and it was a guarantee.

"Um, I'm not sure which I belong to," he admitted. But he didn't say, *And I really don't care*. Still, the kid seemed to know his stuff. "Listen, I was wondering if you carry Irish linen handkerchiefs."

"You bet. Are you looking for pure linen or blended?"

"What's the difference?" Josh asked, already knowing the answer. He wanted to see how much the young man *really* knew.

Brian opened five thin boxes and championed the virtues of each material within. The most expensive was a three-pack of pure linen hankies for $110.49. The packaging showed it was imported for Brooks Brothers from Ireland.

"Have you sold many of these lately?" he asked, holding up Irish linen.

"*I* haven't sold any. But let me check the inventory log," he said, moving to a touch screen register. After tapping it a few times, he shrugged at the results. "We sold a package about two months back. Looks like we mostly move the blended handkerchiefs. But hey, if you buy over 300 dollars of merchandise, I can give you a ten-percent discount on them."

Ignoring the offer, Josh asked, "Is there any reason—other than saying it's pure linen—a person might want to buy these over a linen blend?"

The shop assistant didn't miss a beat. "Well, they say pure linen and pure wool have a natural energy that radiates from them. You know— like how some rocks are naturally magnetic? They say whoever wears pure wool or pure linen is naturally energized and has a better ability to influence people."

"Really," Josh stated flatly.

"Yeah, here," he said, opening the box of linen hankies. "Hold out your hands."

Josh wiped his palms on his trousers then held them out. Brian laid a hankie across each of Josh's palms with reverential care. "There. Now . . . how do you feel?"

Josh couldn't hold back a smirk. "Kind of stupid, actually," he answered.

Brian glanced to either side and leaned forward. "Yeah, that's my feeling too."

He removed the hankies and placed them back in the box. He then balled his fists and placed them knuckle-down on the counter, concentrating. "Other than wanting to impress someone, the only other reason someone might buy these would be for religious purposes."

"Religious purposes?"

The young man shrugged. "Yeah, you know. The Bible says Christ was wrapped in a *linen* shroud with a *linen* napkin over his face. A lot of the ancient burials in Europe and England used pure linen for that very reason. Even some of the mummies in Egypt and Peru are wrapped in linen shrouds."

Josh was impressed. "Where'd you learn all this?"

"I served a mission to Ireland. And I've always been kind of a history buff," he said with another shrug.

Josh took out one of his business cards. As he did so, his blazer shifted to one side, exposing his sidearm.

"Holy crap, is that thing real?" the clerk asked, taking a step back.

Josh handed him his card. "Detective Josh Logan, special investigations."

Brian examined the card. As he did so, Josh set his badge on the counter.

"Whoa. Okay. So maybe I should get my manager," he said nervously.

"No need for that. No one's in trouble here," Josh assured him. "I just needed some information on Irish linens. I've checked the Internet, but all it gives me are cold facts. You've been a big help, Brian. May I call you if I have more questions?"

He gulped. "Uh, yeah, sure."

Josh was about to leave when he noticed the shop's vast tie selection. "Hey, you wouldn't happen to have a Logan clan tie, would you?"

"You bet," the clerk said, brightening.

"I have a girlfriend who thinks I have zero class when it comes to . . . well, everything."

"No worries, detective." He turned and slid a thin box from a high shelf. The cellophane window displayed a stylish tie in the Logan clan's tartan. "This will definitely change that opinion."

Josh looked at the price tag and blinked hard.

"Plus, it's 100 percent pure wool. Just think of the energizing influence you'll have when you wear it," Brian added with a wink.

Josh pulled out his wallet. "Sold."

CHAPTER 33

REBEKAH CLIMBED THE FOUR FLIGHTS of stairs to Josh's office. His desk faced away from the entrance to the office space. As she stepped inside she heard Nick say, "Boss, CK at your six."

Josh spun his chair around. "Finally! Man, I'm starving."

Rebekah stopped short and stared at his tie. "Where in the world did you get that?"

"Just picked it up this morning. You like?"

"It's, um . . . very classy." She stepped forward and rubbed it between her finger and thumb. "Hmm, 100 percent wool, right?"

"Yep."

She read the fob on the back. "Hand-made in Scotland. Very nice, Clouseau. I am duly impressed. But . . . well, it isn't really you, is it? Your style is more jeans and button-downs, not herringbone and oxford cloth."

"Hey, change is good, right?" he argued. "Besides, I can't have you always showing me up, now can I?"

She smoothed the tie against his chest and turned her attention to Nick. "What gives, Lonardo?"

"Not much, Becks. You?"

"Same old, same old, ya know?" She enjoyed bantering with the East Coast immigrant as if they were standing in downtown Brooklyn. "So fess up. Who's CK?"

"It's you, angel face," he said without missing a beat.

"Uh-huh. And what does CK stand for?"

"'Cute Kid,' of course." His smile was wide and mischievous.

"Uh-huh. And why don't I believe you?"

He held his palms up. "Beats me."

"You've got the fort, Nick," Josh said to him. "I'm going to a crime scene up north."

The junior detective looked from Josh to Rebekah and back again, all the while with a Cheshire cat smile stretched across his face. "Well, yous guys have fun."

Josh escorted Rebekah to the parking garage and opened the door of his Escape for her. "Where'd you park?" he asked.

"In a metered spot out front. It's okay; I have my ME's tag on the dash. I love government immunity."

"I believe that's called an abuse of power."

"*Au contraire, Monsieur Clouseau.* Am I not on official business involving the state medical examiner's office?"

"Yes, but—"

"But nothing. I am actually saving the government money by carpooling with you, thereby only accruing one charge for the mileage to Tremonton instead of two." She loved the blank looks he got when she had him in an intellectual corner. It was such a cute blank look. "Well don't just sit there," she continued. "Let's roll. I'm starving too."

As they drove north, Josh told her what he'd learned about linen from Brian at Edinburgh Castle and about the shop itself.

"So he basically confirmed everything you'd learned earlier," Rebekah said, thinking she might have to check out the import shop herself. She'd always wanted a nice plaid wool skirt.

"Yeah, but I think there may be something to this religious angle."

She was skeptical. "So our nut job is getting instructions from a higher power? God is telling him to harvest the blood of old people to do . . . what?"

"I still don't know." He chewed at his lower lip. "This might sound morbid, but I wish I could speak to one of the victims before they were embalmed."

She snorted. "No, morbid would be interviewing them *while* they were being embalmed."

His look conveyed just the emotion she'd hoped to elicit.

"When was the last time you had a psych evaluation?" he asked.

"It's required for all state morgue personnel," she said matter-of-factly. Just then an image of Robert Lansing flashed into her mind. "Speaking of which, I still haven't told you about the run-in I had with Robert the other night."

He frowned. "Is he still hitting on you?"

"Oh, that part I can handle, sweetie. Never fear, you captured my heart long ago. And I know I've captured yours," she said, patting his knee. "Anyway, he came in around midnight last Thursday totally plastered. Drinking on the job is a termination offense, but there's no way to prove *where* he was drinking. I told security there wasn't any alcohol in his office because I felt sorry for him. But when he was threatening me, he said—"

"Threatening you?" he interrupted harshly.

"Well, perhaps 'threatening' is a little strong. How about 'taunting'? He had a knife, but he didn't use it in a hostile manner—at least not toward me. He was going on and on about how he's a doctor too and that he knows how to use a blade and such. I've always suspected he was jealous over the glamour associated with my job," she said, smiling slightly.

"Glamour," Josh echoed in a monotone.

"Truth be told, I don't think he can stomach the sights and sounds and especially the smells of the autopsy room."

"I can empathize with his limitations there, babe."

"I know," she said, caressing her fingers through the hair above his ear. "But it's kinda cute watching *you* turn green. It just makes Robert look more toad-like."

"Thanks."

"Anyway, he also said something about being able to 'find the blood too.' At the time I thought he meant being able to perform an autopsy; but the more I've repeated it in my head, the more I focus on two words. He said 'I can *find the* blood.' Not, I can *work with* blood or *deal with* blood; he said *find the* blood. You think he was talking about AB-positive?"

Josh was quiet for a time then mumbled, "Creepy."

"Yeah, that's what I thought. Then, after he said that, he said 'I'll still be here when you're gone.' It wasn't until yesterday that I wondered if he was talking about the centenarians in some way. You know, like when *we're* dead *he'll* still be alive?"

"Huh. You mean, he thinks he's a centenarian too? Or that he has something in common with them?"

Her head cocked to one side, still perplexed. "Yeah. But why would Robert allude to that? Why not come right out and say it?"

"I have no idea, Becks. But we'll definitely put him on our list of people to interview." He glanced at his watch. "Our appointment with Agnes Baugh's daughter is at three o'clock. Let's grab some lunch first," he said, pulling off I-15 at the Brigham City exit that led to Maddoxs.

Talking about Robert Lansing had somehow quelled her appetite. Hopefully, once they were in the restaurant, the aroma of grilling meat would bring it back. "Oh, speaking of appointments," she said, recalling her crazy morning, "I set up an appointment with Damien Slade later this evening. He's the LPN at Avalon Manor who got to know Lester Johnson before he was killed. I thought it would be best to meet with him away from work so he wouldn't feel so intimidated. They have this Nazi director there who looks like a linebacker for the Raiders and has a temperament to match."

"Sounds like a good plan," Josh said, pulling into the restaurant parking lot. "You want me to go with you?"

She smiled at him. "You're so sweet. But a big burley man like you might intimidate him even more. He's kind of a wimp and he stutters. I'm pretty sure I'll be fine."

"You're the boss," Josh said, leaning over and stealing a quick kiss before exiting the car.

CHAPTER 34

BETH MORTIMER HAD AGREED TO meet with Josh at her mother's house. The huge cottonwoods in her yard cast an afternoon shadow over the small bungalow and surrounding perennials, giving it a comforting, Americana appeal.

"Quaint," Rebekah said as they stopped at the curb. "Reminds me of my grandma's place in Heber. Talk about tiny. I hated going there because it always smelled terrible. And the only thing she ever had to drink was Yoo-hoo."

"I love that stuff. And I think the house has a cozy design," Josh said, leaning forward to look past Rebekah.

"You mean 'claustrophobic design.' I bet the place has one closet-size bathroom for the entire house."

"Sounds perfect. Less to clean."

She rolled her eyes. "Yeah. Ask any parent with more than one daughter and see how 'perfect' one tiny bathroom is."

They exited the SUV and went up a cracked cement walkway. Mrs. Mortimer opened the door before they knocked. "Detective Logan?"

"Yes, ma'am," he said, showing his badge. "This is Rebekah Smith from the state medical examiner's office."

"I'm pleased to meet you, Mrs. Mortimer," Rebekah said, showing her credentials.

Beth Mortimer smiled graciously and stepped back. "Come in, please. It's insufferably hot out there. And please, call me Beth."

They entered the small living room and sat on a small sofa with doilies on each arm and one centered on the back cushion. The room was filled with an eclectic mix of knickknacks, including a collection of penguin figurines that entirely filled a large highboy display case.

Rebekah felt a tad awkward, knowing she hadn't been invited to this meeting, but she *did* have a valid reason for being there. Even worse, she feared that asking Beth about the kidney she received from her mother would trigger another mood swing. She had to keep things light.

Following the direction of Rebekah's stare, Beth explained, "Mom loved penguins. She said looking at them kept her skin cool in the summer and her heart warm in the winter."

Rebekah smiled courteously. "My mom had a thing for warthogs."

"Goodness gracious," Beth said, placing her hand on her chest.

Josh stealthily elbowed Rebekah in the ribs.

"Mrs. Mortimer," he said authoritatively, "as I mentioned on the phone, we'd like to ask you some questions about your mother."

"Oh! Wait just a tick," Beth said, groaning to her feet and ambling out of the room.

Rebekah exchanged a look of bewilderment with Josh. "I didn't expect her to be near 100, too," she whispered.

"Stop it," he whispered back. "What's gotten into you?"

"I think it was that half-pound buffalo burger I ate at Maddox. I feel like I'm on a protein overload."

Beth returned carrying a serving tray with three tall glasses of lemonade. "I thought a cold drink would help keep us cool."

Josh leapt up and took the tray. "That's very kind of you." He placed the tray on the coffee table and sat back down. "Now, I apologize for the indelicacy of these questions," Josh continued, "but I need to ask if your mother was acting strangely before her passing."

"Oh, *pshaw*," Beth said with a wave of her hand. "There was nothing indelicate about my mother. She was pioneer stock from the get-go. She gave birth to me in this very house and an hour later was out helping Dad cut hay with me strapped to her breast. I saw Mom every day before she passed on, and there was nothing out of the ordinary I noticed. She took walks when it wasn't too hot, but most of the time she sat in this here rocker watching her dumb game shows." She jabbed her thumb at the TV, showing her disdain.

"Did she mention meeting anyone new recently?" Rebekah asked.

"No . . . not that I can recall."

"Any strange phone calls or mail?"

Beth frowned. "No. I collected all her mail and weeded through the junk. But it was all the usual monkey business. She didn't mention any strange phone calls."

"Do you know of anyone new in the neighborhood or see anyone new?" Josh asked.

Her brow furrowed. "No."

"Have the neighbors mentioned anyone new?"

"Not that I can recall."

Josh and Rebekah exchanged a second glance. The looks were not filled with hope. "Was your mom much of a socialite?" Rebekah queried.

"Good heavens, no. Oh, she didn't mind company, but she rarely left this house. Even her walks were just around the block. The last time she went anywhere was when she turned 100 and we went down to city hall for a big celebration. It made the local paper and the *Deseret News*. She hated it. It was the same night as some silly dance show she always watches, so she was pretty upset about missing it."

"Detective Logan knows just how she feels," Rebekah said with a mischievous grin. "He hates missing *American Idol*."

Josh frowned and shook his head. "That's not exactly true, and it's irrelevant." He scooted to the edge of the sofa. "Thank you for meeting with us, Mrs. Mortimer. You've been very helpful. We'd better be on our way now."

"Oh. Okay. But I don't know what help I've been."

"You've been a great help. I want to leave my card in case you think of anything else later on. Call me day or night."

"You sure? I mean, Rebekah, you won't mind?" she asked with a raised eyebrow.

"Mind?" Rebekah wondered.

"Yes, well, aren't you kids married? I know I wouldn't want another woman calling my husband, especially at night—and especially if he was as handsome as Detective Logan."

It was all Rebekah could do not to laugh thinking of Mrs. Mortimer secretly flirting with Josh in the still of the night. "Oh *pshaw*," she said, mimicking Beth's earlier exasperation. "Detective Logan welcomes *any* calls he can get from women. Besides, we're not married."

"Really? You're *not* married?" she said, truly astonished. Leaning forward, she fixed Josh with a piercing glare. "What is wrong with you, young man? She's smart as a whip and cute as a bug's ear." Without missing a beat, she waved it away. "Good gracious, do forgive me. It's none of my business."

Groaning to her feet, Beth ambled to the front door. "Well, thanks for stopping by. You kids come back anytime."

"Thank you, Mrs. Mortimer," Josh said, exiting.

"Yes, thank you, Beth," Rebekah echoed.

Before Rebekah passed the lintel, Beth gently grabbed her wrist. "Listen, honey. There's no such thing as Mr. Perfect. God didn't make men that way. So if you find Mr. Close Enough, grab him but quick."

Rebekah gave her a quick hug. "Thanks, Beth. I'll keep that in mind." She joined Josh in the Explorer, barely suppressing a huge grin.

"What'd she say to you?" he asked.

"Just good-bye."

"Oh." He started the SUV. "She's right, you know. You *are* cute as a—"

"If you value your life, you won't finish that sentence," she warned.

He didn't.

CHAPTER 35

DURING HIS SHIFT AT AVALON Manor, Damien spent more time covering his tracks than assisting residents. Mossberg had left for the day, so it was easier to skulk around in places he had no business being. Her office was locked; therefore, he could not access any personal notations on Lester Johnson's passing. He grinned, thinking he could fill quite a few pages himself if they really wanted to know.

Luckily, Avalon Manor did not have in-room security cameras. That would have created some hassle for sure. Mesa Roja had a low-tech surveillance system that had necessitated some extra planning. But because he harvested late at night, he was able to work around it. Besides, he doubted anyone ever reviewed the overnight CCTV recordings anyway.

Confirming that no one was watching him, Damien performed a few menial tasks, removed a few more bits of evidence, said hello to a few of the residents he'd befriended, and went to lunch at two. He ate at a local sushi bar known for very fresh sushi, sashimi, and a house specialty, fish blood soup. He loved the concept of drinking fresh blood—not as some silly vampire wannabe, but as someone fully aware of the life-giving, life-sustaining functions of the liquid. Blood did *everything*. It transported nutrients and waste, oxygen and carbon dioxide; it delivered medicines and removed toxins; it was self-regulating and self-regenerating. No wonder it played such a vital role in longevity.

After work, Damien went directly to his basement to check on his computer hits and refrigeration units. Oh, and on Mr. Doe, too. Surprisingly, the sedated man was still alive. Barely. His blood pressure was ninety-one over forty, his heart rate was at 127 bpm, his respiratory rate was shallow and sounded . . . wet. The LPN could do a white cell count to check for infection, but he knew what he'd find; it would be through the roof. It was only a matter of time before the homeless man went to his spirit home. So why prolong the inevitable?

He stopped the flow of AB-positive blood into, and the drainage of B-positive out of, the old guy. He then removed the respirator and watched as the man's breathing slowed. His heart rate increased but ejection fraction dropped significantly. Not a good combo if you wanted to live. A moment later, Mr. Doe's eyes fluttered open. They were rheumy and distant.

"Where am I?" he asked in a scratchy, shallow voice.

"At the end of your r-rope, old-t-timer," Damien said with poorly masked glee.

Mr. Doe closed his eyes. "Son, I've been there for years."

The LPN placed his hand on the old man's wrist and gently squeezed. "You'll be at peace soon. Any last words?"

Doe's eyes reopened quickly. Damien saw in them the unmistakable horror of complete understanding. He patted the man's wrist and spoke in a voice filled with tenderness. "I know this may c-come as a shock t-to you, but your life is p-p-pointless. I mean, what g-good are you to society anyway? You contribute nothing, so why s-should you receive anything in return?"

"I ain't *askin'* for nothin'," the man exclaimed, his voice hoarse with fear.

"And that's exactly what y-you'll get. No f-food, no water, and . . ." He cupped his hand over the man's mouth and with his other hand pinched his nostrils closed. "No air."

The homeless man struggled against the straps securing him to the table to no avail. Breath would not come to him because Damien wouldn't allow it to. The younger man leaned in so close that the tip of his nose almost touched that of the transient's. His eyes matched the wideness of Mr. Doe's. But Damien's eyes were filled with excitement and anticipation; the older man's with abject terror.

Damien whispered, "And no life."

Mr. Doe mumbled under Damien's hand. It sounded like a plea, just shy of a scream. Damien could not help but smile. It was an open-mouthed smile, a grin stretching from ear to ear, filled with ecstasy. The old man's eyes folded shut, but he continued to struggle.

Damien's smile vanished. "Open your eyes!" he screamed, still millimeters from the man's scruffy face. "Open your eyes. I want to see life leave your b-b-body!"

The man's eyes batted a few times, as if laboring to reopen, but they never fully did. His body went slack. He stopped struggling.

"No! N-not yet. I want to s-see it. I want to see the p-passing!"

Damien pulled away, removing his hands from the man's mouth and nose. With a breath as gentle as a soughing breeze, the old man's chest slowly collapsed, never to rise again.

The LPN was shaking, no longer from excitement but from anger. He'd been robbed. He had been robbed by an old derelict, a homeless nobody whose body did not accept the pure blood he was trying to give it. To refuse such an offering was tantamount to blasphemy. The man was impure, unholy, un*worthy*. There was no doubt about that. But not allowing Damien to watch his life's essence leave his body was just— just—just—

Damien screamed, shaking with rage. He cocked his fist and punched the dead man in the face. "You're so s-selfish," he bellowed. "You're selfish and r-rude. J-just like all the kids who u-u-used to m-make f-fun of me for s-s-stuttering." He punched the corpse again. And again. "Don't laugh at m-me! I can tell you're l-laughing. Stop it, stop it, stop it!"

He spun around and moved to the wide stainless-steel sink. Taking deep breaths, he forced himself to calm down. He was filled with molten bitterness. Nothing was working. Every time he got close, something else would go wrong. His mentor told him to have patience, that in the end he'd be rewarded. But sometimes being patient was too difficult to endure. The trouble was he knew *why* the experiment kept failing. His mentor insisted on transfusing only vagrants—people who would not be missed when they disappeared. But they were always sick and malnourished; no transient was ever in tip-top condition. To endure something as drastic as a full blood transfusion, you had to be healthy to begin with. The trouble was taking someone like that would stir up a missing persons investigation. And yet, did that really matter? Investigations were always instigated when he harvested from centenarians—and nothing ever came of those.

Damien returned to the dead vagrant and gently stroked his stubbled cheek and jaw. "I'm sorry, old m-man. Please forgive my outburst. I've been under a l-l-lot of stress lately. You c-contributed all y-you could. And we thank you."

He leaned down and kissed Mr. Doe's forehead then set about unfastening the restraints. "Now, let's get you back on ice so I can tidy up a bit. I need to prepare for the next volunteer. She'll be here in just a few minutes."

CHAPTER 36

"So what are you thinking?" Rebekah asked as they passed the Tesoro refinery.

"I'm thinking our boy is still actively seeking out centenarians and has lived in the state close to a year."

"Wait—you got all that from Beth Mortimer?"

He cast a quick glance in her direction. "Agnes Baugh's name and age were mentioned at least once in two in-state newspaper articles a year ago. He was either scanning the local papers or got a hit on a random web search."

"You sure?"

"When you did your search for Utah centenarians, how were they listed? You probably got a ton of hits from newspaper articles with human interest stories, right? And that was the majority of Nick's results, too."

She thought back to her printouts and Lonardo's. He was right. "Good one, Clouseau."

"Thanks. I think this guy is—" The buzzing of his cell phone interrupted his line of reasoning. He pressed the Bluetooth feature on his steering column, enabling the hands-free function. "Detective Logan."

"Hey, Detective, this is Brian. From Edinburgh Castle?" the voice stated.

"Yes, Brian. What can I do for you?"

"You said to call if I thought of anything else. Well, I did. I don't know if it's anything significant or not, but it has to do with the handkerchiefs you were asking about."

"The Irish linen ones."

"Yeah, those. Remember when you asked if we sold many? Well, when I looked on the computer, I was looking under in-store sales, which showed just the one transaction. But when I looked at the total turns for that product, it showed we sent six packages via mail-order a couple months ago. We sometimes do that, especially when the buyer is out of town."

"So you sold eighteen linen handkerchiefs to out-of-town customers?" Josh asked.

"No. That's the weird part. They were all mailed to an address in South Salt Lake. The guy paid postage for overnight shipping too. He probably could have *walked* here in less time and saved a ton of money."

Josh exchanged another look with Rebekah. Her eyes were wide.

"Go on," he prompted.

"Yeah, well, that's it, sir," the young man said, as if ashamed he didn't have more information.

"You wouldn't happen to have the address you shipped them to, would you?"

"Oh. Yeah," he chuckled, "I guess that would help. It was a P.O. box in an express mail store, not a physical address. But it was still only a mile or so away." He gave them the address number and promised to keep looking for other clues.

"Thanks, Brian."

"You bet, detective. Hey, did you show that tie to your girlfriend yet? And did it work the magic you were hoping for?"

"He sure did," Rebekah piped in.

A heavy pause filled the line. "Um . . . is that her, detective?" Brian whispered, as if that would keep the communication secured between Josh and himself.

"Yes, that's her. And it's okay. She loves the tie."

"Hi, Brian. I'm Rebekah."

"Um . . . hi."

"So what's this magic you're talking about—some druidic enchantment woven into the tartan that'll turn me into a wanton animal?"

The pause was thick with embarrassment this time.

"It's okay, Brian," Josh said. "You can take the fifth amendment on that one if you want. Thanks for your help with the handkerchiefs."

"And with the magic tie," Rebekah added eagerly.

He disconnected and grimaced at his passenger. "You're ruthless, you know."

"What?" she cried with feigned innocence.

"Never mind. Look, I'm going to follow up on a few things at the office, and you've got your meeting with that nurse. You sure I shouldn't go with you? I don't mind."

"You're sweet. But I'll be fine."

"Do you want to meet up later this evening?"

"Dinner at your place?" Rebekah asked.

"Wait—I did breakfast."

"Oh yeah. Well, we can do my place . . . but only on one condition."

He raised an eyebrow.

Her eyebrows moved up and down in a provocative dance. "Promise to wear your magical tartan tie."

He sighed in exasperation. "You *are* ruthless."

CHAPTER 37

REBEKAH HAD ONLY A FEW minutes before her meeting with Damien Slade. Her original appointment was for 7:00. He had called her cell phone and said his shift had changed; he wouldn't get off work until 7:30. She had no reason to doubt him. He asked that they meet in the parking lot in front of Bonwood Bowl in South Salt Lake. It was a very public place, so she didn't mind meeting him there, even at that late hour. She called Josh and explained the situation. He wasn't happy about it, but he understood the need to follow a lead when it was hot.

"Just be careful, Becks. That's not a family-friendly part of town, especially at night."

"I'll be fine, sweetie. I'm only going to talk with this guy for an hour or so, then we can get together to compare notes. Besides, it doesn't get dark until ten this time of year. And this guy may have the answers we're seeking. Like I said, I get the feeling he knows a lot more than he's letting on, but he's afraid to say anything at work."

"Okay," he agreed, but he still didn't sound happy. "Call me the minute you're done. I don't know about you, but I'm still full from lunch, so maybe we can catch a movie or just watch a DVD to give our minds a rest. I've found stepping away from a problem sometimes gives me a better view of it later."

"Great idea, Clouseau. Just nothing with more explosions than dialogue, okay?"

He gave a short chuckle. "Whatever you want. See you tonight, Becks."

Rebekah parked on the street-side of the lot and watched people enter and exit the popular bowling alley. Like Josh, she wasn't very hungry, even at that late hour. It was undoubtedly the huge Maddox buffalo burger she'd eaten. It may even last her well into the next day.

At 8:15 there was still no sign of Damien. She began to wonder if he'd been detained at the assisted living center. Perhaps Ms. Mossberg had given him some menial task before clocking out. It then occurred to her that she forgot to mention what kind of car she drove. And he hadn't mentioned his either. She accessed her phone's log, but his last call came from Avalon Manor. Calling him there would only get him into trouble.

She stood next to her Accord to make herself more visible. She scanned the parking lot, but no one was looking in her direction. She tried to picture Damien's face but had a hard time remembering anything about him except his red hair and thick glasses. The man was just so . . . plain.

She decided to take a quick look inside the bowling alley. The cacophony of heavy polyurethane balls sailing down hardwood aisles, slamming into pins, of pins smacking against their neighbors, and of cheers and groans from the numerous patrons hit Rebekah like a solid wall. The only refreshing thing about the place was that it was air conditioned. She looked around for a few minutes but couldn't locate the shy LPN. She didn't approach the service desk. They were swamped with customers, and she suspected Damien didn't frequent the place anyway.

Returning to her car, she began suspecting he was a no-show. Perhaps he'd gotten scared. Poor guy. She stepped to the sidewalk and looked up and down Main Street. The sun had barely set, but she knew the sky would remain light for some time. Even so, the street lamps had come on, and many drivers had already turned on their headlights. The heat of the day was still intense. Ripples of heat moved along the surface of the street like frantic spirits trying to avoid the traffic. A fine sheen of sweat beaded on her arms and neck.

She leaned against her car and waited. An evening breeze picked up but offered scant reprieve. She pinched her blouse and peeled it away from her skin. Her watch read 8:36. Fashionably late. Frustrating. A few men and women walked along the sidewalk, giving her cursory glances. One man altered his course and headed directly toward her. He was older and sported a poorly dyed seventies hairstyle and a trimmed mustache. Rebekah then realized her purse was still in her car, making her pepper spray beyond quick reach.

"Warm evening," the man said, wiping his brow with a hankie.

"Uh-huh," was her uninviting response.

"You're not making it any cooler, being so hot yourself," he said with a grin.

She rolled her eyes. "Really? That's the best you got? It's a whole new century, pops. That line might have worked three decades ago but not tonight."

It took a full minute before the man realized she'd just shot him down. He shrugged and headed into the bowling alley. She released an exasperated sigh and continued looking up and down the busy street.

At 8:50 she decided to leave. Maybe he'd forgotten. Perhaps his stutter was accompanied with an attention deficit disorder. Or maybe he'd changed his mind. That meant she'd have to make another visit to Avalon Manor—which she was loathe to do.

She turned to open her car door and saw the reflection of someone moving up behind her in the driver's window. She let out a chirp of fright and spun around, fists up, ready to defend herself.

"I'm s-s-sorry, Miss Smith!" Damien said, holding up his palms. "I didn't m-mean to frighten you."

He was still dressed in his scrubs. His hair was messy and he wore dark glasses, even though night shadows were thickening all around them.

"Holy cow," Rebekah gasped, lowering her fists. "You startled me."

"I'm very s-sorry, ma'am."

She patted her chest. "It's okay, Damien. It's good exercise for the blood pressure."

He smiled gratefully. "Thanks. And I'm s-sorry I'm late," he offered. "I got d-d-detained."

"That's okay. You're here now." She glanced at her watch. "Since you got off work so late, would you like to go get something to eat while we talk? You must be starving."

"Okay. But I feel b-bad making you wait even m-more. W-would you m-mind going back to m-m-my place so I can change?" he asked, tugging on his smock.

Even in the waning light she could see a rosy blush rush up his neck and flush his cheeks. It must have taken every ounce of courage for him to ask a woman back to his place. It was probably the first time he ever had. He didn't strike her as much of a player. "Sure. Do you live around here?"

"Just around the c-corner," he said, jabbing his thumb over his shoulder.

Rebekah considered her options quickly. This was probably the best chance she'd get to talk freely with him. He could change quickly, then they could hit one of the many fast food places nearby. She retrieved her purse from her Accord.

"Pick wherever you'd like to eat. It's official medical examiner business so it'll be my treat," she said, locking her car.

His eyebrows slowly raised above his dark glasses. His voice took on a strange tone. "It'll be just as much m-my treat as yours."

Was he flirting with her? Not likely. Guys like him would rather endure a root canal without Novocain than engage in innuendos with a pretty woman. She wasn't sure what to make of the exchange, but she didn't want to ruin their tenuous association.

"That's good," she said, forcing a smile.

Damien led the way behind a large building that had too many shadows for her liking. The breeze died in the neglected, vacant space, leaving a sticky atmosphere that reeked of garbage and decay.

"Charming neighborhood," she said before she could stop herself.

Damien kept walking, as if he hadn't heard her. His gait seemed brisker than before. Maybe he felt as vulnerable as she did. He turned down a narrow alley and kept walking. Trash and organic refuse lined the junctions where blacktop and sidewalk met building foundation. Above, the dark purple sky was framed in black by irregular cornices and haphazard rooflines. A large crow sitting on the corner of one rooftop belched out a warning caw. The abrasive sound ricocheted down the brick and stucco walls with enough force to make her flinch.

"Are you okay, Miss Smith?" Damien had stopped and was staring at her through his pitch-black sunglasses.

She hugged herself in spite of the heat. "Yeah. I just don't care for close spaces. Are we getting close to your place? We could always go back and get my car."

"No need. We're alm-most there."

He continued his pace, exiting the alley onto an area that looked like an old parking lot surrounded by old buildings. A very small house encircled by blacktop and unkempt shrubbery stood at the back of the lot. No light diffused from the structure, not even the amber glow of a doorbell button. Damien jerked his head toward the house and continued on.

At the front door, he removed a set of keys and opened three different locks.

"Can't be too c-careful these days," he said, as if justifying the redundant security.

"I agree," she said nervously, feeling her purse for the pepper spray within.

The first thing Rebekah noticed was the lack of air conditioning. It had to be close to a hundred degrees in the apartment-size house. The tiny living room was furnished with a mismatched armchair and a sofa. Shag carpet the color of bile ran from the front door to the small kitchen at the far end of the space. There was a rickety old swamp cooler in a small window above the sink, but it wasn't turned on. No pictures adorned the walls. Too bad. Rebekah would have even welcomed a velvet-backed, paint-by-number portrait of Elvis over the faded, orange paisley wallpaper. It was a headache waiting to happen.

"Um, where do you sleep?"

"The bedroom's next to the b-bathroom," he said, pointing to a space sectioned off from the living room and kitchen. "I know it's small, b-but since there's only me, I don't m-mind. Besides, the r-rent is cheap."

"Yeah, well, you get what you pay for—" She stopped abruptly, covering her mouth with her hand. "Oh my gosh, I am so sorry I said that, Damien. I didn't mean anything by it, I promise."

"That's okay," he said, lowering his eyes. "I know it's not m-much. But it suits m-my needs." Then, looking toward kitchen, he added, "I . . . b-better change n-now."

"Any chance of turning that thing on?" she asked, pointing at the swamp cooler.

"Oh sure." He switched it to "cool" and gave the top a thump with his fist. The unit screeched to life and rattled enough to wake the dead. After a minute or two it fell into a rhythm that sounded less like the exorcism of demons and more like a cat with its tail in a vise. It wasn't much of an improvement. No wonder he kept it off. "Gotta b-bump start it," he said loudly with an apologetic smile. "Please, have a seat. I'll b-b-be right back." He then disappeared around the corner.

She set her purse on the sofa and peered out the small front window. The vacant lot and the nondescript backs of the buildings weren't much to look at. The window was a single-hung design with a semicircular latch. She twisted the latch and heaved the window open. With a cross current going, the house finally began to cool. Even the swamp cooler seemed quieter with less strain on its system.

"Are y-you okay in there, Miss Smith?" Damien called from his bedroom.

"You really should call me Rebekah. 'Miss Smith' makes me feel so old."

"O-okay. Thanks."

Rebekah heard the opening and closing of drawers and the shifting of boxes. She also heard him grumble and curse occasionally. She couldn't figure why it was taking so long to change his clothes. Was he putting on a tux?

"So, how long have you lived here?" she asked to fill the awkward silence.

"Oh, n-not long. A year. M-maybe two."

That didn't seem right. She distinctly remembered his employment profile stating he'd only worked at Avalon Manor a couple months. Before that he was working in Colorado. It didn't fit. Something was missing.

"Are you from Salt Lake?"

The rustling continued. It sounded like he was searching for something. She assumed it was his clothes; but in such a small place it was hard to imagine how he even moved without tripping over everything he owned. "No, no. I'm originally from M-Manhattan, in New York. I m-moved down south for s-school then—Ah-ha! Here it is."

She heard the closing of a drawer.

"Here what is?" she asked.

"This," he said, rounding the corner. Dressed in sweats and tennis shoes, Damien held a 9-mm pistol. It was pointed directly at her face.

CHAPTER 38

JOSH WAITED IN HIS APARTMENT, feeling like he should be going somewhere but not having a specific direction in mind. His instincts told him Rebekah was getting in over her head. This kind of criminal investigation was *his* line of work, as were the risks that came with digging up dirt on suspects. It was one thing to do Internet searches and visit public places like the assisted living center; but meeting with a new witness at night in an unsafe location could prove dangerous.

He shook his head, needing a distraction. He hadn't picked out a DVD for them to watch because he wanted Rebekah in on the decision. Instead, he connected to his department's network and pulled up the file on Paxton Harris. Something there didn't jibe either. Smoke shopkeeper Chet was obviously a bigot. He hated the Asian family next door, claiming they used unfair business practices, but as far as Josh could see, they'd done nothing illegal or unethical.

He read over the affidavits of everyone who worked in the dollar store. Contrary to what Chet claimed, they were *not* all from the same family. They were all Hmong but weren't all the same nationality. Josh knew Hmong was an ethnic group comprising Chinese, Vietnamese, Laotian, Thai, and a few other Asian nationals. It was like using the term "Southerner" in the U.S. for people from Louisiana and other states around Florida. The combined testimonies and individual alibis of the Asians pointed to their innocence. Still, even alibis could be faked.

He mentally rehearsed the conversation he'd had with Chet. *Paxton never gave me no flak . . . to speak of. He had his own battles . . . I tried not to get involved . . .* Chet had claimed he didn't know what went on . . . but then how could he have "tried not to get involved?" And what did "no flak to speak of" mean?

Josh typed up a bunch of questions revolving around the Paxton Harris murder. Instead of focusing on the Oriental Posse, he listed everything that involved Chet. Did he have a valid alibi? Did he own a handgun? Did he have a police record? Did the smoke shop claim anything was stolen around that time—perhaps something Chet tried to reconcile before the owner found out? Had the Asian family ever lodged any complaints about him or the smoke shop? Josh added a few more thoughts then sent a copy to Nick's e-mail, asking him to follow up on them.

He glanced at his watch. It was a quarter past ten. Surely Rebekah's interview with the nurse—Damien Slade?—couldn't be taking *this* long. His instincts said she had overstepped her safety zone.

He texted her. *Hey, Becks, are we still getting together tonight?*

He waited for a quick reply but none came. He went to his cupboard and found an unopened Pop-Tart. Iced Blueberry. Rebekah would disapprove, but he needed some quick energy to keep him alert. He could just turn on the TV and vegetate for a while, but he didn't want to risk falling asleep.

Munching on his treat, he paced his living room, trying to organize the jumbled thoughts in his mind. Things should be adding up, but they just weren't. Just as he finished his second Pop-Tart, his phone buzzed.

Hi darling. Everything is fine. I can't meat tonight. Sorry.

Josh stared at the screen. His brow furrowed. His instincts were piqued. *Hi "darling"? Can't "meat" tonight?* She never misspelled words. She might interchange words or misuse them to create a pun or one of her cynical comebacks, but in normal communication she was a stickler for proper grammar and spelling. It could be a random slip, but he doubted it. *Darling?* She never used that endearment—at least not on him.

He texted back, *How did your interview go?*

Fine. She was very helpful.

She? Now he *knew* something was wrong. Rebekah was in trouble. Someone else was using her phone—or she was using it under duress. Was it Slade? It had to be. The nurse was meeting her right after work. Since he worked in Sandy, it was safe to assume he lived near the bowling alley. He decided to give the mystery-texter one last challenge.

He typed, *Did you enjoy your omelet this morning?*, knowing they'd eaten French toast.

Yes, thank you.

Hope I didn't use too many onions.

It was perfect. I love onions.

Good. Have a good night, my darling.

You too, darling.

Josh closed his phone and collapsed onto his couch. Trepidation eeled in his stomach. If anything happened to her, he'd never forgive himself. He should have gone with her—should have insisted on it. He shouldn't have taken Loren to Mexico on their honeymoon. He suddenly felt like he took Rebekah for granted. He should have done more to protect Loren . . . and now Rebekah.

Josh jumped to his feet and began pacing anew. He wasn't going down the path of unrequited regret again. The road to hell was paved with woulda-shoulda-couldas; it was riddled with potholes of self-loathing and doubt. He wasn't doing that anymore. From now on he'd be a man of action, not remorse.

He called dispatch and had them put out an immediate APB on Rebekah and her car, focusing on an area fifteen miles in circumference around Bonwood Bowl. She was thought to still be somewhere in Salt Lake County. She had medium brown, shoulder-length hair; dark brown eyes; five foot seven; trim, athletic build. He sent a picture of her via his phone to be included with the APB.

Having covered everything he could from a legal standpoint, he made sure his gun was loaded, slipped an extra magazine in his pocket, and headed out the door.

CHAPTER 39

REBEKAH'S GAG WAS SOAKED WITH her saliva. The material had a strange taste; not cottony or wool-like; rather, it had a woodsy, grassy taste. She tried to move but couldn't. Velcro straps around her arms, legs, and ankles secured her to a kitchen chair. She remembered feeling the jab of a needle just after Damien had made her sit with her back to him. Then she'd blacked out.

Having just awoken, she still felt woozy. Whatever he'd injected was taking its time wearing off.

As if reading her mind, he held up a syringe and said, "It's Versed. It's a rapid-onset sedat-tive with a short d-duration. It's very handy in situations l-like this."

That was when her cell phone buzzed in her purse. Damien retrieved it and smiled.

* * *

"Well, that was fun," Damien said as he looked at the phone's screen one more time. "I assume Josh Logan is a c-close friend of yours?"

Rebekah scowled at the duplicitous man, hating him for having deceived her—hating herself for having been deceived. Her wrists burned where the straps dug into her flesh. The gag pulled angrily at her mouth, preventing her from speaking. So why was the idiot asking her questions?

"A b-b-boyfriend perhaps?"

She felt tears burning the edges of her eyes, but she refused to let them fall—just as she refused to acknowledge Damien's questions.

"More?" he asked as he moved closer. "A lover?"

He slowly drew a section of her hair between his fingers, letting it fall sensuously against her face. She jerked from his touch.

"Can't say I b-blame him. Lucky m-man. You are very pretty. What does he do for a living? Is he a d-doctor or something?"

The LPN had placed a cookie tin on the kitchen table. The gun lay next to the tin. Rebekah had a clear view of everything the sociopath was doing. She felt like throwing up as she watched him text on her phone. It wasn't hard to guess who was on the other end. Would Josh recognize it wasn't her texting back?

The fog in her head was still thick but was clearing rapidly.

Damien pulled a drink from the fridge: a bottle of Yoo-hoo. With her throat on fire and sweat beading on her face and body, even that watery beverage looked appealing. She began grunting, nodding at the brown and yellow bottle.

"Oh. Are you thirsty?" he asked.

She nodded vigorously.

"Promise you won't scream?"

She nodded again.

"I'm not w-worried about anyone hearing you. We're p-pretty isolated between these b-buildings. I just hate the noise."

Rebekah nodded once more, slowly, with understanding.

He tugged at the gag knotted behind her head. It hurt dreadfully as he peeled it away, but she didn't make a sound. When he set the cloth next to the gun, her eyes went wide. Her gag was made from two linen handkerchiefs tied together—the same kind that were found on the corpses of Agnes Baugh, Silas Snow, and Lester Johnson. That could only mean she *had* found their killer. But it seemed so inconsistent. Damien Slade came across as incapable of such heinous acts. And even if he was, he didn't appear to have the intelligence to come up with a flawless mechanism with which to drain a person of every drop of blood without leaving a scrap of evidence behind. The man was simply too . . . well, simple.

Clearly, that was how he remained incognito. Perhaps he actually *was* intelligent. Perhaps under the stuttering, introverted exterior thrived a brilliant yet delusional sociopath.

"Are you right- or l-left-handed?"

"Right," she said, wondering why he asked.

He removed the strap on her left wrist and handed her the Yoo-hoo bottle. Ah—less coordination in that hand. Pretty smart. She took a small sip and let it slide down her throat. It was instantly refreshing. She managed a second, larger gulp before he tore it from her hands.

"No need to b-be greedy," he said with a half-chuckle, half-curse. "You're a guest, b-but it's rude to be g-gluttonous."

A guest? Did he not know she was on to him? Or was he holding her captive for some other reason? Was he going to assault her sexually, or worse? The bile rising in her throat tasted like she still had a mouth full of linen. Only this time it was soaked with blood—thick, rancid, clotting blood. She took several deep breaths to quell the gorge.

"What do you want with me?" she choked out, fearing she already knew the answer.

"Oh, that's g-going to take some exp-p-plaining. And I'm not s-sure you're sharp enough to unders-stand," he said as he refastened her wrist to the chair.

She swallowed painfully. Her heart was racing. She knew that whatever he had in mind wasn't going to be pleasant. There was a good chance she would not live through the night. Rebekah was not too proud to beg for her life. And yet, when he accused her of being "not sharp enough," her headstrong nature took over. *Fight fire with fire, right?*

"Listen, you stuttering dweeb, even drugged up on benzodiazepine, I'll pit my brainpan against yours any day," she managed to say with surprisingly little garble.

The LPN looked stunned. His eyes registered shock to the point that they misted over. Then steadily, vehemently, his surprise morphed into a glare of pure hate. His jaw clenched and bulged; his nostrils flared. He turned his head slowly, mechanically, as if hinged on a servo. Rebekah followed his line of sight to a wall clock. It was almost eleven. He held the stare for an inordinately long time then turned back with the same robotic efficiency. His eyes were vacant, glassy orbs.

He opened the tin box on the table and removed a syringe and a vial. Calmly, he drew two mLs of the liquid into the syringe.

"What—can't face me like a man?" Rebekah growled. She knew there was no way to avoid what was coming—and that made her livid. "Gotta drug me? Afraid a *girl* will best you?"

Damien rounded the table and plunged the needle into her right shoulder. The medication burned as he depressed the plunger too quickly. Within seconds her vision began to swim and sounds began to echo. Just before she blacked out, he stuck his face extremely close to her ear.

"Thank you for v-volunteering," he whispered.

CHAPTER 40

Sunday

IT WAS WELL PAST MIDNIGHT and Josh was running out of steam, but he refused to quit. He always knew something like this could happen. Lightning *can* strike twice in the same spot. He was not a pessimist by nature, nor was he prone to a doomsday mentality. But the loss of Loren had left an irreparable gash across his soul. Even if new tissue grew over it, the scar would still reside just under the surface, burning the flesh, constantly reminding him of the potential for heartache. The only time he didn't feel the pain was when he was with Rebekah. So why hadn't he taken steps to be with her forever? Just as before, he had no response, no rationalization, no reasonable excuse. Nor did he want one. All he wanted was to get her back safely, remove the threat of the centenarian killer, and then ask her to spend her life with him.

He was not going to lose—again.

Josh had been casing a three-block radius around the bowling alley for hours. The APBs on Rebekah and Slade had yet to produce anything. Slade's last known address was an apartment in Kearns. The Kearns police verified that he had not lived there for over a year. The landlord had no forwarding address or current phone number. That was not a good sign. He could subpoena the information from Avalon Manor, but his instincts told him the nurse had supplied them with false demographics.

Josh parked his SUV in the large bowling alley lot and went inside. The place was just minutes from their one o'clock closing. The overhead speakers were playing a country-western tune sung by a girl half his age but who was making ten times his income. A vacuum whirred in the far corner of the hall, where the lanes were already closed. As he approached the service desk, he removed a photo of Rebekah and his badge.

"I'm Detective Logan, Salt Lake Police, special investigations. Have you seen this woman this evening—perhaps within the last few hours?"

The man at the counter looked at the photo with half-interest. "Nope." His *Bonwood Bowl* shirt was embroidered with his name.

"You're sure, Rob?"

He sneered. "Look, detective, Saturdays are our busiest nights. We've had hundreds of people through here. You'll notice three of our lanes are still being played. It's all we can do to keep our heads above water. Now if you'll excuse me," he said, leaning to one side to acknowledge the person behind Josh.

Angered by the situation and by the employee's ambivalence, Josh was temporarily speechless. The man behind him stepped forward and set a pair of gaudy green-and-red bowling shoes on the counter.

"Thanks, Rob," he said. "The lanes were sweet tonight."

"Glad you had a good time, Kent," he replied.

Josh leaned forward. "Excuse me, Rob, I don't mean to be a pest, but I'd really like you to look at this photo again and concentrate on whether or not she was here. It's very important."

Rob sighed heavily and looked at the photo.

"Her name's Rebekah Smith," Josh added.

Rob shook his head. "Sorry, man. I got nothin'."

"Hey, wait a minute," the patron said, glancing at the photo. "I saw her a few hours ago."

Josh turned to the man. "You sure?"

"Oh yeah. Pretty gal like her. She was out in the parking lot, right along Main Street. She was leaning against a car, like she was waiting for someone. I walked by and commented on the weather—and she blew me off before I got out my best lines."

Josh frowned. "You tried to pick her up?"

"Hey, I see a foxy lady all by herself, that's my signal to go to work."

"Huh. Well did you see anyone else approach her?"

"No. I didn't hang around. I'm enough of a gentleman to know when to tip my hat and leave. She was all woman but tough as nails. I hope she's all right."

The man seemed sincere. Josh couldn't fault him for hitting on Rebekah.

"Yeah, me too. Do you recall what kind of car she was leaning against?"

"Not really," he said with a shrug. "I was focusing on *her* chassis more than the car's, if you get my meaning."

Josh had to force his fist to unclench. "Sure do. Thanks for your help."

He left the building and walked to the edge of the parking lot. He believed the guy's story; it sounded just like Rebekah. But there was no sign of her car. He was convinced Slade had moved it. But to where?

Leaving his Explorer locked, Josh began to walk the area around the bowling alley once more. He had a flashlight in hand, his shoulder holster unclasped, and a fervent prayer on his lips.

CHAPTER 41

REBEKAH AWOKE TO A HEADACHE. The room in which she lay was significantly colder than Damien's small house. And it was dark, gloomy. The humming of small fans worked its way past the throbbing in her skull. The only lights she could see were a few blurry LEDs on some kind of machine. Her mouth was pasty, her throat raw. She wanted to close her eyes and sleep for as long as possible, but her memory was crystal clear, and the images in her memory prevented her from wanting to ever close her eyes again. She forced her eyes open wide—not sure if she was still dreaming. *Wake up!* she screamed in her mind. *You have to stay awake!* She needed movement, action, something to get her blood circulating and the sedative out of her system.

She tried to sit up but discovered she was bound to a table. It was a cold, hard table. Sleuthing with her fingertips, she deduced it was a metal table—just like the ones she worked beside in the morgue. The realization made her breath catch painfully in her chest. It was an *autopsy* table. She'd worked countless hours next to just such a table, but she never dreamed she'd be *on* one. At least not while still alive.

She flexed sequential parts of her body and learned there were six nylon straps securing her to the table: one across her ribcage and arms, one across her pelvis, and four smaller ones securing each ankle and wrist. Luckily, her head was not strapped down. Rebekah focused on the soft LED glow coming from what looked like a large refrigerator. A chest freezer stood at the base of the fridge. Fixating on a green display, she read, *-320° F.* Really? A subzero cryo-freezer? Why would Damien need something that cold? Under the temperature readout, the unit displayed the date and time. *03:49.* She'd been asleep almost four hours? Five? She blinked hard a few times, forcing her eyes to adjust to the darkness.

Lifting her head, she saw a Formica countertop stretching end to end along the opposite wall with a sink situated in the center. Open-fronted cupboards lined the area above the counter. She could just make out three life-size busts atop the cupboards. It was too dark to see much more than their silhouettes, so she had no idea who they were. But she doubted they were Larry, Moe, and Curly. And she prayed they weren't actual human heads.

She laid her head back down and took several long, cleansing breaths. Panic would get her nowhere. The good news was that she was still alive. But whether that would remain "good" or not was the important question. She strained her hearing, listening for indications that someone else was in the room. She didn't even know *where* the room was, but the coolness of the air, the darkness of her surroundings, and the musty, limy odor of old cement convinced her she was in a basement. Damien must have carried her down there then left. She felt alone.

Tugging against her restraints, the strap on her right wrist felt a little looser than the one on her left. Pressing the heel of her thumb into her palm, she was able to narrow the diameter of her hand enough to twist it through the loop. The stiff nylon scraped her skin, but she didn't care. Gritting her teeth, she shrugged her right shoulder and contorted her body, working the arm from under the torso strap. It dug through her light blouse and into her flesh with every move, but she used the pain to help her concentrate until she had freed her arm.

She rubbed the tears from her eyes and raked her fingers through her hair in an effort to help her stay awake. Shaking her arm to get circulation flowing, she felt along the chest strap, trying to find a latch or Velcro release. There was nothing within reach. It must be under the table, she reasoned. The strap across her left wrist seemed extra snug. Bringing her chin to her chest, she saw an IV running into her left median cubital vein. She had no idea what the sociopath was draining into her, but she knew it couldn't be good. Taking a steeling breath, she withdrew the needle from her blood vessel then, using her thumb, she applied pressure to the injection site until the bleeding stopped.

Rebekah's head dropped back to the table. She closed her eyes as a sudden wash of drowsiness swept through her. It'd be okay to rest . . . just for a minute. Just until she could get past the surge of sedative metabolite . . . or whatever was making her so lightheaded. It felt so good to rest after all her exertions.

Once again, she inhaled deeply through her nose and exhaled slowly from her mouth. She opened her eyes as wide as she could—if only to prove she was awake. She *had* to stay awake. She had to free herself. If he found her partially free, he'd secure her tighter next time. Or worse. If she could find her purse, then she could get her pepper spray. But if he'd already gone through it . . .

She thought of Josh and prayed he had put everything together: her need to meet Damien Slade so late, the location of her meeting, the strange text messages. *Please, Josh*. With sickening recollection, she knew she'd only mentioned the bowling alley once. Would he remember?

Rebekah closed her eyes and began a silent prayer. But her mind would not stick to the task. It kept wandering between Damien and Agnes Baugh and Silas Snow and Lester Johnson and Josh and of a trip she made to Frightmares at Lagoon as a child and—

Wake up, stupid! she screamed in her head. She slapped herself in the face and stretched her eyelids open with her free hand. She lifted her head and focused on the LED display of the cryo-freezer. *-321° F. 04:18. Oh no. She had fallen asleep again.*

"Get up!" she growled through clenched teeth. "Get up now or you're dead!"

CHAPTER 42

JOSH FELT AS IF HE'D covered every inch of the area on foot. He'd found a transient sleeping behind a dumpster, a family of stray kittens with no mother, and a pair of teenagers making out in the back of a sedan, but no sign of Rebekah or her car. He told the teens to go straight home; he called dispatch to send out animal control the following morning and a patrol unit to take the transient to the homeless shelter.

Walking back to the bowling alley, he saw a Cadillac CTS parked right next to his SUV. The sour light cast from a single flood lamp mounted atop the bowling alley put both vehicles in dark relief, but even in the low light Josh could tell the Caddy was extensively tricked out. Very little traffic cruised Main Street at that early hour.

He drew his sidearm and held it in tandem with his flashlight. The Caddy was a glossy blood-red color, with a lowered suspension and windows tinted so dark they were probably illegal. When he was within twenty feet, the Caddy's running lights flashed once. Josh froze. Both doors opened simultaneously. Two young men stepped from the vehicle followed by two more immediately after. The group moved to the front of the car and stood four abreast. Although none carried visible weaponry, he had no doubt they were loaded to the teeth. The lights from Main Street revealed that they were all in their early twenties and were all of Asian decent. None of them were smiling.

Josh lowered his flashlight and pistol so the beam wasn't shining in their faces, but his gun was still pointing in their general direction. "I'm just heading to my ride," he explained in an even tone, nodding at his Explorer.

"We figured already," one of them said.

Josh didn't move. Overhead, thickening cloud cover saturated the night air with sticky summer humidity. The lot was silent, deathly still.

"I'm Detective Logan, special investigations. I'm looking for a car that was stolen from this parking lot."

"We figured that, too," another young man said. "It's parked in the Enterprise Rent-A-Car lot, about five blocks up State. 2008 Honda Accord, right?"

Josh's grip tightened on his gun. "Yes."

The young man who just spoke gave the others a look and jerked his head to the Cadillac. They nodded and got back inside. The last kid in made a point of pulling a micro Uzi machine gun into plain view from the folds of his loose shirt just before closing the car door. The power windows whirred open. Message received.

"Has the car been stripped?" Josh asked, feeling no more confident with only one gangbanger in view. He could not see into the car's interior, but there was no question he was in two or three gun sights.

The guy shrugged. "Don't think so."

Josh lowered the firearm and kept the flashlight trained on the kid's feet. "Okay. Thanks for the info."

"Thought we might be able to help each other."

Josh considered the negotiator thoughtfully. "Okay. How can I help the O-P?"

He smiled. "Street word says you're smart. Guess they were right."

"Thanks."

"Some dude dropped the Honda off next to the other sedans in the lot. Blends right in. Gotta give him credit for that move. We figured you was lookin' for it when you parked here and started poundin' the streets."

"Any specifics on the thief?" Josh asked.

The Asian shrugged again. "Just some average white dude. All you people look alike. After he abandoned the car, he walked back here and disappeared. Figure he's got digs around here."

"Yeah. That's what I figured too. So why is the Oriental Posse helping me?"

"Just heard you was fishin' in our pond, checkin' out the old Pax Harris case, right?"

"That's right."

"I assume you're lookin' for someone in particular."

"It's a start."

"It's a dead end."

Josh's hand tightened around his gun again.

The young man noticed the action. "Not that kind. At least not yet." He stepped back to the passenger side of the Caddy. "Here's the meat and potatoes: the Oriental Posse didn't kill Paxton Harris."

"So who did?"

"You're a smart dude. You'll figure it out. But I will tell you this: you've already met him."

Josh frowned. "Okay. So you've given me two perks. What do you want from me?"

"Just back off the O-P. That's all."

"And what if I can't do that?"

The Asian stared silently at him for a few moments. "You can."

Josh holstered his gun. "I can't promise anything. But I'll think about what you've told me. For what it's worth, I see very little evidence pointing in your direction."

The young man nodded and slipped into the Caddy.

As Josh unlocked his vehicle, he said, "You boys head for home now. It's well past your bedtime."

The kid laughed, said something in an Asian language, and laughed even louder. The others joined in. Josh didn't think it was all that funny. The Cadillac pulled out of the lot onto Main Street and cruised away in no particular hurry.

Josh then drove to Enterprise. Sure enough, Rebekah's car sat untouched in line with a few other look-alike sedans. The car was locked. He called it in to dispatch as he mentally cataloged the new information on the Paxton Harris case. He'd get to it when he could. Right now he had more pressing matters.

His watch read 4:30 in the morning. He was beat. But he couldn't stop until he knew Rebekah was still alive.

CHAPTER 43

Rebekah couldn't loosen the nylon strap across her ribcage. Her left wrist was still fettered, as was every other part of her body except her right hand and arm. She craned her neck again to look around her. To one side were the cooling units; to the other was a wheeled surgical cart similar to the ones she used in the morgue. And it looked like it was within reach. Stretching, she could just skim her fingertip past its chrome surface. She shifted to the limit of the restraints and tried again. Millimeters were all she needed to grab the cart. She had no idea what was in the recessed tray, but it had to hold *something* useful. She tried again and could nudge the cart but not get her fingertip over the lip. For the first time in a long while, she wished she had long fingernails. They were simply not conducive to her job.

Lying back down, she fought to control her anger and frustration. She hated feeling so helpless. She hated having been taken advantage of. She hated being held by a man who defined the very essence of wimpy. The guy was clearly delusional. What was he planning on doing to her? Was he going to fulfill some psychosocial fantasy? Some sexual fantasy? Was he going to hurt her? Kill her?

As disturbing as the what-ifs were, she kept going back to the whys. She doubted he had the smarts or wherewithal to run such an operation singlehandedly. Was he acting under the direction of a superior? Some other adult with a teenage mentality or penchant for slasher films? Or did Mossberg instigate her abduction so she couldn't spread bad press about Avalon Manor?

Letting her anger bolster her energy, she reached for the cart a third time. The nylon strap dug at and tore her flesh. She stretched harder. A plaintive, angry wheeze escaped her throat. At the limit of her endurance, she collapsed. It was no good. She could not slip her stubby fingernail over the lip. Shiny, polished, efficient, the chromed cart seemed to mock her. She turned away as the burn of fresh tears welled behind her eyes. But she wouldn't give up. She *couldn't* give up.

Opening her eyes, she focused on the IV tubing hanging loosely at the tableside. It dangled from an IV tree. Of course! *The needle!* She reached across her chest, grappling at the plastic IV tubing—and got it on her second try. Walking her fingertips to the end of the line, she examined the needle. It was roughly one and a half inches long, 21-gauge diameter. It just might work. It *had* to work.

She twisted the needle from the Luer-Lok system and, pressing it against the table, bent it about a third of the way down, forming a hook. She shifted on the table and again reached for the cart. Stretching to her very limit, she was able to slip the bent needle over the lip of the tray and pull it toward her. When it was easily within reach, she used her fingertips to identify what lay inside. Bandages, Coban elastic wrap, Betadine swabs, and . . . *there*! A scalpel. She felt its sharpness by sliding her thumb perpendicular to the edge. It was pretty dull as scalpels go, but it was just what she needed.

Forcing herself to remain calm, she began to saw at the nylon strap on her left wrist. It took about six minutes to slice through the multilayered material, mostly because it was at an awkward angle and she couldn't see what she was doing. She shrugged her left arm out from under the chest strap and flexed it to encourage circulation. The needle wound was bruised and sore, but it didn't start to bleed. The clock on the cryo-freezer read *04:46.*

Damien was probably upstairs, fast asleep, she reasoned. She had to keep quiet. She didn't know if he was an early riser, but even most early risers didn't get up before five. That gave her about ten minutes. Was that enough?

The chest strap took another five minutes to cut. Again, it was at an uncomfortable angle, and she couldn't see what she was doing most of the time, but at least she had the use of both hands now. Once it was cut, she was able to sit up. It felt glorious. She quickly released her feet then gingerly rubbed her ankles, wrists, and ribcage. Each wound felt like a swath of road rash. It hurt to move, to even take a breath.

Before searching for a release mechanism on the pelvic restraint, she looked around her prison. By now her eyes had adjusted to the meager lighting. Everything was varying shades of green and gray. There was little detail, but she could mostly tell what was what. It looked like an autopsy room, minus the overhead operating lights and the clean tile floor. A refrigerator designed for storing the deceased abutted the wall beyond the small cryo-unit. Two evenly spaced, squat windows were notched into the ceiling junction on opposite walls of the basement. Only slivers of light penetrated the glass. It was too dark to see what, but she guessed they were masked with something. Pushed against the back wall sat a second autopsy table similar to the one she occupied. A sheet lay draped over it. The fourth wall at the end of the basement boasted a set of large double doors—her salvation.

Rebekah began to feel under the table for a release. Finding a Velcro junction, she removed the remaining restraints and gingerly lowered herself to the floor. The cement was cold but invigorating. She took a wobbly step toward the doors before her eyes were drawn back to the second table. Cloaked in shadow, the sheet formed the mounded shaped of a corpse. Her mind screamed to leave it alone; it was none of her business. But her unquenchable curiosity overrode her cerebral warnings. She tiptoed up to the table and lifted the shroud from the feet. The material felt like a blend of linen—very light and delicate. Sure enough, there was a body underneath. It was too dark to deduce the state of the corpse, but it seemed very fresh. The feet showed no telltale signs of lividity or early decomposition. She pulled it back a bit farther and noticed the body was dressed in light clothing resembling pajamas. Strange—but she'd seen stranger. She repositioned the shroud and moved to the head. Pulling back the cloth, she immediately detected the clean scent of soap. Perhaps the body had just been prepared for burial. The corpse was male. It was too dark to see details, but the skin looked too fresh to have been dead for more than twenty-four hours. She took a step to one side to allow for the meager light to splash across the face. The instant it did, the corpse's eyes opened.

She screamed. A hand shot out from under the shroud and grabbed her wrist. Too startled to make sense of the action, she screamed again. She froze, unable to fight back as she stared unbelievingly at the dead man who was coming to life. And then she realized he hadn't been dead, only sleeping.

"Shhh," the LPN hushed her. "You scream l-loud enough to wake the d-dead."

CHAPTER 44

By FIVE IN THE MORNING, Josh was running on fumes. He'd combed the neighborhood a dozen times but saw nothing that even hinted at Rebekah's location. Sitting at a bus kiosk, he accessed his office computer though his smartphone and looked for reports on different combinations of Damien Slade's name. He got a number of hits but nothing of a criminal nature. The guy appeared as innocent as he looked.

He rubbed his eyes forcefully. He was losing focus faster than he could generate it. A warm south breeze did little to improve the situation. A business marquee across the street claimed it was a balmy seventy-eight degrees. The humidity was miserably high. He was sweating profusely, but he didn't care about offending anyone. Few people were awake at this hour anyway.

He yawned then stretched and touched his toes a few times. As much as he hated it, he knew he needed chemical intervention. He walked to a Maverik convenience store a few blocks away for some artificial energy.

Inside, a woman with unnaturally blonde hair, black jeans, an Iron Maiden tee, and a dingy company vest looked up from an *LDS Living* magazine. Josh blinked and looked again, certain he was hallucinating.

"Well, hello there," she said, tucking her hair behind a prolifically pierced ear.

"Hey," he replied with a lift of his chin.

He went to the cooler looking for a can of Rock Star, Monster, or Tribe. Normally he didn't imbibe energy drinks; the crash that followed the caffeine high could only be countered by consuming another can. "Hair of the dog," some called it. It just wasn't worth it. But this *was* an exceptional circumstance. He grabbed a tall Rock Star from the cooler and a bag of chocolate-coated mini-donuts from an adjacent rack.

"My kind of breakfast," the cashier said, grinning. "Working a late shift or an early one?"

"Late. Very late."

"You look beat, sweetie. You sure that Rock Star's gonna do it for ya?" She flashed him a smile that suggested a lot more than friendly customer service.

"Yeah. Caffeine, sugar, and carbs. All the things my girlfriend says will kill me. Ought'ta be just the thing to help me finish my investigation."

Her countenance faltered. "Oh. Donuts. I shoulda guessed you're a cop."

"Detective. But I'm really a nice guy. I'm currently working on a homicide case." He pulled out his badge and laid it on the counter. He pulled up a downloaded a photo of Damien Slade on his phone and sat it next to his ID. "Have you ever seen this guy around here?"

She looked at the picture without touching it. Using the eraser end of a pencil, she turned the phone around for a better look. "Maybe . . . yeah, I think so. He's one of those guys who looks like he wouldn't make any difference to anyone about anything. But when he locks eyes on you your spine crawls. He oozes creepiness, you know?"

"Yeah. Good description."

She shrugged. "You work a shift like this, you see all kinds, sweetie. Luckily, we don't get many like him in here. Mostly we get bums looking for cheap wine coolers and beer, or tourists who can't find their way back to the Interstate. But every once in a while, one of the weird ones comes in and stares at me when he thinks I'm not looking—or worse, stares at me when I *am* looking." She shivered involuntarily. "That's when I hate my job."

"Must be a great place to work," he said in a sarcastic tone.

"It pays the bills," she said with a flick of her eyebrows. "Plus I get shift differential working graveyard, so it ain't all bad." She stretched her hands over her head and leaned forward with her hands extended toward Josh. "And every once in a while a cutie like you comes in, which always brightens up my day." Evidently her trepidation of his being a cop had already worn off.

"Thanks. Can you remember anything else about this guy?" Josh asked, pointing to the picture of Damien Slade between her elbows. "Like when he was last in here?"

She studied the photo for a minute. "Yeah. I remember him, all right," she said, straightening. "I haven't seen him in over a month. Maybe longer.

But that's fine by me. See, I ain't afraid of no guy, no matter how big and tough they think they are. But this guy tipped the scale on the creep-o-meter."

"How so?"

"He asked some really weird stuff."

"Weird stuff?"

"Yeah. Most guys ask where to find a good time in this lifeless town. It's the classic lead-in to asking me out. I've heard it a million times." Again using her pencil, she pushed the phone to the edge of the counter, as if wanting to distance herself from Damien's gaze. "This guy asked if my grandparents were still alive and if so, how old they were, and where they lived."

Josh was suddenly more awake now—and he hadn't even opened his energy drink. "What did you tell him?"

"I told him it was none of his business."

"Just like that?"

"Well," she shrugged and played at faking a blush. "I may have added a colorful word for emphasis."

"And how did he respond?"

She rubbed her arms vigorously. "Well, this sounds kinda crazy, but he gave me this cold, creepy look, like he was wanting to . . . to steal my soul. And he says, 'Finding the *chosen* is precisely my business.'"

Josh nodded, retrieved his phone and his badge, and pulled out his wallet to pay for his snacks. "Okay, thanks. How much do I owe you?"

Her flirtatious manner vanished as she rang up the sale. Josh said to have a good morning and headed for the door.

"Wait. There's one more thing," she said.

He turned with raised eyebrows.

"Well, is he a doctor or a nurse or something?"

His eyebrows inched higher. "What makes you ask that?"

"Because he also asked me what my blood type was."

Josh felt his blood chill. "What did you tell him?"

"I said I didn't know."

"Did he believe you?"

She shrugged. "I guess. He left right after. Haven't seen him since."

He nodded. "Thanks for the info."

"Did it help?"

"Yeah. More than you know."

The hint of a smile returned. "I'm here almost every night, sweetie. You need anything else—" she leaned forward again "—*anything* else, you come on back, you hear?"

Josh wagged a finger at her and exited, anxious to begin his search anew.

CHAPTER 45

A LARGE WELT HAD FORMED over Rebekah's left eye. Damien's pistol hadn't broken the skin but had hit with enough force to leave a scar. The wound made her head swim. She was disoriented, nauseated. The swooshing of blood through her ears sounded like the rushing of whitewater inside a tunnel; the pulsing of her heart sounded like sonic booms. She didn't remember being hit. He obviously blindsided her. Her skin was tight and wet over the welt. She couldn't see or feel any blood—she was surprised none had been spilled. But she was certain it would be. Very soon.

She refused to give up but *needed* to give in—at least until her head cleared. The soft hum of a refrigeration unit now filled her ears. She was cold. Very cold. She opened her eyes but could see nothing. At first she wasn't sure she *had* opened her eyes. She forced several long blinks but sight eluded her. She was in complete darkness. She breathed in deeply. The air stung her nostrils and added to the pressure behind her damaged brow. But the aroma of the chilled air gave her a clue as to her whereabouts. It smelled of refrigerant and . . . and death.

She was very familiar with that scent. She encountered it daily at work. It was so commonplace that she hardly noticed it anymore. Until now. Here, it seemed out of place, because she wasn't dead. And yet she was in a place reserved *for* the dead. Damien had put her in the cadaver refrigerator.

As painful as it was, she breathed in the chilled air, knowing it would help clear her head. Surprisingly, she could move her arms; they weren't restrained. She could tell she was on a sliding platform designed for easy on-and-off loading of human remains. A light sheet was draped over her. It was thin and offered minimal warmth. Feeling beneath the shroud, she discovered she only had on her underwear. No wonder she was so cold.

She quickly pushed aside the question as to how she'd lost her clothing. The answer was obvious. Dwelling on it would only add to her misery.

Rebekah slowly, hesitantly moved her hand out from under the shroud; not afraid of touching something in the blackness but that something might touch back. The cold metal ceiling of the fridge was a mere foot and a half above her. It was crusted with a prickly layer of frost that stuck to her fingertips. Feeling to her right, she found the wall a few inches away, equally frosted. With her left hand she reached in the opposite direction. Instead of encountering a wall as expected, her fingers touched skin—dead skin.

She gasped and jerked her hand back. Her breathing shallowed and quickened. There was a corpse lying next to her in the narrow, dark refrigerator. She gritted her teeth and willed herself to remain calm. She was not afraid of the dead bodies; she touched them almost daily. But that was always under bright lights in a sterile environment, properly masked and gloved. She had no idea who was lying next to her, inches away. The familiar smell of death turned to a stench. Her stomach roiled, her scalp wound amplifying her queasiness. Her panting echoed off the ceiling and walls, sounding as if the corpse was struggling to draw breath. *Don't you dare go there*, she scolded herself. *Don't scare yourself witless when you need all your wits to get through this.*

She reached over her head and pushed against the door. It was latched from the outside. She wriggled upward, trying to get as close to the door as possible. Then she felt below the platform for the emergency release installed to prevent accidental entrapment. There wasn't much room, but she was able to wedge her arm between the lip of the table and the door. *There!* She felt a flat knob on a short rod. She tried to push against it, but the angle made it impossible to get any leverage. If she could turn around and lie on her belly, she could slip her foot between the table and door and press the knob with the ball of her foot.

Rebekah twisted her torso and arms until she was facedown, her hips and legs following. The thin sheet was trapped underneath her. Every time her bare skin came in contact with the frosty metal walls, she sucked in a sharp breath. She rested a bit, gritting her teeth and thinking of her next maneuver. It was not going to be pretty. She was going to have to crawl over the cadaver next to her. Using her elbows, she shifted a few inches to one side. She did her best to avoid contact with the corpse, but it proved futile. With only a thin sheet between her face and the cadaver, the stench of death amplified to a noxious reek. She wriggled as quickly as she could, but she was so cold she could barely move. She needed to get past this part before she lost her nerve . . . and quite possibly her lunch. The frigid walls and ceiling bit at her exposed skin. The pressure she exerted against the corpse caused a release of gas from its mouth, which worsened the stench exponentially. She gagged but continued to squirm until she had turned 180 degrees.

Then, wedging one foot onto the safety release, she took a fortifying breath and pushed. The knob depressed a full three inches, accompanied by a muffled clack. Bright light shot into the refrigerator as the door swung open. Frosty fog condensed and billowed away from her. The warmth of the room caressed her feet. It felt glorious.

Rebekah knew she had to move quickly. If Damien was still asleep, the noise of the door opening would surely awaken him. If he was already awake, then hopefully he'd be too shocked to react to her sudden escape. But she was head first in the claustrophobia-inducing cadaver fridge. She had no choice but to exit feet-first.

Placing her palms against the icy back wall, she pushed with all her might. With an initial bump over a thin threshold, the wheeled tabletop glided into the bright room.

"Well, good m-morning," Damien's cheerful voice declared. "Wow, first the res-straints on the table, now the ref-frigeration unit? You are full of surprises, M-Miss Smith. But that's okay. I have a few for you t-too."

CHAPTER 46

JOSH WAS AT A LOSS. Frustrated, he texted, *What have you done with Rebekah?!!!* but he didn't send it. Doing so would reveal that he knew she was in trouble. Better to remain covert until he got a better handle on the situation. His Rock Star was gone and he was down to his last mini-donut. Neither snack had given him the energy and focus he desired. Instead, he felt queasy and jittery. His lack of sleep and high anxiety only added to his misery.

He got out of his SUV, did some push-ups in the Bonwood Bowl parking lot, and walked back to the Maverik store. He could have driven, but he needed fresh air to clear his head. He knew Rebekah was in imminent danger, but there was little he could do until he knew where she was. Slade could have taken her anywhere. She'd obviously been subdued. He also considered that the nurse might not be working alone—but he doubted it. The guy had "loner" written on everything he did.

A Salt Lake City patrol car was parked in front of the convenience store. Josh entered and saw an officer he recognized purchasing a one-liter bottle of Mountain Dew and a box of mini-donuts. He smiled, thinking of his snack a few hours earlier. The fake blonde had been replaced by a young man with almost as many earrings as she'd had.

"Does your wife know you eat that junk?" Josh asked from behind the officer.

The uniform turned with a whimsical scowl. "Hey, Josh. What're you doing on the streets this early on a Sunday?"

Josh glanced at his watch: 6:11 a.m. "Never went to bed, Wyatt. I'm on a case that's got me flummoxed."

"Oh. Hey, listen, my wife doesn't know about this addiction," he said as he paid for his treats, "so I'd appreciate it if you kept it under your belt."

Even though Josh was in excellent shape, he grabbed his stomach and pretended to jiggle it. "You mean *over* my belt."

"Exactly," the lawman chuckled, patting his own belly—which was considerably larger than Josh's. They exited the store. "So does your sleepless night have anything to do with the APB on your girlfriend?"

"Yeah. I have reason to believe she's being held against her will."

Wyatt's normally cheery face turned hard. "You serious? The APB said she was missing, not abducted."

"Yeah, I know. But I've uncovered some info that says otherwise. I found her car at a rental place up State Street. No sign of her. Last I saw her was around six yesterday evening. She was meeting a retirement home nurse named Damien Slade to question him about some things the ME wants to know. Then I got a text from her, only it wasn't her."

Wyatt's eyes narrowed. "Someone pretending to be her using her phone."

"Exactly. I haven't heard from her in twelve hours. She promised to get back to me after meeting with Slade, but she never did. I've talked to a few witnesses who say they saw both Rebekah and Slade in the area around Bonwood Bowl last night, then *poof*, they disappeared. I called in the APBs and a tow to take her car to the impound . . ." His voice trailed off as he again wondered if he'd done all he could do.

"And you've been casing the area ever since."

"Yeah," Josh said, unable to keep the exhaustion from his voice.

"Josh, dude, you look like someone opened a can of hell and you fell out. Let me call in some manpower and we'll canvas the area."

"Without a search warrant it'd be a waste of resources," he said, knowing it'd be nearly impossible to get a warrant with such minimal evidence, especially on a Sunday.

Wyatt nodded, twisted open his Dew, and took a large swallow. His eyes then brightened. He unclipped the radio from his epaulette. "Dispatch, Sergeant Olson here. Get me Ballard in SDU. Yeah, that's him. Yes, I know it's Sunday. Call his cell phone. Okay, thanks."

Josh didn't recognize the man's name or the unit. He could only hear one side of the conversation because the patrolman wore an earpiece. Josh gave his friend a questioning look. The patrol officer responded with a raised index finger.

"Hey, Tommy, this is Wyatt Olson. Yeah listen, I need a favor, stat. You know Detective Logan in special investigations? Yeah, that's him. His gal's gone missing since yesterday and—" He paused, being cut short. "No, they didn't have a spat. Highly probable abduction. Evidence suggests forcible kidnapping. It's unofficial at this point, but he doesn't want to wait until we have a body to initiate an investigation." Another pause. "Yeah, my thoughts exactly. Any chance you can get Cletus to work on a Sunday?" He nodded as he listened to the reply. "Yeah. Okay, thanks. I owe you one. Her car's at the impound. Just brought in last night. There might be something you can use there. It's a . . ." He looked at Josh with raised eyebrows.

"2008 Accord. Dark blue. Tags Delta, India, Echo, November, Echo, Romeo."

"Did you get that?" Wyatt asked, then frowned. "How the heck should I know what 'DIENER' means? Look, just meet us at Bonwood Bowl as soon as you can, okay? Yeah. Thanks, buddy. Wyatt out."

"Who's Ballard at SDU?" Josh asked.

"New kid from Louisiana. He's in the service dog unit. The guy's mutt is amazing. It's a purebred bloodhound."

The puzzle pieces locked into place without effort. "Now why didn't I think of that?" Josh wondered aloud.

"Because you're slammed, man. You look only slightly better than road-kill." He glanced around. "Did you drive here?"

"Walked. I needed the air."

The patrol officer jerked his head toward his cruiser. "Come on, get in. Let's go sniff out your bad guy."

"How does this Ballard kid know me?"

"You're kidding, right? Everyone knows you're hooked up with the Crypt Keeper. Man, even my wife will tell you she should be a swimsuit model instead of a morgue tech."

Josh harrumphed. "Yeah. Rebekah's an enigma, that's for sure."

Wyatt opened his door and pushed the button to unlock Josh's. "Well, let's just hope we can find her before she becomes a statistic."

CHAPTER 47

DAMIEN SAT ON AN AUTOPSY table eating cracked wheat from a steaming bowl. He smacked each spoonful with gluttonous elation. The pretty Miss Smith shielded her eyes from the bright lights and curled into a ball. The thin sheet barely stayed on her.

He scooted off the table and tactfully pulled the shroud over her exposed parts. She was a lady, after all, and should be treated as such. He gently stroked her hair away from her face and sucked air between his teeth when he saw the bump above her eye. "Geez, d-did I do that?"

The woman didn't answer. She was probably still in shock. That was to be expected. None of his volunteers ever understood the magnitude of their service. He hated having to treat her so harshly. It brought back dark memories of Anguilla Island and his medical school fiasco.

Damien retrieved a cold compress from the refrigerator, wrapped it in some linen, and gently touched it to her forehead. She flinched and whimpered.

"Oo, I'm sorry. That is one nasty g-goose egg you have. Hold this c-compress to it; it'll help reduce the inflam-mation. I'd g-give you some ibuprofen for the p-pain and swelling, but it thins the blood. That could really m-mess things up." He gingerly daubed the welt with the cool cloth. "There. Now that's b-better, isn't it? I wish this didn't have to happen. Didn't your m-mother ever teach you never to make f-fun of someone's disab-bility? You shouldn't have called me . . . what y-you called me."

She slowly opened her eyes and looked up at Damien. She had very pretty eyes. In fact, her whole face was very pretty—with the exception of the large bruise. He'd always loved large, doe-like brown eyes. There was an innocence about them that resonated with him. They were soft and pleading. She mouthed a word he couldn't hear.

"I'm sorry?" he said leaning closer.

"Why?" she croaked.

"Why?" he said, standing. "Because it is my destiny."

Her body began shivering. It was reaching the end of its endurance. The time in the fridge had lowered her heart rate and core temperature to a point where she would be docile for some time. Her movements would be slow and measured. That's just what Damien wanted. He hated the thought of having to fight her. If she would accept her place in the grand scheme of things, she'd have a better chance of a successful outcome. It was the same principle many religions called faith. Supposedly, faith could heal all wounds.

He scoffed. If that was true, then the entire world must be one faithless rabble. People died of disease and ailment every day, every minute. Faith did nothing for them. But he could! His plan would *preserve* life. If only he could find the right formula. His mentor kept promising new antigens that would not spawn antibodies. If just one volunteer would accept the protocol—just one!—their success would be heralded as history-making. His mentor had promised a new compound last weekend, but he had yet to deliver it. Damien knew better than to pressure the man. He worked at his own pace. Damien merely had to have patience and be ready with plenty of AB-positive blood. Oh, and fresh volunteers.

Rebekah mumbled again. He leaned close.

"Water, please."

He pantomimed shooting himself in the head with his index finger and thumb. "I am so s-sorry. How inconsiderate of me. You m-must be starving too. Gotta keep your energy up. I've seen time and again volunteers who d-don't make it a day b-because they are in such l-lousy shape. But not you, Miss Smith. Y-y-you're in great shape."

He instantly blushed and turned away. "Oh my gosh. By that, I didn't mean that I looked at you while—I mean, I was m-merely prepping you for the t-transfusion. It's a n-necessary step, you understand. I wasn't trying to—I mean, I didn't intentionally l-look—oh my gosh. I—I—swear I— Oh never mind. I'll g-get you some water and something to eat. But first I need to make sure you d-don't do anything stupid again."

Pulling up straps from under the table, he tied her down securely. He'd replaced the ones she'd cut. The woman groaned when he cinched them tight; but because she'd proven to be very resourceful, he was making doubly sure she couldn't escape again. He then draped a blanket over the shroud and tucked it in gently under her chin.

"This should help you warm up. Sorry ag-gain about the time in the fridge. I hope Mr. Doe didn't b-bother you too much." He smiled and snickered. He could be so funny at times. "But you're probably used t-to dead p-people. That's what you d-do all day, isn't it? You carve up dead people?" He shook his head and made a few tsk-tsk sounds. "Not the job for a p-pretty lady like you. Now, I'll be right b-back with something to eat. If you rem-main quiet and be still, I'll bring something special. Okay?"

She didn't answer but her eyes registered understanding. She then mouthed some more words. He bent to listen.

"Drop dead."

He stood and laughed. "Oh, I d-don't plan on doing that for a long, long time. I'm hoping you d-don't either, but you n-never know. We'll both find out by the end of t-today."

CHAPTER 48

OFFICER BALLARD SHOWED UP IN a pickup truck with a dog kennel secured in the bed. He was a lanky man in his mid-twenties. He wore a police shirt that seemed a size too big, blue jeans, and a tie skewed drastically to one side. The kid had an open face that radiated sociability. Before saying hello, he rounded the bed and opened the kennel door. A large, tawny hound dog, complete with floppy ears and droopy jowls, stuck his head out of the opening.

"Com'on outta there, boy," the young officer said with a heavy Southern drawl.

The dog looked down and licked his chops nervously. He looked back at his master and whimpered. The animal had more wrinkles than a dried-up raisin, and the heavy bags under his eyes exposed close to half an inch of red, periorbital tissue. He looked down again and whimpered some more, obviously not wanting to make the two-foot leap to the ground.

"You lazy bag'a bones," Ballard said as he hefted the large dog off the truck. "Sorry 'bout the bad first impression," he said to Josh and Wyatt. "This here is Cletus. He may be a big baby, but he's the best in the bid'ness. He was top tracker back in Beauregard Parish. Nabbed many a bad guy across the Southern states, we have. Why, this ol' boy can sniff out an ounce of crack sealed in plastic at the bottom a ten gallons a' dead crawdads."

"Josh Logan, special investigations," Josh said, extending his hand.

"Heard a lot about you, Detective. Word is *you* could give ol' Cletus here a run for his money."

"Only in looks," Officer Olson jumped in.

Josh took the jibe good-naturedly. "'Beauregard,' you say? That's just west of Acadia and Lafayette, isn't it?"

The young man beamed. "Why, yessir, it is. Little town, name a' Eu Claire. You been ta Lous'ana before?"

"I served a church mission there. But I never went out west. I was stationed in Jefferson, Orleans, St. Bernard, and St. Charles parishes. Helped a lot with cleanup after Katrina."

"So did me and Cletus, didn't we boy," he said, tousling the big dog's ears. "They had us lookin' for dead persons, missin' persons, missin' body parts, missin' pets, just about ever'thin'."

"I'm sure he was indispensible," Josh said, also giving the dog a scratch. "So what's a Southern boy like you doing in the Rocky Mountains?"

"Well, sir, that there's a long story," he said, stretching out the word *long*. "See, Cletus here is pert old. Goin' on sixteen in human years. He got him the rheumatics in his knees 'n' hips 'cuz a all the humidity an' rain an' such. Only, he can't retire 'cuz he hates sittin' 'round. Get's all depressed and such. So the vet says he's gotta move to somewheres high 'n' dry. Well, sir, there's no such a place in the South. Then I sees an ad on the National Law Enforcement website, says y'all are lookin' for a bloodhound ta join the force in Salt Lake City, an' I figure there's not many places higher 'n' drier. So we up and moved."

"Tommy, did you get a good enough scent sample out of Miss Smith's car?" Wyatt asked.

"Yessir, we sure did. There was a pair of mittens in her glove box. Lord knows why she'd have mittens this time a year," he said, scratching his head.

"Wait three months. You'll understand," Wyatt said with a wink. He then glanced at his watch and added, "Listen, I gotta run. You boys be okay without me?"

"Yes, and thanks," Josh said. "I don't know why I didn't think of this."

"Because you're not as smart as me," the patrolman said, patting Josh's shoulder, "or as good-looking. But I do like that tie."

Josh had completely forgotten he was wearing the tartan neckpiece. "Thanks, Wyatt."

"Y'all take care now, ya hear?" Tommy added.

As the cruiser drove off, Josh asked, "So, Officer Ballard, how does this work?"

"It's Tommy. An' it's easier than skinnin' a gator. I've already acquainted Cletus with the gal's scent."

"Rebekah."

"Okay, with Rebekah's scent, assuming the mittens are hers."

"May I see them?"

Tommy unzipped a fanny pack and removed the woolen gloves. "Don't touch 'em. Cletus knows my scent but no one else's. He thinks anythin' other than me is what he's a'lookin' for."

"No need. Those are hers, all right."

"Good deal." He knelt in front of the bloodhound and held out the mittens. "Here ya go, boy. 'Member these? This is who we need ta find. Get ya a good ol' sniff. That's right. That's right. Good boy. Now, go find her."

The dog let out a woof Josh found surprisingly deep. His tail wagged with enthusiasm. His nose hit the ground, and he started a wandering zigzag across the parking lot. At one point he stopped and backtracked then returned to the spot he turned from. He looked up and around then went back to sniffing. After covering a few other areas, he looked up and let out another bass woof.

"He's got 'er," Tommy announced proudly.

"Already?" Josh was truly amazed.

"Yep. Okay boy, go get 'er."

The bloodhound took off in a steady trot, all the while sweeping the ground with his nose. He led the two lawmen on a route that passed the bowling alley two blocks before turning into a narrow alley. Josh had already looked down there, but he tagged along without comment.

They entered a small courtyard bordered by the backs of large buildings. At the far end of the open space stood a small house, partially hidden by weeds and shrubbery. Josh had noticed it before, but he didn't think anything of it. The place looked abandoned.

"Now, *that* looks promising," Tommy said softly. "Put it on stilts an' stick it in a swamp an' I might just get a little homesick. It's got bad juju written all over it. Better slip back in the alley in case someone's in there with her watchin'."

Cletus stood his ground and sniffed the air. He then resumed his trek directly toward the small house. At the base of the front stoop he stopped and looked back at his master. Tommy waved him back, which he obeyed without pause.

"Your gal's inside," Tommy said with a nod toward the house.

"Are you sure?" Josh didn't doubt the dog's abilities; he simply needed affirmation for his own self-doubt. Had Rebekah only been a couple blocks away from the Bonwood Bowl the whole time? It made him feel like he'd wasted his whole night. He could have—*should have*—rescued her hours ago! And that thought made him livid.

"I guarantee it," Tommy said, tousling the bloodhound's ears and neck again. "Good boy, Cletus. You're a good boy." To Josh he asked, "Should we call for backup?"

Josh stared at the house. His guts told him to call for assistance. But he feared by the time it came it'd be too late. Plus, he needed a way to vent his anger. He shook his head. "You wait here. I'm going in."

CHAPTER 49

DAMIEN GLIMPSED THE DOG SNIFFING around his front stoop. At first he thought it was a stray, a mangy mongrel looking for scraps of food. But on closer inspection he realized it was a real bloodhound. He never cared for dogs in general, but he'd done enough experiments using dogs that he was familiar with many breeds. He preferred cats as pets. The concept of nine lives appealed to him. But the name bloodhound carried significance too—something that went beyond species definition. He watched the dog turn and head into a shadowy alley.

No matter. He had work to do. Having recently showered, he still needed to dry his hair. If the dog returned, he'd give it some table scraps—if it proved friendly. If the dog proved to be mean, he'd give it some table scraps laced with ibuprofen. The common OTC medicine would shut down its kidneys, and it'd be dead by the next morning.

Damien got to wondering why a purebred was wandering the backstreets of South Salt Lake unattended. Surely a dog like that would be worth a pretty penny. He remembered it was wearing a collar, meaning it belonged to *someone*. But who?

Just as he was about to turn away, he saw a man leave the alley, making a beeline right to his front door. He was dressed semi-casually: sport coat, jeans, and a tie that reminded Damien of bagpipes.

He felt panic cinch his nerves. He couldn't tell if the man was the dog's owner or just someone needing directions—but the determination in his stride said his intent wasn't friendly chitchat. Damien moved quickly to the kitchen. He could exit out the back door and sneak down to the basement, but that would not identify the man. And his curiosity was overpowering his trepidation.

The man knocked. Damien counted to ten before answering. He took a steadying breath and opened the door.

"Yes? C-can I help you?"

"Morning. I'm Detective Logan from the Salt Lake special investigations unit," he said, holding up a badge. "Are you Mr. Damien Slade?"

"Yes, Det-tective," he said, using the corner of a bath towel to wipe the inside of his ear. The rest of the towel remained draped over his left hand and forearm.

"I apologize for the early hour, but I need to ask you a few questions. May I come in?"

Damien hesitated. The detective's tone was hard, bordering on angry. "Um . . . okay, sure," he said, stepping back. "As you can see, I'm g-getting ready for work. I hope this won't take long. P-please, have a seat."

The lawman entered but didn't sit. "I'll be brief. A woman was reported missing last night from this area. Witnesses say she was seen with a man matching your description in front of the Bonwood Bowl two blocks from here." He pulled up Rebekah's photograph on his phone. "Have you seen this woman?"

Damien frowned at the picture. He tilted his head at varying angles, hoping it would come across as confusion. "I-I'm sorry, Detective. She's very p-pretty so I'm sure I would rem-member seeing her."

He pocketed his phone. "So you're saying you haven't seen her?"

"N-no, sir."

"Ever?"

"No, sir."

"Mr. Slade, you are lying to me," the man almost growled. "That is considered obstruction of justice, and I have every right to haul you in right now. I have confirmation that she interviewed you *twice* at Avalon Manor, your place of employment."

Damien's felt the blood drain from his face. He lowered his eyes. "I-I-I am so ashamed," he said remorsefully. "You're right. I-I-I have seen her . . . at w-work. I was j-just scared. I thought m-maybe Ms. Mossb-berg sent you. She's my b-b-boss. She's n-never liked me because of m-my stutter. I thought that . . . well, I was j-j-just scared, that's all." He made sure to put a whimper of desperation in his voice and to stutter extra severely. That usually endeared people to him—or at least made them feel guilty for giving him a hard time. "I d-did m-meet with her. Her n-name is R-R-Reb-bekah Smith. She works at the c-c-coroner's office. But I haven't seen her since, I p-p-promise. W-why? Is something w-wrong?"

Detective Logan's eyes hardened to match his tone. He reached behind his back and withdrew a set of handcuffs. "That is another lie, Slade. I happen to know she met with you last night. Put your hands on your head and interlace your fingers. You're under arrest."

"But—but—but I haven't d-d-done anything," he whined. "Y-you have no p-proof."

The man chuffed. "Proof? You want *proof*, you sick freak?" His voice rumbled like a volcano about to erupt. He punched a number on his cell phone. Five seconds later a phone began to ring from his kitchen.

Damien felt his heart skip a beat. He knew he couldn't fake his way out this time. He hated complications like this. Still, it proved who the woman's boyfriend was. That might actually simplify things.

"You have Rebekah's phone," he hissed. Damien could almost taste the venom in his words. "Put your hands on your head! Now!"

The nurse tried to suppress a smile but couldn't. He knew he had the upper hand, even though this man was bigger and unquestionably stronger than he was. The fact that the detective had the law on his side didn't matter. Damien answered to a higher law.

He whipped the towel off his arm, revealing the handgun underneath. He raised it to point directly at Josh's face. "I think n-not, Detective L-Logan. Drop your phone and put *your* hands b-behind *your* back and c-cuff your wrists tog-gether. N-now, if you please."

It was so gratifying to see the look of astonishment and loathing on the lawman's face. Slowly, with bitterness seething from his eyes, the detective complied with his demands.

When Damien heard the ratcheting of the cuffs, he said, "Thank you. Now turn around so I c-can see."

Logan did.

"Tug them apart so I can tell they are secure."

He did.

"Now d-drop to your knees."

"What have you done with Rebekah?" the man demanded.

"Do as I say and I'll s-show you," he promised.

Logan cautiously knelt down. "I have backup outside waiting for me. Give up now and it'll go easier for you."

He laughed. "You lie ab-bout as well as I do."

"I'm not lying. Did you see the dog? It's a bloodhound. It sniffed out Rebekah to this exact location. I know she's here."

"Right you are, d-detective. She *is* here. But I b-believe you're here by yourself. Well, there may be the dog's t-trainer," he said, glancing out the porthole on the door, "but if you really had b-backup, they would have come with you. Standard police p-procedure says you can-n-not enter a p-potentially hostile environment alone. And yet here you are. Now, before we c-continue, let me apologize in advance," Damien said, feeling very pleased with himself.

"Apologize for what?" the man grumbled.

"For this." He wound up and slammed the heel of his gun on the back of Logan's head. The big, tough lawman crumpled with only a slight grunt.

CHAPTER 50

DAMIEN DRAGGED JOSH DOWN THE wrought-iron steps behind the house into the basement. He wasn't very gentle about it. After all, he was under a time constraint. Rebekah was strapped securely to her autopsy table in the center of the room. He had locked the wheels so she couldn't reach anything to help her escape again. He'd also placed a linen bag over her head. She was such a resourceful woman. He was certain the transfusion would work this time. The new chemical had yet to arrive, but he was so confident she'd accept the AB-positive blood that he decided to proceed without it.

With significant effort, he hoisted the unconscious detective onto the second table, stripped him to his underwear, and strapped him down securely. It was stuff he did daily at the nursing home—well, except for the strapping down part. He then covered him with a linen shroud and treated the bump on the back of his head.

"What's going on?" Rebekah asked through the linen hood over her head.

Damien removed the hood with an indelicate tug.

She squinted at the light and began to cough. "It's—about—time! Ack. I almost suffocated in that thing."

"S-sorry. It was all I had. The only other option was to put you b-back in the f-fridge with Mr. Doe."

"Thanks for the courtesy," she said with indignation.

Damien smiled. "I brought you a present."

"If it's a gun, make sure it's loaded with hollow points so I can watch your head vaporize when I blow you away."

"You're such a j-jokester," he chuckled. "No wonder he likes you so much."

She frowned. "Who?"

"Your boyfriend. Detective J-Josh Logan. He's a pretty good l-l-looking guy. I bet his sandy b-blond hair and b-blue-green eyes turn a lot of heads. Doesn't that m-make you jealous?"

Rebekah's eyes widened for an instant then hooded. "His hair is dark brown."

"No. I'm pretty sure it's blond." Damien moved to the second table and pulled back the shroud. "See?"

She gasped.

"Oh. Well his hair *is* a little red in the back," he said, picking up a cotton pad soaked with blood and dropping it into a trash can. "As soon as his scalp stops b-bleeding, I'll wash out his hair. Then he'll be b-blond again."

"What did you do to him?" she demanded.

"J-just conked him on the head a bit. He'll have a headache f-for a while but he'll be fine. He c-came looking for you. It's all very romantic. Foolish but rom-mantic."

Tears welled in her eyes. He couldn't figure why. This was such an exciting time.

"Don't b-be sad. He'll be able to witness your t-transformation."

She paused. "What transformation?"

"Oh, come now, Miss *Diener*. I'm p-probably the only g-guy you've met who knows what that means. As a c-coroner's assistant, you've seen all this equipment b-before," he said with a sweep of his hand. "If you're so smart, you t-tell *me* what I do down here."

The look in her eyes belied the fact that she *did* know. Damien felt incredibly confident about the whole situation. It was one more proof that what he was doing was a good thing, even a righteous thing.

"I have no idea what you're talking about. I file paperwork in the ME's office, that's all."

He sauntered over and caressed her cheek with the back of his fingers. She recoiled from the tender action. So unappreciative. "Miss Smith. Reb-bekah. M-may I still call you Rebekah? You may still call me Damien. When I hid your c-car, I noticed your license p-plates. And the questions you asked at Avalon Manor were n-not the kind a p-paper-pusher would ask. I believe you're actually interested in m-my research. Am I right?"

The woman stared at him with a mix of disbelief and consuming guilt. He saw her jaw muscles flex several times, as if she was deciding whether to answer or keep silent. He sat on the edge of her table, one leg dangling off the lip, the other supporting him from the floor.

"I have a feeling you're going to tell me anyway," she growled.

Using the back of his fingers again, he stroked her exposed arm tenderly. He couldn't understand why she was being so headstrong. If *anyone* should appreciate what he was trying to accomplish, she should. Maybe she was having trouble seeing the big picture. Well, that was excusable. A lot of people were not as enlightened as he was. Perhaps the situation took her by surprise. She *was* strapped to an autopsy table wearing nothing but her underthings and a linen shroud. Still, that was how she prepared all *her* patients. Why should *his* patients be any different?

She pulled away from his caress. "Stop touching me, you freak."

"Freak? Well, I g-guess I m-might seem that way to the unenl-lightened. Anyone who knew what this was all ab-bout would consider me a genius. Maybe even a saint."

With raised eyebrows he waited for her response, but none came. She refused to look him in the eyes. He patted her shoulder. "Allow me to exp-plain. See, everyb-body wants to live forever. I believe I have found the k-key to do just that."

"You're insane."

"So was Alexander Graham Bell for thinking he c-could send voices over wires. So were the Wright B-Brothers for thinking they c-could fly." Her expression remained filled with hate. Oh well. That would change. "Do you read the Bible, Rebekah?"

She said nothing.

"K-keeping silent is so childish. The more we communic-cate, the better you'll understand."

After an infantile pause, she grumbled, "Yes, I read the Bible."

"Do you remember how old Methuselah was when he died?"

"Nine hundred and something."

"That's right. The Bible says the first m-man, Adam, l-lived nine hundred thirty years. Noah was n-nine hundred fifty years old, and Methuselah nine hundred sixty-n-nine years."

"Wow, neat," she said with zero enthusiasm.

"So why did they live so long? Or did everyone b-back then live as long?" She frowned. "I don't know."

"Well," he continued, folding his arms, "there are nearly as many sp-peculations on why they l-lived so long as there were years lived. Some p-people believe the earth's atmosphere and g-gravity were different back then. Some say there was less p-pollution and f-f-fewer carcinogens; or that today's radio and m-microwaves have a m-mortalizing effect; or that evolution has caused our genes to m-mutate from Adam's pure genotype. I'm not sure I believe any of th-those theories, do you?"

She stared at him for a time before answering. "I haven't given it much thought."

"Really? I assumed someone in your l-line of work would think about it all the t-time. You deal in d-death, after all."

"I deal *with* death, not *in*. There's a difference. You're the one who's obsessed with dealing *in* death."

"Oh, that's where you're wrong, Reb-bekah."

"Yeah? Try and tell that to Agnes Baugh, Silas Snow, Lester Johnson, and countless others you've butchered."

Damien felt a thrill tingle up his spine. His heart fluttered in his chest. "I am *so* flattered you c-cared enough to follow my work. I *knew* you were exc-ceptional. With you assisting in my next trial, I know milestones will b-be met."

"And I knew you were insane," she spat. "Not brilliant, not a genius— certifiably insane. I would rather die than assist you."

Damien smiled and cupped her face in his hand. "You just might."

CHAPTER 51

JOSH FELT AS IF HE were clawing his way up a muddy slope. Each movement took every ounce of strength he had. Though he could see a dim light above him, the source of the light was still a mystery. He continued to struggle. He knew something was wrong, that without his immediate intervention, someone would die. *Rebekah!* It was Rebekah who was in trouble.

He tried moving but couldn't. The mud. No—it wasn't mud. It felt like ropes or a belt of some kind. Then he heard voices. One man, one woman. He needed to get out of the pit. He groaned and tugged against his restraints. Slowly, the fog in his head was supplanted with a throbbing pain. But with the pain came clarity. He remembered everything.

"Welcome back, Det-tective Logan."

Josh endeavored to open his eyes, but a sharp glare made him proceed very slowly. It was as if his pupils didn't want to adjust to the harshness. Still squinting, he turned his head toward the man. He saw Slade casually sitting on the edge of a gurney. He could also see Rebekah lying on the gurney; her eyes were filled with a remorse almost too painful to witness. She was covered in a pale sheet—just as he was. Using the limited movement of his hands, he felt the soft material covering him and the cold metal surface on which he lay. He did not recognize the room, but it looked very much like a basement.

"Where . . . ?" he croaked.

"You're in my lab," Slade said with unmasked pride.

"Why . . . ?"

"Because you stuck your n-nose in where it didn't belong. Just like Reb-bekah, here. But I've c-come to realize she was d-destined to be here, so her case is excusable."

He wanted to close his eyes, but he was afraid of losing contact with Rebekah, even if that contact was only visual. He could tell she was frightened. In addition to remorse, her expression belied terror and angst. But it also held a measure of annoyance. He inwardly smiled at that. It was so typical of her. When she was not in control of a situation it irritated her like a pebble in her shoe. Still, this was no laughing matter. She was defenseless—as was he.

"I'm so sorry," he whispered toward her.

"I don't think sorry is g-going to cover it, detective," Slade replied.

"He was talking to me, you moron," Rebekah snapped brazenly. Apparently, she was not afraid of the man or of the situation. Or she *was* afraid and was doing her best to appear otherwise.

Slade tenderly brushed Rebekah's hair back. "She *is* quite b-beautiful, detective. I can see why you're s-so in love."

Rebekah tried to bite his hand, but he pulled it away just in time.

"Oo, and feisty, too. Are you sure you're m-man enough to handle her?"

Josh's throat felt like he'd swallowed battery acid. His head pounded mercilessly. He wanted to excoriate the little man with every foul word he knew—and improvise a few new ones on the spot. But all he could manage were weak, scratchy sounds.

"He's more of a man than you'll ever be," Rebekah answered for him. "You're just a puny, stuttering dweeb."

Slade gave a forced pout that threatened to break into a grin. "D-dweeb? What—are we in the sixth g-grade now?"

"Bite me," she hissed.

"Really?" Slade looked over at Josh. "Do I have your permission to c-comply?"

"Don't touch her," he managed to croak harshly.

The LPN's eyes twinkled. "Oh, you mean like this?" He forced his palm down on her cheek so she couldn't turn away from Josh, then bent down and nibbled playfully at her neck. She struggled but couldn't move. Tears pooled in her eyes and trickled onto the table as his lips and tongue slid across her skin.

Josh was livid. Ignoring the blinding pain, he fought against the fetters restraining him. Finding his voice, he yelled, "I said don't touch her!"—but his words sounded more like the screeching of a rusty hinge than a threat.

"Oh. Not like that?" Slade asked innocently. "Then how ab-bout this?" Opening his mouth, he bit down on the slope where her neck met her shoulder.

Rebekah's eyes registered sudden, intense pain. She screamed.

Josh yelled at him to stop, but all that came out was a hoarse wheeze. Slade rocked his head, intensifying the torture.

Rebekah gasped between screams. Unrelenting terror filled her eyes. Her body shook as if convulsing.

"Stop! Please!" Josh finally belted out.

Slade backed off and turned to him. Fresh blood circled his mouth and trickled down his chin. Rebekah whimpered softly, tears still trickling from her eyes.

"I don't know what it is you want, but please don't hurt her anymore," Josh pled. His voice had a sandpaper quality. He tasted blood.

Slade adjusted his glasses then went to a sink and poured a glass of water. He brought it to Josh and tilted his head so he could drink. "You sound t-terrible. Here, sip this."

Josh didn't resist. He allowed the man to assist him until the glass was empty. Slade's movements were surprisingly tender. The water felt life-saving. "Thank you," he said.

"You're m-most welcome," Slade responded kindly. "Now, since we're all f-finally under c-control, we'll have no more outb-bursts or insults, okay? We're all grown-ups and should act ac-cordingly, don't you agree?"

"Yes," Josh said, looking at Rebekah's trembling form. He felt so weak, not so much from the hit on the head but because he had allowed this demented little man to get the better of him. He should have had him reveal his hands first off. But he fell for a ruse as simple as feigning dizziness. What an idiot.

Slade soaked a cloth in water and daubed it soothingly on Rebekah's lower neck. She flinched and whimpered. "Shh, there, there. It's okay. Just c-cleaning this up a b-bit. I'll put some Betadine on it. It's pretty deep, but I don't think it'll n-need stitches."

He spoke in hushed, caring tones, like he was speaking to a child who had scraped her knee. The gentleness in his voice was eerie, disturbing. Josh sensed Slade truly felt the compassion he was rendering—as if he had no clue that *he* was the one who had caused the injury. It made him sick to his stomach to watch the way he cared for Rebekah, touching her, caressing her, soothing her. He could only imagine how Rebekah felt, knowing she needed the care but detesting the one giving it.

Josh hated being helpless. He had no idea what Slade intended to do to them, but it wasn't a far stretch to assume they wouldn't live through the day. Who knew what Slade had already done to Rebekah? *That* thought sickened him even more. Presently, her stare was vacant, lost. He tried to encourage her with his eyes, but his attempts felt so inept, so ineffective.

Just as Slade taped a bandage to the wound on her neck, a knock sounded at the door to the basement. Before they could yell, Slade had Josh's gun pressed against Rebekah's temple and his gun pointed at Josh's head.

"If you make a sound, I'll b-blow her head off," he quietly hissed at Josh. To Rebekah he whispered, "If *you* m-make a sound, my dear, I'll shoot him in the face."

CHAPTER 52

THE KNOCK REPEATED, LOUDER THIS time. "Police. If y'all can hear me, open up."

Josh knew it was Tommy Ballard. He had forgotten the kid would be waiting for his return. That meant he *was* in the basement of the old, run-down house. How had Slade gotten him here without notice? He looked around but could only see one set of double doors—the source of the knocking.

"Hello? Anyone in there?"

Slade was steady as a rock. Josh had no doubt the guy would hold true to his word. He dared not utter a sound lest Rebekah die. And he knew she was thinking the same thing—lest she be responsible for *his* death. Slade had played it exactly right to keep both of them silent. Everything depended on what Ballard did next.

"Come on, now, I heard all y'all's voices, so I know y'all're in there. B'sides, old Cletus done sniffed y'all out. He says Miss Smith is in there with y'all. So come out with your hands up, nice 'n' easy like."

Slade scowled at Josh. With a gun still pointed at each prisoner, he moved to Josh and whispered in his ear. "I'm going to wheel you c-closer to the door. You will say exactly what I t-tell you to say or I will shoot your g-girlfriend in p-places that will cause so much pain she'll wish she were d-dead."

Josh nodded slowly. Slade then whispered something in Rebekah's ear. She nodded too.

"Detective Logan? If y'all can hear me, shout out a holler. If not, I'm gonna bust down this here door. The law says Cletus pointin' to a door is the same as bein' in hot pursuit, an' I can enter forcibly if need be."

Slade grabbed a bar under the tabletop and pulled Josh closer to the door. He whispered instructions in his ear and finished with, "Make it sound believable."

"Is that you, Tommy?" Josh called out.

"Detective? Yeah it's me. Y'all okay in there?"

"Yeah, I'm fine. I'm just looking around. It's kind of dark so I've got to move slowly. I'd open the door, but there's a big padlock on this side."

"Well, can y'all hear me okay?"

"Yeah, I can hear you just fine now."

"How come y'all didn't answer me before?"

Slade pressed a gun to one of Rebekah's knees. Josh continued: "This is an old building. The walls are pretty thick. I was in a room on the other side and guess I didn't hear you."

"Do you have your gal?" Ballard asked.

Slade shook his head slowly.

"No, there's no sign of her."

"Y'all sure, detective? Cletus never misses."

"Well she must have been here at one time, but the perp has moved her." He flashed Slade a questioning look. The younger man nodded.

"Then what'ch'all doing in there?"

"Just looking for clues."

"Y'all need some help?"

"No thanks. No need to keep you working on your day off. Go home. I should be finished up at ten thirty-three."

Slade frowned at Josh.

There was a lengthy pause. Josh shrugged.

"Y'all sure, detective?"

"I'm sure. Shouldn't be any later than ten thirty-three. Thanks again for your help," Josh said, praying the new recruit understood the clue he'd just given.

"Well, okay, then. Y'all take care, ya hear? And call me when you find your gal."

"Sure thing, Tommy."

Slade moved to the door and pressed his ear to the wood. After a wait of nearly ten minutes, he climbed the counter and peeled back a section of duct tape masking the window. Angling his line of sight, he took in as much of the outside as possible. Replacing the tape, he did the same thing on the opposing window.

Hopping down, he said, "That was close, but k-kinda thrilling, don't you think?" His eyes danced merrily as if he'd just gotten off a rollercoaster. He wheeled Josh so that he was head-to-head with Rebekah but was facing away from her. "You two wait here. I'm going to make sure he's gone."

He pocketed both guns, unlocked the basement door, and crept out, locking the door behind him.

"What an idiot. Where's he think we're gonna go?" she huffed.

Josh was inches away from Rebekah. It pained him to know he couldn't reach out and comfort her, let alone see her. "Are you okay, Becks?"

"Yeah. But . . . I'm scared." It was the first time he'd ever heard her utter those words. She'd been her usual, resolute, headstrong self while Slade was present. But apparently when he left, so did her resolve.

"I know. I am too. But not so scared that we can't figure a way out of this. Come on, we're both smart. We can do this."

He heard her choke on a gasp of air. "Josh, are *you* okay? Your head looks terrible."

"It hurts like crazy, but I'll be okay. Listen, Becks, we don't have much time. Is there anything in here we can use to get out of these restraints?"

"No. I got out once before because he didn't cinch them tight enough. Now they're so tight I'm going numb."

"Mine too."

There was a long pause. "Josh?" her voice was laced with anguish.

"Yes, sweetheart."

She drew a shuddering breath. "I don't want to die like this." He knew she was at the end of her rope—a rope he'd thought had no end.

"I'm not going to let you die."

"You promise?"

"I promise." How he'd back up that promise, he had no clue.

"I love you, Clouseau."

"I love you too, Becks."

After a second long pause, she whispered, "Do you realize that's the first time you've ever said that to me?"

Confused, he asked, "Said what?"

"That you love me."

"Oh."

She was right and he knew it. Why had he waited so long to tell her? He knew the excuses he'd used in the past were weak. They made sense from a logical standpoint, but in the end they were pathetic cop-outs for soothing his emotions. "Well, it's true. I love you, Rebekah Smith. I have for a long time."

She sighed—then scoffed—like his words had reignited some of her old fire. "A long time? Really? And you wait till *now* to tell me? Great timing, Don Juan. It's a good thing I'm strapped down or I'd kick your butt."

He smiled. "Listen, babe, *when* we get out of this, I give you permission to kick my trash all you want."

"Count on it."

CHAPTER 53

REBEKAH WAS HUNGRY, COLD, AND thirsty. Josh probably felt the same way. She was still very frightened—and chastised herself for being so. Perhaps it was the suddenness in which she found herself in this predicament. Perhaps it was the fatigue she'd endured that lowered her resistance. Perhaps it was the fact that Josh was in the same predicament *because* of her. Whatever the case, she was angry with herself, and she was determined to channel that anger to find a way out of this mess. She allowed the girlish giddiness she felt from Josh's declaration of love to bolster her resolve. She'd always known he loved her. But hearing the words from his mouth made all the difference in the world.

Josh had not spoken for some time. She could hear him grunting and tugging against his restraints, but she couldn't imagine what he was thinking beyond the need to escape. All she could see from her position was the countertop and cabinets, and the three busts on top of the cabinets. She didn't know who they were, even though she could see them clearly now. Such statuary was usually accorded to musicians. But she doubted that's what they were. She guessed they were either obscure philosophers or scientists. It was not a stretch to see the psychotic LPN venerating such men.

"Josh. Can you see the refrigeration units from your angle?"

"Yes."

"There's a readout on the smallest one showing the temperature. Below that is the time. Can you see it?"

"Yeah. It says twelve twenty. Why?"

"I estimate Damien's been gone almost two hours. Any guesses where?"

"He probably followed Ballard to make sure he left the area."

"Do you think he believed you? Ballard, I mean."

"I hope not. But I *had* to sound convincing. Slade is a basket case. I'm no psychiatrist, but he shows every symptom of full-blown crazy. We were taught not to agitate people like that in hostage training."

She harrumphed bitterly. "What did your training teach you about a scenario like this?"

"Not to get into one."

"That's what I was afraid of. Any other thoughts?"

She heard him tug against the restraints a few times. "Afraid not. I wish I had something more positive to offer, but he's got us over a barrel, and my pounding skull is making it difficult to concentrate. Sorry."

"So . . . how *did* he get the upper hand on you?"

With manifest self-loathing, he related what had happened. "The thing that keeps eating away at me is what a lousy mess I've made of this. I feel like a pathetic rookie."

"Listen, Clouseau. You are *my* hero. This has got to be the most romantic thing anyone has ever done for me." And she meant it too. She had loved him for over a year, but seeing him bound and wounded in her behalf tipped the scales of affection.

Just then the door rattled and opened. "Your friend sure sp-pent a lot of t-time on his cell phone, but he eventually left," Damien explained. "I waited to make sure n-no one else showed up. Ap-parently you *were* convincing enough, d-detective. I believe we'll be able to spend a quiet Sunday afternoon tog-gether now, studying the sacred aspects of blood." His tone was barely restrained euphoria. He kept shooting glances toward the stone busts above the cabinetry. "I was g-going to wait for the new c-compound, but I am so excited to get s-started, I think we'll just p-proceed as normal. Is that okay with you?" he asked Rebekah.

She rolled her eyes. "What if I say no?"

He giggled. It sounded childlike. "Oops, y-you g-g-got me. That was meant rhetorically, of course." He turned to Josh. "Do you know what that m-means, detective? *Rhet-torically?*"

"Of course."

"So, then, I guess we'll p-proceed irregardless of what either of you s-say."

"You mean *regardless*. *Irregardless* is a double negative," Josh said with condescension. "Geez, Slade, you've only been in Utah a year and you're already picking up the bad grammar. I bet you say *unthaw* too."

Damien's eyes flared briefly. "Oh, s-so you're a *smart* cop. Well, how much do you know about b-blood? Huh?"

"More than I care to, thanks to you," Josh grumbled.

Damien pulled up a stool and sat, resting his elbows on his knees and clasping his hands. "Okay. Let's hear it."

"Hear what?" he asked.

"What you know about my research."

"We know you're the sociopath who's been harvesting AB-positive blood from centenarians in four or five states," Rebekah said. She wondered if she should reveal everything they'd unearthed. It might scare him into doing something drastic to silence them. Then again, that's probably what he had in mind anyway. "You then embalm each victim with—"

"Donor," he interrupted with a frown.

She bit back a caustic retort. "You embalm them with some oil and spice concoction that has minimal preservative properties, but you don't embalm the body cavity, just the circulatory system. Then you prepare each victim for viewing by placing a coin over each eye—"

"A silver 1917 D and S obverse Walking Liberty fifty-cent piece," Josh broke in.

Damien's eyes danced.

"And then dress them for a viewing and drape a pure linen handkerchief over the face."

The LPN appeared ecstatic. Wringing his hands like a cartoon wolf outside a henhouse, he looked from Rebekah to Josh and back again several times. When neither of them spoke, he held out his hands, palms up. "And?"

"And that's it," she said.

"Seriously? I th-thought for sure someone as sm-mart as you would p-put two and two together and see the amazing p-potential of this work." He seemed truly disappointed. "You were able to f-figure everything else out."

"We know you are responsible for the murders of several centenarians in this state and possibly a dozen more in other states. What more *should* we know?" Josh added.

A flash of offense crossed his face. "There is *a lot* m-more to know, detective."

Damien told them about discovering the key to the Fountain of Youth, including the scrap of parchment he'd purchased in Puerto Rico. As he spoke, his entire body took on an inanimate quality that was trancelike, as if he was experiencing an out-of-body event. His focus turned empty, devoid of life. "The Fountain is not m-m-magic water like everyone believes; it's b-blood. You said you study the B-Bible. Remember when Jesus said He was the 'l-living water' and that if you d-drank from Him, you'd be immortal?"

"That's some *very* liberal paraphrasing," Rebekah said with emphasis.

"Even so, every Christian religion feels it's the b-blood of Jesus that saves them. They also believe He was God or the S-Son of God in the flesh. He was a human and a God at the same t-time because He had a mortal m-mother and an immortal Father."

Rebekah hated being lectured on such a personal subject, but she decided to let him ramble. If anything, it would buy them more time. "Okay . . . ?"

"They say Mary's lineage c-came through Adam then Noah then M-Methuselah, right? And they all lived over n-nine hundred years. So if you m-mix an eternal D-Deity with a gene p-pool of amazing longevity, you get a recipe for im-mortality."

Now she *knew* he was insane.

"Did you know there is n-no record of Jesus ever being sick? And the scourging He endured before His c-c-crucifixion was t-triple that usually given. Normal scourging killed about fifty p-percent of the prisoners who got it. So h-how did *He* live through it? How c-could He go without f-f-food and water forty days? How was He able to r-resurrect from the t-tomb?"

"Because He is God's Son," Josh said firmly.

"And *Mary's* Son—which makes Him p-part human."

Rebekah didn't want to hear anymore. This was getting into sensitive areas of doctrine. He was talking about her Savior with such aloofness that it left her feeling cold inside. Still, she needed to understand his twisted reasoning if she was going to find a way out of this mess. "Go on . . ." she was hesitant to say.

"Well, some scholars say Jesus was m-married and had children. Well, what happened to them? Are there still t-traces of Jesus' b-bloodline on the earth today?" He paused, staring at her with vacuous eyes that seemed to suck the life from her.

"Apparently, you believe there are," she stated flatly.

"I do."

Like a fog lifting from a gruesome battlefield, clarity came to her mind, revealing a scene she didn't want to see, but which she knew she'd never be able to forget. "You think Jesus' blood type was AB-positive," she said in a hard whisper.

"I don't think. I *know.*"

"Is that in the Bible?" Josh asked, trying not to sound flippant.

"Yes. The G-Gospel of John, chapter twenty, v-verses five, six, and seven."

Rebekah frowned. She assumed Josh did too. "I'm not familiar with those passages."

Damien stood and picked up a corner of the cloth covering her. Rubbing it between his fingers, he spoke softly. "Simon Peter arrived at the sepulcher and f-found a linen shroud on the burial p-platform, but no body. He also saw a linen n-napkin set apart from the shroud." He stopped speaking but continued caressing the material as if *it* were the very cloth that had covered the body of Jesus.

"Okay. But that doesn't say *anything* about blood types," Josh argued.

Rebekah was able to think ahead, deducing his line of reasoning. "You're referring to the Shroud of Turin—which has never been proven authentic."

With measured steadiness, his eyes narrowed to tiny slits behind his thick glasses. "The b-bloodstains on the Shroud of Turin match those m-mentioned in each of the gospels: the nails, the spear wound, the c-crown of thorns." As he spoke, his voice hardened with steely intensity. "The age of the Shroud c-carbon dates to AD thirty-three. And it's made of pure linen, which was the m-most common burial cloth of the t-time." His eyes took on a viciousness, piercing and deep. "It *is* the burial cloth of Jesus! The b-blood stains are made from *His* blood. And it's been tested *and* typed."

Rebekah had never seen such rage in a person's eyes before—not the rage of anger but of passion, of conviction beyond measure. She spoke softly, without emotion. "Tested and typed as AB-positive."

He nodded deeply, reverently.

Flip-flopping between comprehension and incredulity, she stared in stunned silence as the final puzzle pieces fit into place. Damien actually believed if a person had AB-positive blood, they were automatically granted unnatural longevity. But he was *way* off the mark. She'd seen plenty of cases where people with AB-positive blood died in their seventies and eighties, some even earlier. Even *if* the blood found on the Shroud of Turin *was* the actual blood of Jesus, it didn't mean having AB-positive blood was a guarantee of long life, let alone immortality.

"You honestly believe by transfusing AB-positive blood into someone not AB-positive, you can increase their lifespan?" she asked with blatant skepticism.

"Of course. It is *the* Fountain of Youth."

She shook her head violently, as if trying to repel the insanity of his conjecture. "Religious underpinnings aside, how have you deactivated the antigen-antibody rejection mechanism?"

His eyes cleared momentarily as he shifted his gaze to various points around the room. They eventually rested on the statuary above the cabinets behind him. "We're still working on that," he softly replied.

"Meaning you haven't," she said caustically.

To date, no one had been able to totally change one blood type to another. And even if they could, it wouldn't automatically mean an increase in health or longevity. That Damien had developed the idea from some shyster in Puerto Rico and from his convoluted interpretation of the Bible was ludicrous. Worse than ludicrous, it was laughable. Only she didn't feel like laughing. Countless people had died at the hand of this disturbed man; countless more would follow if she couldn't end it here and now.

"Damien, listen to me. I don't know about all that stuff on the Shroud of Turin or what Jesus' blood type was. I really don't think it matters. He was the Son of God. He died for our sins and was resurrected so we could live again. That's all we need to believe."

"No!" he barked. "Jesus said whoever drinks of His l-living water will b-be *immortal!*"

"I believe He said they'll 'have everlasting life.'"

"No. The Bible p-promises immortality." His voice had softened slightly but still burned with passion. "P-people who live to one hundred *prove* it's p-possible. It's up to *me* to find out how." He held his hands up to the stone luminaries on the cabinets, beseechingly. "*They* have charged me with this noble resp-ponsibility."

"Damien, please. Listen to reason," she urged. "Not all one-hundred-year-olds have AB-positive blood; and not everyone with AB-positive blood lives to a hundred. You have some very interesting theories, but they don't really pan out, do they? You need to find verifiable, *reproducible* proof."

The LPN turned and favored her with the eeriest expression she'd ever seen. "And that is p-precisely what we are going to d-do."

Without another word, he soaked a cotton swab in Betadine solution and began swabbing the crook of her left elbow.

CHAPTER 54

"Mr. Slade, I beg you to reconsider," Josh said as he watched Damien prepare Rebekah's arm for venipuncture. "Rebekah is as much of a scientist as you are. She works with blood every day. She could help you figure out what isn't working with your experiments, if you just let her."

"Oh, but she *is* g-g-going to help," Slade corrected him.

"I don't mean as one of your vict—as one of your volunteers. I mean as a colleague." Josh's angst intensified as he watched Slade select various needles, tubes, and instruments with calm fluidity. "Listen to me, Rebekah deals with death all day long. She recognizes things that slip by most doctors. If she dies, you will lose all the groundbreaking information she's found on blood incompatibility."

Slade paused and regarded Josh with hooded eyes. "What groundbreaking inform-m-mation?"

Rebekah glanced at Josh in confusion.

"Information she's been working on," Josh explained. "I'm not even supposed to know about it, but it has to do with the different types of blood they encounter in the autopsy room."

The LPN crossed his arms. "I haven't heard ab-bout any of this."

"I'm not surprised. It's brand new. She's been doing studies on the health of internal organs in relation to blood types." He snuck a look at Rebekah. Her eyes held less confusion but not full understanding either. Hopefully she would sense where he was heading with this.

"It's true," she said after a pause. "I've found that when a body rejects a blood type, it happens in the liver first, then the kidneys, the heart, and finally the lungs."

Slade frowned. "I thought it was specifically an im-mune system response. You know, through the l-lymphatic system."

"That's what I thought at first, too," she said, her excitement rising. "Boy, did I feel stupid when I found out what really happens! But it sounds like you are *way* ahead of me."

Even though his frown remained, there was now a glint of pride in his eyes.

"For example," she continued, "what measures do *you* use to prevent immune rejection?"

He shrugged. "We've been working on a comp-pound that destroys red b-blood cell antigen coding so no antib-bodies develop."

"We?" Josh asked.

Damien quickly ducked his head and averted his eyes. "Um . . . well, yeah. I have a m-mentor. He's the one who sends me different comp-pounds to test when I do the t-transfusions." He shuffled his feet then looked up with a fresh scowl. "But he's never mentioned anything about an im-mune response in the liver or any other organ."

"Well, he wouldn't, would he," Rebekah stated cautiously. "No one is aware of what I'm researching on the side. But, after listening to you, I can see I'm obviously on the wrong track. What's your mentor's name?"

Damien opened his mouth—then abruptly closed it and shook his finger at her. "Nice t-try, diener. I just call him Mentor, so you can too. And he's a b-brilliant scientist. He knows what he's d-doing. And I know what *y-you're* doing. You're trying to d-distract me. But it won't work. We are going to d-do this transfusion b-because Mentor said I should."

"He said you should replace *Rebekah's* blood?" Josh asked specifically.

"Well, not just *her* blood. Any v-volunteer will do, as long as I use the n-new compound." He pointed a stiff finger at her. "But she's going to be my n-next volunteer b-because she was s-sticking her nose where it didn't b-belong and g-got m-me in trouble."

"Wow. I wish my deputies did their jobs with as much dedication as you do," Josh said with no small amount of admiration. "You know, Mr. Slade, I misjudged you earlier. You obviously take your assignments seriously and fulfill them to the letter *and* beyond, am I right?"

Slade's cheeks colored and his frail chest puffed out slightly. "I try."

"Oh, you do more than try, my friend. You take every opportunity to *excel*," Josh gushed. He hoped he was on the right track, flattering the unstable young man. He had to try to change the LPN's mind before he went too far. "You're probably the only one smart enough to recognize such opportunities when they come, too. For example, if you had the chance to do your next transfusion on a volunteer who's *never* been sick in his life, and with the backup of an expert on conditions of the body and death, you would, wouldn't you? I bet you would because you're so bright."

"Josh," Rebekah whispered harshly.

Still glowing, the LPN nodded. "I . . . guess I would."

"Exactly. Why waste your time on a busybody like her when you've got a healthy, prime, willing candidate in the same room?"

"What?" Damien blinked.

"Today is your lucky day, Mr. Slade. *I'm* your man. I want to be your next volunteer. I've never been sick a day in my life, I'm in peak physical condition, I don't smoke or drink or take drugs, and to make things easier, I won't even put up a struggle. On top of that, you have Rebekah Smith here, who is the best forensic medical assistant around, bar none."

"Josh!" Rebekah hissed through clenched teeth.

"Besides that, I'm O-*negative*, which will give you the opportunity to test your compound on Rh incompatibility too, right?" He knew the Rhesus factor was more of a concern between mothers and their unborn babies, but he was hoping that would slip by the sociopath.

Damien nodded slowly. He looked at the brown stain in the crook of Rebekah's elbow and at the trocar needle in his hand. His expression bore indecision—with a glimmer of excitement.

"Think about it, Mr. Slade. You have a better chance of success using me as your next volunteer than you do using her. And if something goes wrong with me, *she* can help. If something went wrong with her, I'd be useless."

"*Josh, stop it.*"

"Even you know I'm right, Rebekah," he said to her.

"No, you're not," she snapped. "Damien, don't listen to him. He doesn't know what he's talking about."

The LPN looked back and forth between Josh and Rebekah. His mind seemed torn between Josh's reasoning, Rebekah's rebuttal, and his own preconceived plans.

"Come on, son. Let's do this."

"*Josh, no!*"

Slade's face twisted with uncertainty. Some key element was keeping him from seeing the logic in Josh's argument. Josh had dealt with this kind of unbalanced psych profile before, so he knew he needed more than reasoning to tip the scale in his favor. Having observed Slade's behavior of late, he believed he knew what to do.

Josh waited until the LPN was turned away then gasped loudly. "What in the—? That's—that's incredible," he said breathlessly, staring at the three statues atop the cabinets.

Slade followed his line of sight to the marble luminaries. "What?"

"I don't know who those men are, but I swear they just—just *moved*."

The young man briefly frowned at Josh then returned his gaze to the three statues. "They're j-just stone figures," he said, almost as if he didn't believe his own words—as if he wanted to see what Josh had seen.

"Josh . . . *please* don't."

"No, I swear it, Rebekah. I've never seen anything like it before in my life. I know it sounds crazy. But—but all three of them . . . they just *smiled* at you, Damien."

The LPN's knees faltered. He leaned against the gurney, drew a sharp breath, and gazed up at the statues. "Really?" he asked in a breathless whisper.

"On my honor as a cop," Josh said, forcing each word as if making a solemn vow. "They must approve of my idea. They *know* it makes perfect sense. And so do you. Now, stop stalling and start my transfusion."

* * *

"So how exactly is this done?" Josh asked stoically. His head wound was still pounding, but it was nothing compared to his heart-thumping anxiety. He needed to keep Slade happily focused on his task while he sought desperately for opportunities to escape. "You don't drain all the old blood first, do you?"

The LPN giggled as he calmly swabbed the crooks of Josh's elbows. "Don't be silly, detective. If I did that, y-you'd die."

"Oh. Well I certainly don't want to die. Of course, if I do in the long run, it'll be for a worthy cause, right?"

Slade favored him with an expression filled with admiration. "You're the only o-one who's ever understood that, d-detective. That is so awesome."

"Well, you're a good teacher."

"Damien, he doesn't believe anything you've said," Rebekah cried in a plaintive tone. "Josh, please! Stop this nonsense right now."

Slade scowled at her.

"You know, Mr. Slade, perhaps it would be best to gag her for a while," Josh said, hating himself for making the suggestion—but knowing it was the only way to save Rebekah. "I don't want you to be distracted while you're performing such a delicate operation."

Rebekah gawked at Josh in stunned disbelief. Tears shimmered in her eyes—her face belied a mix of anger, betrayal, and shock.

Slade cleared his throat. "Um, he's right, Reb-bekah. You really need to keep q-q-quiet so I can concentrate. Can I trust you to stay q-quiet?—or should I put you b-back in with Mr. Doe?" he asked, tipping his head toward the cadaver fridge.

With her mouth open but silent, she nodded slowly.

"Good. Thank you," Josh said with a sigh. "So then, Mr. Slade, enlighten me if you will. You drain the old blood at the same time you infuse the new? Kind of an in-one-arm-and-out-the-other proposition—like embalming?" Josh figured the process was pretty straightforward, but he knew stroking the young man's ego would prevent a bipolar flare-up.

"Yep. I go nice 'n' slow so the b-body maintains a steady blood p-pressure. It takes about two days to comp-plete. That's why I sedate the volunteer. It's a fairly t-traumatic event. Embalming usually takes only a couple hours."

"I see. But, if it's all the same to you, I'd rather be totally lucid during the operation."

Slade's brows pulled together. "I . . . I don't know about th-that . . ." he hemmed, rubbing the back of his neck.

As the LPN turned to the marble luminaries, Josh quickly glanced at Rebekah. He needed to convey the urgency for her to play along. But what he saw made his heart ache.

Rebekah stared at him through liquid eyes, as if she wasn't cognizant of his presence, yet held him firmly locked in her gaze. Tears pooled and fell, pooled and fell. Her head shook slowly, almost imperceptibly. He saw in her eyes unparalleled despondency. He hated being the cause of her grief, but he saw no other way around the situation. He hoped he wouldn't have to complete this charade, but if he had to, he would see it to the end. To his end. Curiously, that thought didn't frighten him. In fact, he felt a strange sense of comfort, assurance, even confirmation from his actions. He smiled at her, feeling more love for her than he ever had before.

Slade continued to mumble, still unsure.

"Think about it," Josh continued, focusing on the nurse. "If I'm fully awake, I can describe everything I'm feeling, be it good or bad. I can tell you what hurts or if I suddenly feel stronger and more alive. I bet you've never had one of your volunteers do *that* before."

Damien turned back, his eyes gleaming behind his thick lenses. "Well . . . that w-would help my research," he acknowledged.

"Great. It's settled, then. Now, what about Mentor? You said he's given you a new compound to try?"

"No. Not yet." Damien's voice revealed his disappointment. "It was sup-posed to be here yesterday. That's when he p-promised to bring it." With a frustrated sigh, he marched back to Josh and wheeled him next to a machine bristling with tubes and wires.

"Mentor brings it by *personally*? He doesn't use a courier?"

"N-no. He doesn't trust anyone b-besides me."

"Well, I can certainly see why. No one else understands the importance of this work like you do, right? Hey, but that's okay. I'm sure it'll be fine. I mean, you're giving me AB-positive blood, which is *immortal* blood, right? How cool is that!"

He hoped he wasn't overacting but knew giving compliments and asking a barrage of questions would slow Slade down *and* keep him happy. More importantly, it kept his mind off the previous decision to use Rebekah as his next volunteer. "So what's *this* machine do?"

"It's an embalming pump I've c-customized for this p-p-procedure. Usually, it pumps embalming fluid in while b-blood drains out. But I've ad-dapted it to slowly introduce fresh b-blood while eliminating the old."

The "medical" contraption was roughly the size of a 100-gallon oil drum and looked like something from a movie about alien abduction. "Wow, that's kind of . . . well, it's huge. This isn't what you used to collect the centenarian blood, is it?"

"Oh no," he chuckled. "I have a smaller unit that fits in my b-backpack. But it doesn't have as good a p-pressure as this beast," he explained, patting the large tank. "So, when I'm harvesting, I have to make sure the donor is dead first. That way the evacuation and embalming goes much faster— usually only a couple of hours."

"But if they're not dead, aren't you afraid poisoning or shooting them will taint their blood?" he asked, feigning deep concern.

"Of c-course it would," the LPN chuckled again. "That's why I always sm-smother them instead. That way their b-blood remains p-pure."

Bingo. Josh glanced at Rebekah. She was glowering at the LPN. Great! Two witnesses just heard Damien Slade confess to first-degree murder and illegally harvesting human blood.

"Oh yeah. Gosh, I'm such an idiot," Josh chastised himself. "Sorry about asking such stupid questions, but this stuff is so fascinating!"

"Oh, I don't m-mind," Slade said with a shy smile. "But we really should get started on your t-transfusion. Once you're started, you can ask me any q-question you like."

Because of the tightness of the restraining straps, the veins on Josh's arms were already distended and easy to palpate. Slade poised the first needle over Josh's right median cubital vein. To Josh, the wide, trocar needle looked like a drinking straw. He'd donated blood several times before, but even those large-bore needles looked hair-thin compared to the one in this psycho's hand. He closed his eyes and held his breath.

"Okay, you may feel a little p-poke now," Slade said in his best phlebotomist's tone. "Do you want me to count to three?"

Just as Josh was about to answer, he felt the thick needle gouge into his flesh. Pain shot up his arm and across the back of his shoulders and neck. His fingers involuntarily splayed apart. He gritted his teeth, forcing himself to remain silent. Slade fastened a strip of tape across the junction of the needle and tubing, securing it to Josh's arm.

"See? That w-wasn't so bad, was it?"

When he could breathe again, Josh said, "What wasn't? Oh! You've already done it? I thought you were going to count to three. Man, you're good. I barely felt a thing."

Slade beamed.

"So is this the inlet or outlet?"

"The outlet. Now let's see how w-well it flows," he said, unclasping a hemostat clamp a few inches down the tubing.

Josh's blood barely trickled into the clear tube, following the pull of gravity. He expected more of a pressurized stream. Apparently Slade did too. His expression was a mix of confusion and frustration.

"Where does the blood go?" Josh wondered, keeping his tone light.

"Just into the floor drain," he answered, still with an unhappy face. "Most m-morticians do it that way. So do a lot of autopsy departments. Isn't that right, Reb-bekah?"

She continued to glare at Slade with utter disdain. She closed her eyes and turned away, not answering him.

"She's probably just hungry and tired," Josh suggested. "She might have to go to the bathroom too. I mean, just consider how long you've had her locked up down here."

"Oh. I hadn't thought of that," Slade admitted. He left Josh's side and placed a hand on her shoulder. "Are you hungry or need to g-go to the b-bathroom?"

Instead of meeting his eyes, Rebekah turned her head toward Josh, as if trying to ascertain his intentions. Josh mouthed *yes* and nodded quickly.

"I thought you'd never ask," she said in a suddenly congenial tone. "I *really* need to go. I've been holding it for hours because I don't want to ruin these beautiful linen sheets." Her voice was forced but not to the point that her words sounded fake.

Damien looked back at Josh, apparently thinking. He rounded the table and checked the drain tube. Still just a trickle. He secured the hemostat clamp and rubbed his chin. Then, returning to Rebekah, he said, "Okay. I'll let you up. But no f-funny business. If you try anything, the d-detective is a d-dead man. Got it?"

She nodded. "Yes. I promise."

CHAPTER 55

DAMIEN PLACED JOSH'S PISTOL IN a tray and set it on the top shelf of the cabinets, just under the marble men, as if asking them to guard it. He then unfastened the nylon straps securing Rebekah to her autopsy table. He kept his pistol in his left hand at all times. He pulled a white lab smock from a drawer and tossed it to Rebekah. He then leaned against the counter and looked down at his shoes. "Don't take t-too long."

When Rebekah sat up, the room began to sway. She quickly wrapped the smock around her shoulders and waited for her vertigo to pass. She was surprised that her captor had averted his eyes. He was the one who had undressed her in the first place. For all his bluster about knowing so much and being so enlightened, emotionally he was very much a little boy.

She slid off the table, testing her balance. Movement caused her abraded skin to sting with renewed intensity. Ignoring the pain, she took a few tentative steps toward Josh.

"What are you doing?" Damien barked, raising the gun.

"I just want to give him a kiss," she said in a voice thick with emotion.

Damien thought for a moment, then nodded. "Keep your hands behind your b-back."

The kiss was brief, but it filled her with more emotion than any kiss ever had before. "I love you, Josh," she whispered, her lips a fraction of an inch from his.

"I love you too, Becks," he whispered back.

She paused, trying to keep her emotions in check. "You sure about this?"

"Yes. Without question."

"Now listen, d-detective," Damien broke in. "I'm going to t-trust you alone for a few m-minutes."

"You have my word," he said without taking his eyes from Rebekah's. "I won't move a muscle. No matter *how long you take,* I'll be here when you get back."

She kissed Josh's forehead then wobbled to the door. Her legs still had some strength but she made it seem otherwise. "I'm sorry I'm so slow," she said to Damien. "My legs feel like spaghetti."

The LPN smiled tenderly. "It's ok-kay. You're doing great. There's some stairs just outside, but I know you c-can do it." He spoke as if coaching a patient in physical therapy.

The light filling the cement service slope was muted but still harsh. The sky was gray and mottled—the color and texture of cadaverous skin. The air was heavy with the threat of rain. The smell of ozone brought the promise of lightning. Shielding her eyes, she used her toes to find the first rise then lifted her foot to the tread and repeated the process, taking the stairs one at a time. Damien followed a few steps behind. The rusty ironwork creaked and shimmied under their combined weight. At the top, he handed her a key with which to unlock the door.

"May I ask you something?" she asked in a caring tone as they entered the small house.

"Okay."

"What if you're wrong?"

"Ab-bout what?" he said with caution.

"About everything. About your research. The whole Fountain of Youth thing."

His eyes registered a flash of anger. "I'm not." He pointed to the closet-size bathroom off his bedroom. "Bathroom's in there."

"Thanks," she said entering and closing the door.

The tiny room had a narrow tin shower stall, a stained porcelain sink, and an equally stained porcelain toilet. Much to her surprise—and gratitude—the cramped space didn't stink. Despite the stains, the bathroom was very clean and smelled freshly disinfected. She smirked at the irony that Damien was more pathogen-conscious than Josh. Well, he was a nurse—a sick, sociopathic one, but still a nurse.

She heard him opening and closing cabinetry in the adjacent kitchen. Outside, a distant rumble warned of an impending storm.

"Are you hungry?" he called out.

"Starving," she replied. "I bet Josh is too. He'll need his strength for the transfusion."

She hated having to sound happy about the despicable event. But she trusted Josh enough to go along with his promptings, even if it seemed absolutely insane to her.

"You're p-probably right. Something l-light, though. I don't want him throwing up and asp-pirating in the m-middle of it."

"Oh yeah, that's right. You know, Josh was right, you *are* very bright."

He didn't respond—but she could guess he was beaming. *Keep stalling him. Josh said 'no matter how long it takes.' He wants me to stall him.*

"Hey, Damien? Do you mind if I take a quick shower as long as I'm in here? I smell like the inside of someone's old sneaker."

"You're n-not that bad." His voice was suddenly so close to the door it startled her.

"And you're just being nice. But if I'm going to assist with Josh's transfusion, I'd like to be in my best form. Please? I haven't showered in almost three days, and I'm starting to ferment."

There was a brief laugh followed by a length of silence that about suffocated her. Finally she heard a faint, "Well . . ."

"Ah come on, Damien," she nearly teased. "Look, I could have been done by now. There's no window in here, so there's no way I can escape. Besides, why would I want to? You have a healthy volunteer and we're excited to test your theory about AB-positive blood."

"Well, okay, but make it q-quick. And dry off the walls and floor when you're done. I hate m-mildew."

She turned on the water and jumped right in. The cold spray hitting her abraded skin felt needle-sharp. She gritted her teeth against the pain and thought of how she could prevent this nightmare from progressing. If Josh needed her to stall, she would move at a snail's pace. She shampooed, soaped, and rinsed, humming one random tune after another. As the water warmed, she lathered up again.

"That's enough!" Damien hollered, pounding against the door.

"Okay," she called out. "Just let me rinse off."

When Damien pounded a second time, she shut off the water. She dried off with a towel hanging on a door rack and then wiped down the entire room. It proved difficult because all the surfaces kept steaming up. She dressed and opened the door then proceeded to wipe everything a second time.

"Yeah, I have to d-do that, too," Damien said, leaning against his kitchen counter, frowning at her.

"Sorry. I hope it doesn't mildew."

"Me too. You were in there l-long enough."

"I'm sorry. Do you have a comb? My hair feels like a rat's nest."

He pushed away from the counter and opened a drawer in the bathroom. As he did so, she noticed a dish-drainer filled with plates, a small pot, a couple of glasses, and a drain cup filled with utensils. With glasses fogged over, he handed her a wide-tooth comb.

Standing in front of a small mirror, she began untangling her hair. "Thank you again for letting me clean up. I'm sorry I took so long, but I was afraid I might start attracting flies."

Damien's demeanor lightened with her jesting. "You *are* funny. I c-can see why the d-detective likes you." He pointed to the table. "There's Club crackers and Cheez Whiz. I haven't g-gone shopping in a while; it's all I g-got."

"It's perfect," she said with her broadest smile. *What is it with guys and salty snack food?* "Oh my heck! How did you know this is my favorite kind of Cheez Whiz?" She reached for the can but misjudged her grip and knocked it to the floor. "Oops."

When Damien bent to retrieve it she reached into the utensil drainer, grabbed the wooden handle of what looked like a steak knife, and slipped it into her smock pocket. If Damien saw the move, he didn't react to it.

"It's m-my favorite too," he said, standing.

She picked up the crackers. "Let's take these to Josh, okay?"

He shrugged.

The sky outside had darkened considerably. When Damien locked the backdoor, thunder clapped and rumbled directly over the small house, shaking the windows.

Damien nodded and had her lead the way down the rickety staircase.

CHAPTER 56

JOSH HAD HEARD THE WATER running upstairs and draining down a pipe in the wall. He tried not to think about what Slade might be doing to Rebekah at that moment. The guy didn't seem like the perverted type. He was definitely twisted, classically psychotic, but he was not a sexual threat to her. Still, the calm side of his bipolar nature could hide . . . *anything*.

The moment Josh was alone, he struggled against the restraints but to no avail. He was bound so tightly, it restricted his breathing. The thick needle in his arm still burned. He wondered why Slade had stopped the drain tube. Josh rehearsed what the guy had said: *The transfusion should take a couple days. Embalming takes only a couple hours.* Perhaps the trickle was too much?

About twenty minutes later he heard the creak and clank of the metal stairs.

As Rebekah opened the basement door, a crack of thunder ricocheted down the service slope and into the room. Slade paused in the doorway and looked up at the sky. Sporadic gusts of wind tousled his hair.

"The weatherman *did* say a storm was coming," Josh commented. "See any lightning?"

"Not yet," Slade said, closing the door behind him.

Rebekah set the Cheez Whiz and crackers next to the sink. "Hungry?" she asked, glancing at Josh.

"Ravenous," he answered, watching her for signals.

She coated a cracker with the oily, artificial cheese and took it to him. He almost laughed at what must be going through her mind—intentionally feeding him something she considered the antithesis of food.

"Umm, these are great," he swooned. "Have you had any yet, darling?"

She flashed him a confused frown. "No, I . . . well I'm not really that hungry anymore."

After downing three goop-laden crackers, he asked Slade if he could have some water.

"There's a cup in that c-cabinet," he said to Rebekah.

Rebekah retrieved a cup and filled it from the sink. Slade watched the whole thing from a drafting stool at the computer. He held the gun limply on his lap and alternated between pecking at a few computer keys and watching his prisoners. He seemed bored but not wholly uninterested. It was as if he enjoyed listening to them interact.

Tipping the cup too quickly, she spilled the water down his chin. "Oh! I'm such a clumsy oaf." To Slade she said, "Be a dear and get me a towel, will you please?"

He rolled his eyes and went to the near end of the cupboards. As he did so, she rounded the table to the side where the IV hung from Josh's arm. As soon as Slade's back was turned, Rebekah slid something into his hand. If felt like a standard steak knife: roughly four and a half inches long, maybe an inch tall, with a serrated edge. He palmed the wooden handle so that his wrist concealed the blade. It was little use against a handgun, but it was better than nothing.

As Rebekah meticulously toweled off Josh's face and neck, he tried angling the small blade against the nylon strap. Even if he had a prime angle and freedom of movement, it would be a difficult material to cut. But because the blade was serrated, it just might work . . . Rebekah looked down at Josh with deep concern. He knew what she was thinking: that he was insane. Perhaps. But he didn't know what else to do. What he needed most was time to saw through the nylon strap. He cocked his head a few times toward Slade. He needed to keep him talking, to keep him off balance. Hopefully, Rebekah had sensed that.

"Okay, now that everyone is f-fed and pottied and c-clean, can we g-get on with the assignment?" There was a definite annoyance in his voice.

Rebekah draped the towel over her shoulder. "Right. Do you want me to tap the feed vein in this arm?" she asked, palpating the crook of Josh's elbow.

"You know how to start an IV?"

"Sure. It was part of my lab work at the morgue. Of course, it's been a long time since I've done it on a *live* person, but I think the procedure is the same."

Slade looked like he was about to speak when his cell phone buzzed. He read a text and smiled. "Well, well, this d-day just keeps getting b-better and b-b-better."

"So share the good news," Rebekah said.

He held up his phone, showing them the message on the tiny screen. "Mentor is coming by in a few minutes with his new compound."

* * *

Rebekah swallowed hard and tried to remain smiling. They might have had a chance if Damien had to do the procedure alone. Now, with the addition of another bad guy in the small room, their odds of escaping plummeted with each passing second. She considered using the steak knife against Damien herself, but he always kept his distance from her. And he continually had the gun in one hand.

Think, Rebekah. Come on!

"His new compound?" she asked, moving to the counter, away from Josh. "A new drug of some kind?"

"Yes. Like I said, he's c-close to finding a way to des-stroy the antigens on red blood cells so they n-never code for an antibody from a t-transfusion."

"That's brilliant. I can't wait to meet him." She paused and looked down at her smock. "I um . . . I feel a little awkward having anyone see me like this," she said, gesturing at her sparse attire. The smock was little better than a micro-miniskirt. She flashed him her shyest demure smile. "Any chance I can have my clothes back so I can assist without shame?"

Damien leveled the gun at her. "You're not t-trying any f-funny stuff, are you?"

Like I would tell him if I was. "Of course not, silly. I just feel a bit . . . overexposed. You understand, don't you?"

He lowered the gun and with wide eyes took in the amount of leg that was showing. She wondered why he only just now seemed to notice. She also wondered if Josh had noticed. Then she wondered why she was wondering such foolishness in light of the situation. *Fickle woman!*

"Um, yeah, I can see your p-point." Damien's face was bright red with embarrassment. And yet *he* was the one who had removed her clothes in the first place. *What a weirdo.* He opened a cabinet under the countertop and pulled out a neatly folded stack of clothes—her clothes, freshly laundered and pressed. "I'll face the d-door. I want you to keep t-talking while you're dressing, so I can t-tell how far away you are."

"Damien, I'm not going to try anyth—"

"No argument!" he snapped. "You do it my way or you stay in the smock."

She lowered her eyes. "Okay. I'll do it your way."

"Start t-talking," Damien insisted before moving to the door. Luckily, the position also faced him away from Josh.

"Okay, sure. You know, as long as you're interested in centenarians, I should tell you some of the facts I uncovered," she said as she began changing. "At first I thought their longevity was due mostly to a healthy diet—you know, lots of vegetables and such. But one study I read a few years back looked at what they ate and found the vast number of centenarians had grown up on meat and potatoes." She knew Josh was probably biting his tongue, wanting to comment. But he was keeping quiet for a reason, and she wasn't going to solicit his response. "So, of course, the researchers wondered why these people *were* living well past their prime. So they looked at other factors and found that all of the subjects had been raised in labor-intensive environments: farmers, ranchers, dockworkers, manual laborers, and the like. They almost exclusively lived in the country or semirural settings. Those who lived in a city preferred to walk over riding anywhere. Most of them claimed to have walked upwards of ten miles—roughly 20,000 steps—every day."

"I've read the same thing," Damien said with his back still turned. "B-b-but regular exercise alone won't g-guarantee longevity. There *are* other f-factors involved."

"Oh you're absolutely right," she was quick to say. "I'm just kind of rambling like you asked me to."

"Yeah, but it's i-interesting stuff. Keep g-going."

"Okay. More recent research has isolated certain variants of the FOXO3A gene, showing an increased effect on the life expectancy of humans worldwide."

"I've seen th-that one, too."

"But to date, I don't think anyone has looked specifically at blood *types*. That's why what you're doing is so impressive."

"Wow, you *have* d-done a lot of research," he said cheerily. "I'm imp-pressed."

"Yeah. I feel like a regular Inspector Clouseau."

Josh cast a quick glance in her direction. She was fully dressed now but wasn't going to tell Damien that.

"I know j-just what you m-mean. It's like solving a great m-m-mystery. Keep talking," Damien urged. "This is great."

"Okay," she said holding up her palms to Josh, questioning him on his progress. He nodded several times, as if encouraging her to continue stalling. "Another aspect of long life has to do with the importance of interpersonal interaction. Have you read any of that?"

"Oh y-yes. Most c-centenarians have logged hours and hours in c-community service, beginning at an early age. It gives them a sense of p-purpose and resp-ponsibility in a worthy cause."

"Precisely." She could see Josh working frantically at the restraint under the shroud, but she had no idea how far he'd gotten. *Come on Josh! Move it!* "It gives them a sense of personal value. People need to feel *needed*."

"T-true. But even feeling n-needed, staying active, and eating right are n-not solid guarantees of l-longevity."

"Don't I know it! In my job, I've seen people who lived the life of a saint die in their fifties and those who have embraced the 'eat, drink, and be merry' philosophy live into their nineties. Some people are just lucky. That's why your AB-positive hypothesis is so groundbreaking. Are you thinking of publishing your results?"

"I don't know. Maybe." He paused and shuffled his feet a bit. "I've n-never sought for at-tention. It's . . . it's my s-stutter, you see. P-people make f-fun of it—like you did earlier."

Another peal of thunder rumbled outside, emphasizing his indictment.

"You're right, Damien. You're absolutely right. That was terribly rude of me, and I apologize."

Josh's wrist came free at that moment. He deftly changed the knife to his other hand and smoothed out the shroud, closed his eyes and breathed slow and deep, as if asleep. Damien remained facing the door.

Rebekah continued. "But there's a big reason I said those things, only . . ." her voice trailed off into silence.

"Only . . . what?"

"I . . . I can't say."

"Why not?" His head turned slightly toward her.

"It's okay. You can turn around now."

He did so and gave her a look of anticipation. "Why c-can't you say?"

She placed a finger to her lips, shushing him, then pointed at Josh's sleeping form. "He's been awake so long that he's fallen asleep, but I . . . I don't want him to hear what I have to say." Her voice was soft yet urgent.

"Oh, o-okay."

"Can we . . . can we talk outside for just a minute? It's very important," she whispered.

Damien looked from Josh to Rebekah and back again. "O-okay. Just for a minute. Come on."

He opened the door and stepped outside. A tempestuous wind had picked up, signifying the arrival of the storm front. Rebekah followed him out into the turbulent afternoon and closed the door behind her.

CHAPTER 57

THE WIND BLEW DIRECTLY FROM the south, hot and sticky. It brought no relief from the heat; in the cavity of the service bay, it thrashed and scorched like a blast furnace. Damien held the gun to his side, but his finger remained on the trigger. He pointed to the landing of the metal stairs. "Sit there."

She did. She hoped she looked as frightened as she felt. This was her only chance to give Josh enough time to make his escape. She wasn't kidding about him being awake so long. Although she didn't know it as a fact, she knew it in her heart. That was the kind of man he was. He would risk everything for her. She needed to do the same for him—even if it meant putting him at greater risk.

Raising her voice to be heard, she said, "Damien, I didn't understand at first. I thought you were just some weirdo getting his kicks. I am so, so sorry. But now that I see the big picture, and the importance of what you're doing, I think I understand now." It was a lie, but a necessary one.

Damien's eyes were dark and undefined behind his thick lenses. "Why have you b-been following me, sticking your n-nose into my b-business in the first p-place?"

Her mind whirled, realizing he might know more about her than she did about him. A gust of hot air blew her still moist hair across her face, lashing into her eyes. She held it back and tried to sound sincere. *Make it believable.* "It . . . it was Josh. *He's* the one investigating you. He forced me to help him because I have access to a national medical database."

"Forced you?" he asked with a sneer.

"Yes, Damien. He said if I didn't cooperate, I'd be obstructing justice. I could end up in jail."

"But you're his g-g-girlfriend. He wouldn't d-do that to you."

"You don't know him," she cried. "He . . . he threatens me all the time." It pained her to be lying about Josh like this. He'd suffered a severe head wound because of her. He was strapped to an autopsy table because of her. He offered to take her place—in reality, sacrificing *his life* for hers.

"I don't b-believe you. You're j-just stalling. I saw the way you l-l-look at him."

The clouds overhead had thickened into a malignant, churning mass of black and gray. A clap of thunder slammed into the cement depression, causing Rebekah to recoil. Damien didn't flinch. He stood as motionless as a statue, his face like one of the visages he venerated in his basement lab. His eyes were dark sockets, devoid of life, his red hair whipping and dancing like flames from a torch.

"No, I promise I'm not. He's says he'll beat me if I try to leave. He swore he'd kill me if I ever betrayed him. He said as a homicide investigator, he could make it look like an accident or a suicide. No one would ever question him."

Damien rested the gun on his shoulder, pointing it into the air. But his finger still twitched on the trigger. "Why would he d-do that?"

"He was using me to get to you. He's been following you from state to state, but he needed the information from my office to find out who was committing—" She stopped abruptly and shook her head. "To determine who was harvesting the AB-positive blood. He knows nothing about blood types like you and I do. He doesn't understand the importance of AB-positive blood. When you explained where it came from, how important and *sacred* it is, I finally understood what you were trying to accomplish. It makes perfect sense, Damien. Please let me help you."

A fat spit of rain struck her cheek, followed by another and another. Damien's smock began to speckle as the clouds relinquished their burden. He seemed oblivious to the storm.

"Help how?"

Her mind reeled, trying to come up with something that made sense, something he could not refute. "How many peop—volunteers have you transfused so far?"

He slowly lowered the gun, as if the movement required serious thought and execution. The weapon stopped halfway down, pointing directly at her.

"Why?"

"I'm just wondering what kind of success you've had so far. Since you're still testing, I can only assume something is not working right. I'm sure it's not your fault, but maybe I can help find where the procedure needs adjustment."

His eyes flickered briefly, but his voice remained cold and measured. "Mentor says it's b-because he hasn't found the right c-compound yet. *I* think it's b-because I haven't come ac-cross anyone worthy enough to survive the t-transfusion."

The rain was now coming in diagonal bursts, carried on the wind like salvos fired from a battleship. In the stairwell, Rebekah had scant protection from the frenzied deluge but Damien was fully exposed. His hair no longer whipped about but stuck to his head, its bright color now squiggled down his forehead in crimson rivulets, looking very much like blood.

"I'm sure you're right," she said over the wind and rain. "That makes perfect sense."

He stood silent, staring, the gun hovering motionless.

She felt helpless. She needed to do *something*. Had she given Josh enough time? It'd only been about eight minutes. If she forced Damien to make a decision, he could crack. If she just sat there, Mentor would show up, and their chances of escape would vanish.

"Damien, please." She looked up at the roiling storm. Lightning ripped across the sky, crackling and booming, sounding like the onset of Armageddon. "We're going to get electrocuted standing out here," she cried. "Let's get back inside and get things ready for Mentor."

Slowly, he looked up at the dark sky. He closed his eyes and stretched out his arms, swelling his chest to the heavens. He stood there until another thunder clap fractured the sky. Then, as if snapping from a trance, he opened his eyes and chuckled. "This is c-crazy! Let's get inside b-before we drown!"

Damien held the door open for her. She saw right away that Josh was still on the table with the sheet over his body. He appeared to still be asleep. No restraint straps hung from the edges of the table. He had failed.

She walked a few paces to the cabinet from which Damien had removed a towel earlier. Helping herself, she grabbed one for her and one for Damien.

"Just leave it on the counter and go over there to dry off," he ordered, pointing to the far corner of the room.

Another snap of lightning caused the lights to flicker.

"Ever lose power in here?" Rebekah asked, pressing the towel to her soaked clothing.

"Not that I know of," he said, rounding Josh's table. He placed his gun on the counter, removed his glasses, and began running the towel over his head and face.

"But, well, aren't you worried about the refrigeration units losing power?"

"Oh, that. They have b-built-in backup b-b-batteries. They're good for eight hours if the d-doors stay closed."

"Ah." She looked at Josh again. He *must* have fallen asleep. She'd never seen him this peaceful before. It was almost as if he was laid out for—

She closed her eyes and refused to finish the thought. He wasn't dead, and she was going to do whatever she could to prevent that from happening. But thinking of him deceased brought something else to mind. "Hey, Damien? I have to ask, when one of your transfusions doesn't work, what do you do with the body?"

He bent over and rubbed the towel down each leg of his jeans. "Oh, that. You'd b-be surprised how easy it is to d-dump a body around here. There are lots of d-deserts and wilderness p-places only an hour or t-two away. Just ask the det-tective when he wakes up. I bet he's had lots of b-bodies showing up in the middle of n-nowhere all the t-time."

Her stomach twisted—not at the thought of a corpse in the desert, but at the base, compassionless way in which he spoke of someone he'd just murdered. Even when she was dissecting a cadaver, she knew at one time the body housed a spirit from Heavenly Father. That alone garnered a large measure of respect.

"So . . . what about Mr. Doe in there?" she asked, nodding toward the cadaver fridge.

"Oh, I m-may just keep him until we're done with the det-tective. Just in case, you know? That'll save me a t-trip."

Rebekah swallowed a jagged shard of emotion. "Just in case . . . he doesn't make it?"

"Well, yeah. But I feel his chances are b-better than most."

She covered her face with the towel, pretending to dry herself. In reality, she was hiding her true emotions over what was about to happen— over what she was about to *help* happen. She clamped her jaw so hard it popped. She couldn't go through with it. Feeling the rage build within her, she did nothing to subdue it. *Nothing* was *about* to happen because she was *not* going to allow it to. Peeking over the towel, she glanced around, seeking anything she could use. Rebekah turned from Damien toward the telescoping tray on which she'd found the scalpel. With any luck, it'd still be there.

"So tell me about your medical training," she asked casually.

Without warning, a knotted towel dropped past her face and yanked tightly against her neck. The force was so strong she felt something crunch in her throat. She tried to gasp for breath but couldn't. Her hands clawed at the towel, but it was like raking her nails against a steel cable. The towel was twisted into a thick cord that threatened to crush her trachea.

"You m-must think I'm a real idiot, Miss Sm-mith," Damien hissed, his mouth just millimeters from her ear. "I know what you're t-t-trying to d-do."

She grappled at the towel uselessly. The cloth creaked like the ropes on a sailing vessel. Rebekah's vision darkened around the edges.

"You? Offering to help m-me?" he growled. "I heard what y-you said to the d-detective. You would d-die for him. You're j-just waiting for a ch-chance to stab me in the b-back, aren't you?"

He shoved her forward, slamming her against the empty autopsy table. She folded onto the cold, hard surface with enough force to knock the wind from her lungs. Her head smacked against the tabletop with a metallic clang. Using the towel as a handle, he raised her up and slammed her down again and again. Her head felt ready to pop from her neck.

The towel then slackened a bit—just enough for her to catch a quick gasp of air. At the same time, she heard the ratcheting of a pistol being cocked.

"Hands on top of your head, Slade, or you're a dead man!" Josh growled.

CHAPTER 58

REBEKAH SLOWLY PEELED THE TOWEL from her throat. It'd been cinched so tightly that it felt as if it took a layer of skin when she removed it. Blood flowed back into her head, roaring past her eardrums. Because of the severe trauma, her hearing played tricks on her. She swore she had just heard Josh's voice. She pushed off from the table and turned. The room continued to spin even after she stopped. Her vision swayed but was sharp enough to see Josh handcuffing Damien's wrists behind his back. *Josh is free! Josh is free!* her mind cheered. Her eyes burned afresh with both pain and happiness.

"Are you okay?" Josh asked her, standing behind Damien.

She coughed, gagged, but couldn't speak. Her legs felt useless, her throat inoperable.

"Can—breathe—kay?" His words came intermittently. The blood rushing past her eardrums still muddled all sounds.

She gave a thumbs up. It was easier than speaking.

"Do—taste—blood?"

She swallowed and grimaced at the pain. She flashed a "little bit" sign with her thumb and index finger.

"Sip—water—elp." Turning his attention to Damien, he said, "As for—sick piece of—you sit—sorry butt on—table and don't move—so help me—have an accident—break your fingers—at a time."

She was able to fill in the blank spaces between his words. She'd never heard such anger in his voice before. She knew his threats were serious. She hoped Damien did too. On second thought, maybe it wouldn't be so bad if Josh inflicted a few "accidents," just for the satisfaction it would bring.

"You're—reg-gret this," the LPN murmured.

"Shut up," Josh said, slapping the back of Damien's head. He shoved him against the autopsy table. "Sit."

Rebekah stumbled to the sink and sipped some water. It stung and soothed simultaneously. She tipped her head back to let the water trickle down her raw esophagus—but the move made her extremely dizzy. She closed her eyes, trying to keep her balance. A migraine raged just behind her eyes, threatening to split her skull. Its spiky throb was disorienting. She turned her back to the counter and slid to the floor. The room didn't spin as wildly down there as it did when she was standing.

The rain pattered lightly against the blacked-out window panes and the double doors. The main storm front had passed, but its rumbling continued to echo back to the tiny house. *Let it grumble all it wants.* Josh had been able to free himself! The thought made her happier than she knew was possible. The timpani in the heavens now brought reassurance instead of dread. The distant thunder sounded musical, mellifluous.

Josh was speaking again. "You—right to remain silent—you have the right to an attorney—do you understand . . . ?"

She drew her knees up and placed her forehead on them. How had she gotten involved in this mess in the first place? How could anyone possibly think one blood type had any special powers over another? Or that those powers would transfer upon elimination of one type and introduction of another? Or that science claimed to know what Christ's blood type was? Was that truly important? Wasn't *believing* His blood was spilled for them the important thing?—not what *type* of blood was spilt. That's what *she* believed. She knew Josh did too.

Rebekah let her mind drift. Too many questions added to the pain in her skull. Focusing on calming thoughts, she breathed slowly and deeply through her nose, which helped her feel a sweet release of anxiety and tension. More words—some Josh's, some Damien's—drifted through the room, garbled and clearly embattled. That was okay. If Josh needed her, he'd call her name. She'd recognize his voice.

As her head cleared, the voices drastically sharpened, instantly harsh and bitter. Maybe Damien was acting up, being difficult. Maybe Josh was inflicting an "accident"—just to show the LPN he was dead serious. Only . . . it didn't sound like Josh's voice. Or Damien's.

"No sudden moves, detective." The voice was accented, foreign, and strangely familiar.

She frowned, trying to place it. *Pakistani?*

"Please release my assistant and place the handcuff key on the table, Detective Logan. I do not wish to kill you. Thank you. Now lie facedown on the table. Slowly. Hands behind your back. Very good."

She rubbed her eyes and looked toward the doorway. Images slowly morphed from blurry to semi-defined to detailed. She stopped breathing. The speaker met her stare.

"Hello, Sundara. I wish I could say I was happy to see you."

CHAPTER 59

Dr. Sandeep Mahesh walked over to Rebekah and offered to help her stand. "This is as much a shock to me as it is to you, I am certain."

She took his hand and struggled to her feet. He escorted her to the empty table and had her sit. Seeing her neck, he sucked in a breath through his teeth. "Oh my soul! That looks terribly, terribly distressing. May I examine you to check for injury?"

She lifted her chin as he probed the battered areas of her neck. It was painfully sensitive, but what hurt more was the realization that Sandeep Mahesh was partners with Damien Slade. She had never wanted to be wrong so much in her life. Yet Damien was standing beside Josh, handcuffing him at Sandy's command with minimal gentleness. The look in the LPN's eyes matched the feeling in her heart—cold, lifeless.

"Why are you doing this?" she croaked.

"Oh, my dear Sundara. It would take a lifetime to explain," Mahesh said sympathetically. "I am extremely sorry you got caught up in this. I had hoped to discourage your investigation by sending you down false pathways. But, regrettably, I did not act speedily enough. And, like the proverbial cat, your curiosity has ensnared you in a trap from which I cannot release you."

He finished his exam by looking down her throat, using his penlight. He retrieved some Advil from a cabinet and refilled her cup of water. He knew exactly where everything was in the basement lab—another testament to his involvement with Slade. "Take these one at a time so they do not exacerbate the damage to your esophagus. Your trachea is terribly bruised, but I cannot see any permanent damage. Your larynx is raw and weeping, but I can feel no damage to your cricoid or tracheal cartilage. Can you taste any blood?"

Josh had asked the same question with as much heartfelt concern. But Josh's query carried more true sympathy than Sandeep's ever would.

"Not any more," she rasped quietly.

"That is a comfort," the pathologist said. "Sometimes our Damien can get over-passionate in his responsibilities. But he is enormously good at what he does." He went to the fridge and retrieved an icepack. He wrapped it in a linen handkerchief before giving it to her. "Hold this to your throat. The ibuprofen will take effect in a few minutes. Until that time, can I get you anything else?"

"Yeah. A gun."

He laughed good-naturedly. "That, of course, I cannot do. I can sense your distress over this situation, Sundara, but allow me to me explain. Remember when I told you to look for things you know as a means of discovering what you do not know? If you truly examine what we are doing here, you will see that what appears to be brutal is actually life-saving. We are delightfully close to finding an antigen neutralizer that will revolutionize blood transfusions and organ donation. Ponder it, Sundara. Transplanted tissues will never be rejected, the need for blood typing will become a thing of the past, even common seasonal allergies may be totally eradicated."

Tears pooled in her eyes as she looked at the face of the man who had become a second father to her, who had treated her as a daughter, whom she respected and even revered as a role model for all men. The word *betrayal* didn't come close to describing the feeling churning in her stomach. She was physically sick. Her soul felt as if it were tearing in two. This man of infinite wisdom was espousing a noble *idea* but was supporting it with tactics that were despicable and criminally insane.

"Really, Sandy?" Her voice was still coarse—the ibuprofen had yet to kick in—but the ice was helping. "You can't possibly think killing *innocent* people is a good thing."

He wheeled over a drafting chair and sat in front of her. "Sundara. These bodies we possess are merely vessels—temporary structures we inhabit while on earth. You have said as much many times. Even your religion teaches that the spirit within us makes us who we are, does it not? That the spirit *and* the body are the soul of man?"

"My religion teaches that our bodies are temples—and that they should be treated as such," she said with conviction, forcing the words past the pain.

"Precisely. And as temples, should you not do everything possible to help them live long and fruitful lives? Should you not do everything in your means to prolong the life of your body? Is long life not a guarantee of your Word of Wisdom?"

"Long life is a *potential blessing* for treating your body right—by avoiding addictive and abusive substances and through a good diet and regular exercise—but it is *not* a guarantee. And exchanging what we were given at birth with something that might—*might*—prolong life by a few years is *not* the key to eternal life."

"Ah, but I have caught you in a conundrum. Do we not replace blood during surgery or in cases of severe injury? Do we not replace defective heart valves and joints of the body?" His voice softened. "Did you not give one of *your* kidneys to try and save the life of your mother?"

"*Replace,* Sandy! *Replace*, not *exchange*, you ignominious monster!" Rage coiled inside her, begging for the chance to strike. Using her mother's death as justification for his twisted experiment was the last straw. "Replacing a defective part is one thing. Exchanging a perfectly healthy tissue for another one is irresponsible butchery, not research! I can't believe you think you're doing humanity a service. It's reprehensible. How can you even sleep at night?" She was crying now but didn't care. She tasted blood again, but it no longer mattered. Any vestiges of respect she once had for Dr. Mahesh faded into oblivion. "I wish I'd never met you. I wish *you* were dead!" The fury in her voice matched the rumble of thunder outside. "And if you *ever* mention my mother again, I swear you'll wish you were dead, too."

He reached out to pat her leg. She slapped it away.

"Oh, my dear Sundara. Try to see what you do not yet see. I know you do not believe in reincarnation, but it is a part of my culture that I accept as fact. We cannot choose what we will come back as—that is up to the gods. I am very much happy with my body—well," he chuckled, "maybe not *happy*—I do not look like George Clooney, after all—but I am content. And I have a mind full of knowledge and enlightenment that I might not have in my next life. Why should I not do everything I can to prolong *this* life by fortifying *this* body?"

"So it's *not* for humanity," Josh said flatly. "It's for *you*."

Rebekah was so focused on wallowing in Mahesh's muddled way of thinking that she'd forgotten that Josh was fully awake on the other table. Damien had turned him over, strapped him down, and removed the handcuffs. Presently, the LPN was preparing an IV—she guessed for introduction of Mahesh's new compound.

"I feel I must disagree, Detective Logan," Mahesh said apologetically. "While it is true I have personal interests in this research, consider how many people will benefit from such a discovery. Bloodbanks everywhere could carry whatever blood they could get because it would not matter to the recipient. Eliminating the antigenic effect would do away with antibody production, which could save millions. Is this not a truly divine concept?"

Josh shook his head. "If there's one thing history teaches us, it's that a righteous end *never* justifies sadistic means. Hitler convinced a nation that genocide was the necessary means to an exalted end. So did Stalin and Mao Zedong. And just last year there was that fiasco in Hawaii where some nut job almost killed the entire population of that island in Hawaii testing a vaccine he thought would save millions from a bioweapon of his own making. The end always sounds divinely inspired, but you will never succeed if it requires doing the exact opposite."

Rebekah smiled at Josh. Even in this hopeless situation he still championed his ideals. And hers. She wished she could be that strong. "I agree with Josh."

"You w-would. He's your b-boyfriend."

For a rare moment, she was at a loss for words. Needing to say *something*, she asked, "So how did you two pathetic miscreants meet?"

Mahesh laughed. "Always the jokester, Sundara. If you must know, I was on vacation in Puerto Rico. I went to a bar for a taste of local rum and heard this skinny, redheaded American claiming to have found the *real* Fountain of Youth."

"I had a l-little too much to d-drink," Damien admitted sheepishly.

"As I am a lover of old legends, I offered to buy him a drink if he would share his fascinating story with me. One thing led to another and we formed a mutually beneficial partnership. Just think of it: a chance to become legends ourselves."

"So you two think you're saints," Josh growled. "I think you're scum."

Mahesh scooted off his chair. "What you may or may not think is not a matter of consequence, Detective Logan. Because you two are aware of our research, we cannot allow you to leave this laboratory. I am deeply sorry." He examined the straps binding Josh to the table. "He is sufficiently restrained. Please prepare this patient for transfusion, nurse."

"Sandy, no," Rebekah pled. "We can work this out."

"I am afraid not, Sundara. I love you like a daughter, you know this. But I want to live a long, long time, and that takes precedence. There is a property in AB-positive blood that engenders longevity, I am convinced of this. I do not know what it is yet, but I will in time."

He took the pistol from Damien and, speaking to Josh, pointed it at her head. "Do not try anything heroic, detective, or I *will* shoot her. Damien is going to give you my new compound through your IV. It may burn a little, but with luck it will help you survive the transfusion."

"And here I thought you *wanted* me dead," he scoffed.

"No, no. Do not be absurd. It will be incredibly satisfactory if you live, as it will prove my brilliance as a biochemist and as a visionary doctor of medicine. If you try to resist, however, I promise you Rebekah will die right before your eyes. The choice is yours."

CHAPTER 60

JOSH HAD REMOVED THE NEEDLE from his right arm when he'd escaped. He wasn't looking forward to being gouged again. But he wasn't looking forward to dying either—or seeing Rebekah die. The situation *was* hopeless. He couldn't see how either of them could get out of it. He was convinced if he died, so would she. All he could hope for was to buy her some time. If that worked, it would be worth it.

Damien had assumed his caring LPN persona. Josh resolved to take it like a man, but he wondered if maybe asking incessant questions would slow him down like it did before. It was worth a try.

"You don't believe all that stuff the doc said, do you?" he whispered to the nurse.

Damien didn't answer. He swabbed the crook of Josh's elbow with more Betadine solution then palpated the vein until it bulged under the skin. He secured a fresh needle to the drain tube, swabbed it with alcohol, and positioned it over the puncture site.

Josh smirked. "Why all the sterile technique if I'm going to die anyway?"

The LPN gave a friendly frown. "We're hoping you d-don't die, detective. That's the whole p-p-point."

"Oh yeah, you're looking to save mankind. How noble. Too bad others had to die along the way, huh," Josh sneered.

"The greater good, d-detective. It's for the g-greater good. Ready?"

"No." His negative response didn't work. The bite of the wide-bore trocar needle was worse the second time because the tissue was already bruised and hypersensitive. He grimaced and hissed an expletive between clenched teeth.

"Oh, don't be such a b-baby," Damien teased.

"Couldn't you at least hit the same hole?" His arm was on fire.

"I t-tried, but I guess I m-missed. Sorry."

Josh looked over at Rebekah. She had her head in her hands. Her shoulders rose and fell with each rasping breath. Mahesh was seated casually in front of her, the gun pointed loosely at the ground. *Keep them talking. They need to be distracted.* He remembered some of the things Rebekah had shared at the onset of this madness. *Try it.*

"So you're a Hindu priest?" he asked the doctor. "A panda?"

"A pandit," Mahesh chuckled. "But yes, I am an ordained pandit. How did you know?"

"I heard a rumor."

Rebekah's head snapped up. "Wait—*you* are a pandit? No wonder you knew so much about the embalming oil—" She stopped and gasped. Her expression was instantly one of unbridled fury. "You knew because *you* made it, didn't you? You made it and gave it to this stuttering ignoramus to use after harvesting centenarian blood to make amends for taking an innocent life."

Damien's face darkened. He glowered at her. "Stop s-s-saying that."

"Stop s-s-saying what?" she goaded him. "That you used the oil this alchemist-wannbe gave you—or that you're an ignoramus?"

"Sundara, be nice to the young man."

"Why—so he'll kill us less dead?" Her civility was at zero, her rage off the charts. "You two are so evil I wouldn't be surprised if you were spawned by Satan himself. I detest you both."

"Sundara, I—"

"You what? You think I'm being irrational? Insensitive? You think I'm letting my emotions muddy my thinking?" She was yelling now. Josh heard the pain it caused her throat, but she didn't back down. She stood with her arms held slightly away from her body, posturing for a fight. "You've taken an idea with merit and totally blown it out of proportion to suit your own narcissistic aggrandizement." She turned to Damien. "That means to overinflate your own ego. Probably because n-n-no one else will."

Josh couldn't believe she was mocking a person's disability. She was way above that kind of juvenile behavior. Something must have snapped inside her. Rather than trying to delay the inevitable, he sensed she was intentionally aggravating it.

Scowling at Rebekah, Damien rounded the table and, without any forewarning, rammed the second needle into the vein in Josh's other arm. Josh grimaced noisily, his head involuntarily thrashing back and forth.

"Stop it, you freak!" she yelled.

"That is enough, Sundara! You are behaving like a child." Mahesh's tone was sharp, full of censure.

"*I'm* behaving—" Her voice caught, unable to finish the sentence. She looked at the ceiling and roared. "You are so blinded by your own arrogance that you can't even see what a hypocrite you are. You profess to be Hindi yet you openly venerate AB-positive blood because it was supposedly Christ's blood type. You use pure linen because that's what the Shroud of Turin is made of. You even place coins on the eyes of your victims because that's the way it was done in Jesus' day. But you're not even Christian! Talk about being a hypocrite."

Mahesh's smile was rife with condescension. "Oh, my dear, misguided Sundara—"

"No! You do *not* call me that anymore. My name is Rebekah Smith. And I'm leaving. Right now. If you want to stop me you'll just have to shoot me." She marched to Josh's side and glared at Damien. "Back off— or you'll be on this table nursing a lot worse than a bruised ego."

Mahesh pinched the bridge of his nose and inhaled deeply. "Rebekah, please. Calm down and listen to reason. I am so close to the correct formula—the compound that will change medical therapy as we know it. Detective Logan is a very healthy young man. We shall transfuse him with the new compound—but at the slightest sign of rejection, I will stop the procedure. You have my solemn word on that."

"Your word means nothing to me anymore."

She turned her back to the pathologist and began removing the tape holding the first trocar to Josh's arm.

"Rebekah, I beseech you to stop. This research *must* progress."

"I'm not listening to you anymore, Sandy." She slid the needle from his arm and pressed on the wound to stanch the bleeding. "Find some other guinea pig. We're leaving."

"I cannot allow that," Mahesh said in a firm voice.

With her back still turned, she growled, "Oh yeah? Try and stop me."

"As you wish."

The gunshot in the small, cement-lined basement was deafening.

CHAPTER 61

REBEKAH AWOKE TO A PAIN so intense she could barely think straight. Her left leg felt like it was melting from within. Her thigh muscles twitched relentlessly, cramping and seizing, and her hamstring seared with molten agony. She was lying faceup. Her lower back ached, her head pounded, her throat was excruciatingly raw. She could hear the drone of an electric motor, louder than the ones cooling the refrigeration units. She heard occasional whispers—men's voices. And she heard a heart rate monitor sounding out an unhealthy cadence.

She opened her eyes, squinting at the harsh fluorescents overhead. When she could focus, she tipped her head to take in the room. She was still in the basement. An IV drained into her arm; the fluid was clear, thank goodness. It was probably normal saline or Ringer's solution to prevent shock.

Sudden realization overwhelmed her. *I've been shot!* The gut-wrenching duplicity of it threatened to make her vomit. Sandeep Mahesh, her longtime friend, her mentor and confidant, her surrogate father, had shot her! Yet even though the wound was agonizing, the crippling humiliation she felt for having believed he was a good man all these years hurt worse than the bullet.

Josh was still strapped to his table. Three lines ran from his arms: one into his left arm from the machine making the droning hum, the second—the IV filled with Sandy's chemical—also into his left arm, and the other from his right arm into a drain on the floor. The linen shroud was folded down to his waist. The rise and fall of his chest belied rapid, shallow respirations. Sweat beaded on his cadaver-hued skin. The rapid beeping she heard came from his heart rate monitor. She squinted at the readout: HR 143 bpm; BP 223/109; pulseOx 88%. They were not good numbers. She could see the glistening residue of spent tears tracing from his eyes. She knew he'd been crying—probably not from pain, but for her. Every few seconds his body shook violently. Febrile seizures, she guessed.

Rebekah tried to speak but found her mouth unable to form words. Her tongue felt twice its normal size. She could not work up any saliva to quench her thirst or soothe her ruined trachea. She looked at the clock on the fridge. Almost five in the evening. She'd been unconscious for just a few hours.

How much blood had been drained from Josh's body? How much AB-positive blood had he received? More importantly, how much would be introduced before antibody rejection began? From the look of things, it already had. What truly shocked her was that Mahesh and Slade were not even monitoring him; they were busy discussing something on the computer screen. They needed to do something before Josh's heart gave out!

She grunted a few times but made little noise. She *had* to get their attention. Josh was dying! She tried sitting, made it to one elbow, and fell back down. Steeling herself, she tried again and was finally able to sit up. Blackness crept in around the edges of her vision. Head swimming, eyes unable to focus, she thought she heard sirens in the distance. It was probably just the blood rushing from her head. But she refused to blackout. Not now. Not until Josh was safe. Not until this insanity was ended.

Mahesh and Damien seemed oblivious to the sirens. In this section of town, it was probably common background noise. But when the closest one abruptly silenced, Mahesh stood and looked toward one of the masked windows. Another siren closed in and then went quiet. Mahesh moved to the door and opened it a crack. After a moment, he eased outside with the tentativeness of a deer entering a quiet meadow. Damien didn't even look up. He was totally engrossed with the computer display.

Hoping against hope, Rebekah lay back down and pretended to be asleep but kept her ears tuned to the commotion at the door.

A few seconds later, Mahesh reentered the basement. She heard him lock the door. "We have a serious problem," he whispered urgently.

"Now what?" Damien asked.

"The South Salt Lake police are here."

"So?" the LPN sneered. "They'll kn-nock on the front d-door then leave. If they knock on the b-basement doors, we'll just b-be quiet. They c-can't search inside without a search w-warrant, and g-getting a warrant on a Sunday in Utah is imp-possible."

Rebekah heard footfalls approach her.

"Sundara?" Mahesh said softly. She felt his hand press against her shoulder. "Rebekah?"

She groaned and shifted a bit but did not open her eyes. Time seemed to stand still as she waited to hear him walk away. She could *feel* him standing there, staring at her. Yesterday she wouldn't have minded. His attention would have felt like that of a guardian, even a loved one. At that moment, it felt like being watched by a predator, a demon seeking her soul.

She drew in a deep breath and let it out slowly with a slight shudder, as if trying to quell a bad dream. It wasn't far from the truth.

After another minute, she heard Mahesh turn and walk away. "I believe she is asleep. Hopefully, the police will not search down here," he said softly.

A moment later, a dog barked low and deep just outside the basement door. A solid knock sounded an instant after. "This is the police. Open the door, please."

The would-be scientists looked at each other but did not make a sound.

"Mr. Slade? We know you're in there."

With Mahesh and Damien focused on the door, Rebekah slipped off the table to test her injured leg. It had no strength—just as she feared. Testing her good leg, she found she could balance as long as she was holding onto something else. Her throat was still too raw to utter more than a squeak. If she could make something crash to the floor, it'd alert the police, but it would have to be very loud or it might not be impetus enough for them to bust down the door.

The only other sounds were the droning of the transfusion pump and the beeping of Josh's heart monitor—which was beating much faster now. Not good.

"Mr. Slade, this is the police. Open this door, now!"

Desperately seeking something, anything, her eyes lit on the stainless steel sample tray in the open cabinetry, directly below the three marble busts. She knew it held Josh's gun. It was too high to reach but she could use something to knock it down. Her aluminum IV stand was on casters. She clenched her teeth and pulled the needle from her arm. She then quietly removed the IV bag and wheeled the stand across the short space, using it as a crutch as she hobbled on one leg.

"We have a warrant for your arrest, Mr. Slade. Open up now or we'll be forced to break down the door."

Looking at Mahesh, Damien shook his head slowly. "It's a lie," he barely whispered.

Josh's heart rate increased even more. His entire body convulsed against the nylon restraints. The heart monitor sounded a cautionary buzz, indicating imminent cardiac failure.

Just as Rebekah reached the cabinets, one of the wheels on the IV stand squeaked. Both Damien and Mahesh spun around. Using the counter to support her, she thrust the aluminum stand up, missed the tray, and accidentally hit one of the statues. It teetered and fell to the floor, shattering into several indistinguishable pieces.

"No!" Damien cried, tears instantly filling his eyes. He lunged toward the shards, screaming, collapsing to the ground, hands hovering above the pieces as if unsure where to begin reconstruction.

"Mr. Slade?" the officer called.

Rebekah struck at the tray again, this time knocking it off the shelf. It clattered to the countertop, ejecting Josh's pistol. The gun skittered across the counter, just out of reach. She leaped for it at the same instant Mahesh went for Damien's gun by the keyboard. But the sudden pressure on her injured leg resulted in blinding pain, and she crumpled to the floor weaponless.

The pounding on the door intensified; the handle rattled noisily. "Mr. Slade, please stand away from the door! We're coming in!"

The heart monitor blared a klaxon warning.

Clambering to a knee, Rebekah groped along the countertop. She could feel herself screaming even though little sound was being made. The heart monitor alarm pierced her eardrums like a red-hot spike. Mahesh grabbed Damien's gun just as the door splintered from something slamming against it. The sound distracted him—just long enough for Rebekah to wrap her fingers around Josh's gun. She pulled it off the counter, aimed, and fired—simultaneously with Mahesh. The twin shots fractured the air in the cement-shrouded room. They both cried out. Rebekah's ears rang with high-pitched tinnitus as the pain in her leg was superseded by a new pain in her left shoulder.

A second attempt on the double doors burst them open. Officers entered with guns drawn. Commands were shouted, radios crackled. Damien still cried openly on the floor, searching for the missing pieces of his demigod. The dog barked endlessly outside the door. More officers entered the room yelling.

The tumult was the deafening, nausea-inducing. But the one sound that permeated all the rest was Josh's heart monitor registering a flatline with one steady, ominous note.

CHAPTER 62

REBEKAH DRIFTED BETWEEN MUDDLED CONSCIOUSNESS and reliving the last few minutes in graphic nightmares. Dr. Sandeep Mahesh had shot her—*again*! The implausibility of the situation almost made her laugh—*if it didn't hurt so freaking much!*

She didn't remember much after the gunshots. She felt herself being loaded onto a gurney. EMTs and officers inundated her with words of encouragement. She couldn't open her eyes, but she didn't know why. The pain seemed to be everywhere, even in the air she breathed. But at least she *was* breathing. What about Josh? Then the recollection of the flatline warning brought everything into a sobering light.

Through swollen, cracked lips she mouthed some words. One of the EMTs shushed those around them and placed his ear next to her lips. "Say again, ma'am."

"Josh?" she asked in a voice that sounded more like a puff of wind blowing through a rusty screen.

She never heard the answer. Blackness overtook her. Deep inside, she wished the blackness could be permanent.

* * *

The silence was suffocating. She couldn't tell if she was awake or dreaming. Prying her eyes open, she took in the dark-filled room. She'd seen rooms just like this before. She was in the University of Utah hospital. Subdued light filtered through drawn curtains of the private quarters. An inch-wide strip of artificial light showed her door was slightly ajar. No noises came from the adjoining hallway. A countertop to one side overflowed with flower arrangements. Her bed was in a slightly inclined position. A single IV dripped into the back of her right hand. Bandages swaddled her left leg and shoulder. A fog of anesthesia clogged her mind. She wasn't very comfortable, but at least she was being cared for.

As her eyes adjusted to the dark, she saw a figure slouched in a chair near the window. She couldn't distinguish any identifying features but she sensed it was a man. She had a million questions to ask—the foremost being what had happened to Josh. Just the thought of him warmed her heart . . . but the rest of her was filled with the chill of dread. For over a year now she knew she'd been *in* love. But until the events in Damien's basement, she never realized just how much she truly *loved* Josh Logan. Thinking of him dead pained her physically more than her wounds.

She begged the Lord to let him be alive. She knew it'd be nothing short of a miracle. The flatlined heart monitor had sounded his death knell. Still, she continued to pray, opening her heart and soul until at some unrealized moment she fell asleep.

* * *

Rebekah heard voices. Opening her eyes, she saw a woman in a long white lab coat talking with the man still slumped in the chair. Rebekah blinked a few times to make sure she was seeing right. The man looked past the doctor and made eye contact.

"Good morning, Rebekah," beamed Robert Lansing. "You know, even beat to a pulp in a hospital bed, you're still a stimulating sight for sore eyes."

For the first time ever her skin didn't crawl at his come-on. Her throat was extremely dry, but she managed to squeak out a thank-you. The doctor adjusted Rebekah's bed to a sitting position and handed her a cup of ice chips.

The physician's nametag read Dr. Pinkston. After a few preliminary questions, she said, "You may have as much ice as you like, but until we're sure you can swallow without choking, nothing more. Sorry. Knowing your background in medicine, I'm sure you understand."

"Yes. Thanks, doctor," she said weakly but with good spirits. The ice was already helping. "I've heard your name before. They say you're the best trauma specialist there is."

"They're probably right," she said with a wink. "I've heard your name too. They say you run circles around everyone in the morgue. I'm impressed."

"Thanks."

Robert Lansing stood and brushed out his slacks. "You'll be happy to know that Dr. Pinkston also worked on Josh."

Rebekah's eyes immediately widened and filled with tears. "He's . . . alive?" she dared to ask.

"Yes. But it was touch and go for a while," the doctor admitted.

"How much blood was transfused?"

The doctor blinked. "You know about that?"

"She was in the room when it happened," Lansing explained. "The guy that shot her was the mastermind behind Detective Logan's transfusion experiment, as well as several deaths nationwide."

"Dr. Mahesh," Dr. Pinkston said rhetorically.

"Yep. Who'd have guessed? Talk about drumming up your own business." Lansing followed up the inappropriate comment with the inappropriate onomatopoeia, "*Ka-ching.*"

The man will never change, Rebekah mused. "So what are Josh's chances, doctor?"

"Oh, I think we've got him pretty stabilized. He received about two liters of AB-positive blood. That's almost half his total volume. Fortunately, there was no antibody reaction with his blood."

"But he was diaphoretic and convulsing. He—he flatlined. I saw it!" she said, disbelieving.

"That's true," Dr. Pinkston concurred, "but the police and EMTs were able to resuscitate him and get him here before he coded again. I believe his body just shut down because the speed at which Dr. Mahesh transfused his blood put undue pressure on his system. He had lots of internal bleeding that took some time to stop. As far as we can tell, none of his major organs were damaged."

Rebekah closed her eyes. "Thank you," she said with heartfelt gratitude.

"You bet. Now, you really should be getting more rest. Robert here assures me your job is safe, so stay here as long as you need."

"That's right, darlin'," Lansing said, sitting on her bedside and placing a hand on her knee. "I don't want to see you again until you're completely healed."

The feeling is mutual, she thought behind an appreciative smile.

"As for your wounds, you should heal just fine," Dr. Pinkston continued. "The bullet to your thigh entered through your semitendinosus muscle, barely missed the femoral artery, just nicked your femur, and lodged in your quadriceps. It'll be sore for a long while, but regular PT will bring it back to full use. The GSW in your shoulder is not as pretty. It shattered your left clavicle then passed on through your trapezius and stopped two millimeters before exiting. I excised it then used the larger bone fragments and some of our new bone mesh to reshape your collarbone. Again, the PT won't be any fun, but it'll sure help it heal faster."

"Thank you, doctor. When can I see Josh?"

"Ha! I told you they were an item," Lansing chimed in with his hand still on her knee.

She would rather not have him touching her, but it no longer felt as greasy as it did before. From the look of his clothes, she guessed he'd spent the entire night in the chair in her room. Maybe two nights.

"Josh is still in ICU. Let me get back to you on that," Dr. Pinkston said, heading toward the door.

"Well, now that I know you're okay, I'd better get back to work, too," Lansing said with a squeeze to her knee. "Lots to do back at the bone yard."

His mention of work brought up something that had bothered her for some time. "Hey, speaking of being okay with things: the other night, when you said you'd still be there when I was gone . . ."

He lowered his gaze and cleared his throat. "Yeah . . . I was hoping you'd forget about that. I was feeling down and had a bit too much to drink that evening . . ."

"Forget about that part. I just want to know what you meant. 'I'll still be here when you're all gone,' 'I'll outlast you all' . . . or something like that."

He shrugged awkwardly. "I guess I was just trying to throw my weight around. As administrative head of the department, I have the final say on who works there and who doesn't. So while some may end up quitting or being fired, I'll still be there when others have gone. I know it sounds juvenile, but I wasn't in my best form that night, and I apologize if I scared you."

She couldn't bring herself to harbor animosity over his indiscretion. "No harm, no foul, Robert."

The relief on his face was unmistakable. "Thank you. Now I better get back and do what they pay me to do. I gotta find us a new head of pathology, after all."

Rebekah nodded. "I guess it's no surprise Sandy is in jail, huh?"

"Actually, Dr. Mahesh is already back at the morgue," Lansing said just under a chuckle.

"What?" Rebekah wheezed. "But you said you have to find a *new* ME."

He gave her an exaggerated wink. "He's not there as an employee . . ."

CHAPTER 63

THE NEXT DAY REBEKAH GOT a surprise visit from Nick Lonardo. "W'sup, CK?"

"Oh, you know, trying to dodge bullets, failing miserably. You?"

"Oh, ya know, findin' evidence nobody else can, trackin' down bad guys, keepin' a smile on the ladies' faces."

"Any luck with that last bit?"

"About fifty-fifty," he said, laughing. "But I keep tryin'. That's what's important, ya know?"

She smiled warmly. For all his egocentric, Italian-Stallion obnoxiousness, he really was a likable guy.

"So, yous seen Josh yet?"

Her smile waned. "No. They say he's in and out of consciousness. His vital signs have stabilized, but he can't seem to get his circadian rhythm back."

"Come again?"

"His day-night cycle. His hormones, his thyroid, assorted chemicals and neurotransmitters can't seem to get on the same page. Half his body thinks it's awake and half thinks it's the middle of the night. It's messing up his whole system."

"Oh. Gotcha. Well, he was awake just now. He gave me some things ta follow up on downtown. The gumba doesn't know when ta stop workin', ya know? So, how's the shoulder?"

"It only hurts when I'm awake, so it's not too bad."

"Right."

"So . . . any news from the outside world?" She got scraps of information from the TV and nurses, but they always gave the public-eye version of things. She wanted to know what was *really* going on.

He stepped to her doorway and checked out the halls. He then closed her door and pulled a chair next to her bed. "I'll tells ya what I told Josh. They's matchin' evidence with murders in the states Slade worked in. Turns out he was pretty smooth in his methods, but they've tied that embalmin' oil he used back ta a single manufacturer in Pakistan. Possible connection to Mahesh right there. And the angle Josh was workin' with the linen handkerchiefs? Turns out he was right. They's all from the same factory in Ireland," he accentuated with a snap of his fingers. "Forensics has just gotten clearance to go through Mahesh's office *and* his home files. His wife's havin' a cow over it. But if Mahesh was as dirty as he's lookin', she wants nothin' ta do with him, you know what I'm sayin'?"

"Well, that should be easy. Last I heard, he was faceup at the morgue," she said without much humor. It still hurt her to think about how much she had revered the man. And the fact that she had killed him.

"Dead as a doornail, CK. Did Josh take ya ta the firin' range a lot or somethin'?"

She gave a confused frown. "No, why?"

"'Cause yous nailed the gumba right through the heart. From what I hear, while fallin' to the ground takin' *his* bullet." The admiration in his voice was obvious. "That's one heck of a shot, kiddo—one I'd be braggin' 'bout for a long time."

She lowered her eyes. "Killing a man is nothing to brag about—even one like Mahesh."

"Says you." Always a little slow on the uptake, Nick cleared his throat and gave a playful nudge on her good shoulder. "Hey, don't let it get ta you, Becks. Yous was fightin' for your life. *And* Josh's life, too. Self-defense all the way, baby."

"It goes a little deeper than that," she said softly.

An awkward pause filled the air as she fumbled with her emotions. Nick sat there looking like he knew he'd said something wrong but for the life of him couldn't figure what it was.

Pushing back her melancholy, she decided to rescue the guy. "So what happened to Slade?"

Nick instantly brightened. "Oh, man. That guy is one sick puppy, ya know what I'm sayin'? He's already booked for the murders of the three old folks in-state, plus a couple of transients, *and* the attempted murder of yous and Josh, right? But get this: he's confessed ta *everythin'*—like he's proud of what he's done. Says he's found the *real* Fountain of Youth." Nick rolled his eyes. "An' here I thought it was just a legend all this time," he accentuated with a slap of his palm on his forehead. "Oh, and the half-dollars on the eyes thing? He chose those because of the mint marks. D and S, right? For 'Damien Slade.' Talk about leaving a whacked-out calling card."

Rebekah smiled for Nick's sake. She didn't find anything funny in what Damien Slade had done. "Josh and I counted at least six other deaths across the nation that sound like his handiwork."

"Yeah, we're lookin' into those. Thanks for lettin' me get into your apartment ta grab all those papers I gave yous guys. You got a real nice place, ya know?"

"Thanks."

"Yeah, well, anyway, Slade's under psych eval right now down at county. But we got a mountain of evidence against him plus more ta come. And we got his own confession, so even if he *is* found nutso, I doubt he'll ever walk."

"Good to know," she said, suddenly feeling very weary again. "Hey, thanks for coming by, Nick. I'll let you know the minute I hear anything on Josh."

He nodded and stood.

"Oh, one more thing," Rebekah said. "How did the police know to come to Damien's house?"

"Oh, that. We got this new kid, Ballard, from Louisiana? He's got one of them bloodhounds, right? Sorry-lookin' fleabag named Cletus."

Rebekah frowned. "I was rescued by a dog named Cletus?"

"Yeah, sort of. See, Josh knew yous was in the area, but he couldn't find ya, so this dog sniffed yous out."

"This just keeps getting better."

"Oh, that doesn't mean yous smells funny or nothin'. This dog can sniff out anything, good or bad. So they get him on your trail and he leads them ta Slade's place. Turns out he's home, so Josh goes in the front door, and that's the last this Ballard kid sees of either of them. He waits for a while then decides he'd better go check things out, only there's no answer upstairs. Cletus leads him 'round ta the back, an' he hears something comin' from the basement door. He gives a knock an' Josh answers, says everything's okay, and tells Ballard to go home."

"Yeah, I was there for that part."

"Right, right. But do ya remember Josh sayin' anything strange?"

Rebekah thought for a moment. She didn't want to ever replay *any* of those moments in her mind, but she did want to get some closure on exactly what happened. She shook her head. "Like what?"

"Josh gave Ballard a clue, the sneaky bast—I mean the sneaky guy. Trouble was, the kid didn't get it right away. That's why it took a while for backup to come. But it ain't really his fault."

"What clue?"

"A police code: a ten thirty-three. Ballard says Josh told him he'd finish up at ten thirty-three, right? In Utah, a 10-33 means 'officer down or injured.' He was tellin' Ballard he was in trouble, like a hostage situation, you know?—only Ballard didn't get it right away 'cause not all police codes are the same from state ta state. But when he finally *did* get it, he came runnin' with a truckload'a backup."

"Just in time, too," she said with a twitch of her eyebrows. She looked up at him, feeling very grateful for his friendship. "Thank you for telling me the truth, Nick. I really appreciate all this."

"No problem, CK."

She reached out for his hand and gave it a squeeze. "Keep in touch."

"Try an' keep me away." He opened the door and paused, suddenly looking very sheepish. "Um . . . speaking of telling the truth . . ."

"What?" she prompted.

"Well . . . just thought yous should know. 'CK' doesn't mean 'Cute Kid.' Later, dollface." And with that, he winked and left the room.

CHAPTER 64

Two days later a nurse wheeled Rebekah into Josh's room. It wasn't so much a room as a nook divided from three other nooks that faced a nurse's command center of monitoring devices, file cabinets, and computers. Four such nooks lined each wall surrounding the central station. Each bed held a critically infirm patient—some conscious, some comatose, some at various stages in between.

It was the first time they'd seen each other since the incident. That was five days ago. She tried not to gasp when she saw him.

Josh looked pale and gaunt, but when he saw her, his mouth widened into a grin. "Hey, Becks. Wow, you look terrible." His voice was shallow but expressly happy.

"Thanks, Clouseau. You look like you should be in a fridge at my office," she replied.

He huffed. "Luckily, I feel better than I look. How about you?"

"I feel exactly how I look, but they tell me I'll live."

He sighed heavily, as if a huge burden had just been lifted from his shoulders. "I can't tell you how good it is to see you. When they told me you'd been shot twice . . ." His throat closed off before he could finish the sentence.

"I *was* shot twice. That's why I'm just as glad you're seeing me and not viewing me."

"Amen to that," he whispered.

She tried to sound upbeat, but her heart pounded with anxiety. She had so much to say to him. And she knew she had to say it right away before she lost her nerve. The emotions she carried were crushing her. She chided herself for being so weak. It was just plain silly to be so scared. They could banter small talk for hours—it was one of their favorite pastimes.

They could discuss anything: their jobs, things they liked or disliked, movies, books, gospel principles—it didn't matter. But the one thing they studiously avoided was their life *together*. It was time for that to change.

She wheeled next to him and took his hand in hers. She immediately felt her throat close off as her vision blurred with tears. "Josh, there's something . . ."

"What is it, Becks?" His voice conveyed a tender assurance that everything would be okay, regardless of what she needed to say.

"You—" She swallowed hard and looked at their joined hands. Her eagerness and angst battled just under the surface of her resolve. "Josh. You . . . you *died* for me."

"I did? Wow. Well, I guess that means I'm now talking to an angel—which is something I've known all along."

"Please don't kid, Josh," she said, her voice cracking. "This is serious."

His smile fell. "Oh. Sorry."

Now guilt was added to her jumbled emotions. "No, don't be sorry. I just need . . . Look, I know we're always joking around, and I love that about our relationship, but . . . but I need to know something. So I need for us to be serious, just for a moment. Please."

His eyes registered a flash of hurt. "I'll do my best."

"No, no," she quickly demurred. "That's not what I mean. I—" She gritted her teeth and growled. "Aaaargh, why is this so hard?"

"What, hon?"

"Being open . . . being totally honest."

"Rebekah. Sweetheart. I will tell you whatever you want to know, and you can do the same without fear of repercussion." His voice was filled with that soothing richness she loved. "No joking, no smart remarks, I promise."

She forced herself to meet his eyes without shying away. "Why—?" she asked in little more than a whisper. It was all she could muster before her voice betrayed her.

"Why what?"

"Why did you die for me?"

He pulled her hand to his face and tenderly brushed her fingertips against his lips. "That's easy. Because I love you."

The tears pooled and ran. "Why?"

"Because you're . . . amazing. Because you're everything I wish *I* was but I'm not."

She struggled out of the wheelchair and fell against his chest. She didn't care how awkward the position was, nor did she care what the ICU nurses might be thinking. Her left arm was still secured against her chest, and it hurt to put pressure on her shoulder, but that didn't matter either. She was holding the man she loved. The rest of the world could vanish around them for all she cared. And for a moment, it did.

* * *

Throughout the next week, Rebekah became a regular face in the ICU. No one seemed to mind. Josh's health improved exponentially. She took it upon herself to see that he got the best of everything. He welcomed the attention from her, but he didn't much care for it from anyone else. He didn't like hospitals and made a point of mentioning it every day. Why couldn't they just give him a couple of pills and send him home?

"Josh, honey, listen, medicine is never cut and dried, black and white. Let me decide when you're ready to go home."

He sighed remorsefully. "You're the doc."

"So you're calling me 'doc' now?"

"Yeah. You're certainly smart enough. Besides, I kinda like the sound of it."

She leaned back. "Well, it's better than CK, since I don't even know what it *really* means."

Josh's face flushed. "What did Nick tell you?"

"It's not Cute Kid. Come on, Clouseau. Total honesty now."

The words tumbled out: "It's Crypt Keeper. But it's all Nick's, I had nothing to do with it, nor do I call you that."

"Ah." She looked at the ceiling, as if contemplating the moniker. "I like it."

He swallowed. "Good. But I still prefer to call you doc."

She toyed with a fray of yarn from his bedspread. "Yeah, along that line . . . I should tell you I've made up my mind."

"About what?"

She took a deep breath and spilled her news. "About going back to school. Robert stopped by again and said there's a spot open on the dean's list at the medical college he's holding for me for this fall if I apply by next week. They still have my MCAT scores from the last time I took it, and I have a slew of doctors who'll vouch for my abilities as a med student."

He sat up straighter and took her hand. She felt a slight tremor as he cupped his hands around hers. "Then I guess we'd better hurry."

Her head cocked to one side. "Hurry with what?"

"With our wedding plans. You're going to need someone to support you through med school, and I can't think of anyone better suited to put up with your quirkiness than me."

Her mouth opened then closed then opened again. Tears burned at her eyes. Her hand matched the trembling of his. She threw her good arm around him and squeezed tightly. Placing her lips close to his ear, she whispered, "You have no idea what you're getting into, Clouseau."

"Let me worry about that, doc."

* * *

Nick Lonardo showed up later that evening. "Yous was right, boss. I followed up on the Harris case just like yous asked. We got a warrant ta check out the smoke shop an' that grease-ball Chet. His real name's Marion Chesterfield. Got a rap sheet long as your arm. He had an unregistered 9mm under the cash register. Ballistics was able to match it to Harris's GSW. Don't know why they missed *that* before. Anyways, we's take him in an' he starts singin' like a canary just ta save his own pathetic skin, ya know what I'm sayin'? Turns out the shop's a front for drug trafficking. Harris was inta the small stuff but wouldn't do meth or coke. Chet says when his boss tried ta push Harris, he threatened ta go ta the cops. The next night, *wham-o*, the kid gets nailed. They knows they's in O-P territory, so who better to blame it on, right? We's chasing down the boss now. Man, oh man," Nick said, snapping his fingers with gusto. "Yous was right on the money, *pisano*."

Josh sighed heavily. "While I don't share your enthusiasm, I am glad to have closure there. Keep me informed on where it goes, will you?"

"You got it, boss."

The Italian left the room whistling loudly. When the nurse on staff shushed him, he transitioned smoothly into pick-up mode.

Josh simply smiled and shook his head. *Some things will never change.*

CHAPTER 65

FIVE WEEKS LATER, JOSH AND Rebekah sat at their living room window gazing out over the vast expanse of the Salt Lake valley in all its fall splendor. They quietly munched thin-crust vegetarian pizza and drank Hires draft root beer. As usual, their conversation drifted from one topic to the next. They made a conscious effort to avoid dwelling on the events of that summer, but because Josh was coming due for a mandated annual physical, the subject returned.

"I don't think you'll have any problems," she assured him. "I mean, how many guys can bounce back from the dead and still look as handsome as you?"

"Just goes to show what a good physician you'll make."

She smiled and bumped her shoulder against his. "Yeah, about that. The next four or five years are going to be pretty crazy, Clouseau. You really think we can handle it?"

He wiped his fingers and mouth with a paper napkin. "I think you and I can handle just about anything, as long as we handle it together."

"I'm glad you feel that way," she said, snuggling against him. "I was just thinking: do you remember all that stuff we learned about centenarians?"

"How could I forget?"

"Well, we tended to focus on the *physical* aspects of their longevity. But there was something even more crucial to longevity that we didn't address."

"And that is?"

"Companionship, interpersonal interaction, the need to *feel* needed. Like losing yourself in the service of others. Did you notice not a single centenarian we reviewed was ever divorced? That's not to say their lives were filled with marital bliss 24-7. But I bet *enduring* hardships was what strengthened them as individuals and as couples."

Josh took a breath to speak, but she quickly held up her hand. "Before you say anything, I know there're a number of legitimate reasons to end a marriage. But people today don't recognize the benefit of putting in an honest effort to fix *petty* differences; they just toss up their hands and walk away, thinking the grass is greener elsewhere."

Josh wrapped an arm around her from behind. "Well, then, I promise to never leave you just because you cannot go to bed without the kitchen being completely spotless first."

"And I promise never to walk away because you squeeze the toothpaste from the middle of the tube."

"See? We'll make it together for 100 years . . . and beyond."

She clung to the arm around her. "You really mean that? Even though you're married to a crypt keeper?"

He chuckled. "With all my heart—even if it ends up as a specimen on your desk."

She tipped her head back, stole a kiss, and whispered, "Good answer."

ABOUT THE AUTHOR

GREGG R. LUKE, R.PH., WAS born in Bakersfield, California, but spent the majority of his childhood and young adult life in Santa Barbara, California. He served an LDS mission in Wisconsin then pursued his education in natural sciences at SBCC, UCSB, and BYU. He completed his schooling at the University of Utah College of Pharmacy.

Gregg currently practices pharmacy in Logan, Utah. He and his wife, Julie, have three children and live in Cache Valley, Utah. He has been published in *Skin Diver* magazine, the *Oceanographic Letter,* and the *New Era* magazine. His fictional novels include *The Survivors, Do No Harm, Altered State, Blink of an Eye, and Bloodborne*, four of which were Whitney Award finalists.

Visit him at www.greggluke.com.